L.A. MENTAL

ALSO BY NEIL McMAHON

Twice Dying
Blood Double
To the Bone
Revolution No. 9
Lone Creek
Dead Silver

AS DANIEL RHODES

Next, After Lucifer
Adversary
Kiss of Death

L.A. MENTAL

A THRILLER

NEIL McMAHON

HARPER

An Imprint of HarperCollins*Publishers*
www.harpercollins.com

L.A. MENTAL. Copyright © 2011 by Neil McMahon. All rights reserved. Printed in the United States of America. No part of this book may be used or reproduced in any manner whatsoever without written permission except in the case of brief quotations embodied in critical articles and reviews. For information, address HarperCollins Publishers, 10 East 53rd Street, New York, NY 10022.

HarperCollins books may be purchased for educational, business, or sales promotional use. For information, please write: Special Markets Department, HarperCollins Publishers, 10 East 53rd Street, New York, NY 10022.

FIRST EDITION

Designed by William Ruoto

Library of Congress Cataloging-in-Publication Data has been applied for.

ISBN 978-0-06-134078-9

11 12 13 14 15 OV/RRD 10 9 8 7 6 5 4 3 2 1

TO CARL LENNERTZ,

WHO HAS CARRIED ME

FOR A THOUSAND PAGES

I can feel the heat closing in, feel them out there making their moves, setting up their devil doll stool pigeons . . .

—WILLIAM S. BURROUGHS

L.A. MENTAL

Los Angeles Times, **February 2**

Bizarre Rampage Leaves Judge in Critical Condition

Police were summoned to the Santa Monica home of municipal court judge Allen Berthold by neighbors late last night. Reports of shouting and breaking glass led them to expect a crime in progress, but it now appears that Berthold was alone through the entire incident.

According to a source who spoke on condition of anonymity, Berthold had damaged his house extensively, throwing furniture through windows and streaking the walls with his own blood. "It looked like he'd been running around trying to bash his brains out," the source said. He was unconscious when police arrived, and they have refused to speculate as to a possible cause. He was taken to Cedars-Sinai hospital and is listed in stable but critical condition.

Los Angeles Times, **March 5**

Accused Celeb Heiress in Pool Accident

One of the decade's most sensational murder cases took a twist last night when Pamela Dutton, a onetime Miss California and widow of wealthy philanthropist Clifford Dutton, was found in a coma in the pool of her Beverly Hills condo.

In 2006, less than two years after their May-December marriage (Mr. Dutton was eighty-three, his wife, thirty-six), she was accused of murdering him by pushing him off their yacht. After a highly publicized trial, she was acquitted and the death ruled accidental, leaving her more than $200 million. The verdict was bitterly contested by prosecutors and by Mr. Dutton's family. This acrimony was recently renewed when she announced her engagement to investment banking magnate Warren DeKampe.

No official details have been released, but private sources say that alcohol and drugs don't appear to be factors.

Pasadena Star-News, **April 7**

CalTech Tragedy Saddens, Disturbs

CalTech graduate student Peter Janacek died last night in an apparent suicide by running onto the westbound Foothill Freeway. He was struck by several vehicles before traffic could stop, and pronounced dead at the scene.

Janacek, twenty-six, was a doctoral candidate in astrophysics. Friends describe him as a talented student, cheerful and well-adjusted. He had followed his usual evening routine of going to work in one of the school's labs, although no one has reported seeing him during the last hours before his death.

To anyone paying close attention, the city of Los Angeles seemed to be going insane.

This was not just the usual everyday madness, but people erupting in destructive rampages, all directed at themselves. Over the past year, almost forty such incidents had made the front pages and nightly newscasts, with many more that had not.

Gunnar Kelso sat working at his laptop—copying and pasting online news clips to update the file that he kept of the incidents. It was evening, and he was very much alone in an old log hunting lodge in the mountains outside L.A. His makeshift office was arranged, with a careful appearance of carelessness, to suggest his former life. The bookshelves were stacked with scientific texts and journals, the desk scattered with computer printouts of complex equations and modular graphics. A text in German on the physics of magnetic resonance lay open to his left.

Kelso paused a moment in regret at the third clip, the CalTech student. That had been a mistake.

Perfume, Gerald Wainwright thought—maybe that was what was getting to him, prickling his sinuses and making his head feel like a balloon was blowing up inside.

The party was like a thousand other glossy Hollywood events he'd been to—a plush house in Beverly Hills stuffed with young actors, hangers-on, and a sprinkling of local celebrities and players. A few, like Wainwright, had the money to back up their stature here.

As the vibrant lovelies came around flirting, he basked in their fragrance, imagining how the warm aura would exude from their skin when they were wearing only that and jewelry. But tonight, it seemed he'd had too much of a good thing. He felt euphoric but unsettled. He put down his drink, eased his way out of the crowded room, and stepped through a sliding glass door onto a patio. The night air was cool and fresh from the April breeze, and he walked into it gratefully, letting it wash over his face and into his lungs.

"Hiding from the girls, Gerald?" a woman's voice said from the doorway.

He swung around to look back. The party's hostess, Cynthia Trask, was coming outside to join him.

"Not from you," Wainwright said, although his smile was guarded. She was damned attractive, in her late thirties, but with a cold edge. She made him uneasy, not just because of herself but because of what she embodied—the party's other atmosphere besides the perfume, a subtle undercurrent that the physical senses couldn't pick up but that was just as present.

In a word, Parallax, an organization that bonded together all the people here tonight.

All except Wainwright. So far.

Cynthia closed the door behind her, muting the chatter and laughter from inside.

"The decision's been made," she said. "You're in. Now you start to find out what Parallax really is. But we need a commitment from you." She moved closer to him as she spoke.

"What are we talking?" he said.

"You sign on to the film as executive producer. Make the important things happen. And a good faith buy-in—call it twenty million for now."

Wainwright's eyebrows rose. "That's a little on the steep side."

"This is not a buy-sell arrangement. You and Parallax open up to each other. Power like you never imagined—learn to use it, and you'll get anything you want. In return, you help us with our work. Everyone gains."

Wainwright shoved his hands in his front pockets and stepped away from her, shaking his head. He'd been to a few of these Parallax events by now, sizing up the people while they did the same with him. But he was cynical by nature, and more so from his years in the film industry; the secretive allure that captivated the others had not taken hold on him.

Not twenty million bucks' worth, that was for sure. The sheer brazenness of it pissed him off, and the irritation in his head joined in to tap the mean streak that was never far below the surface.

"Cynthia, I've got a problem with this. I just can't take any of it seriously. All this hinting about how you're somehow tied in with the power of the universe. You know what I see? A bunch of people blowing smoke up their own ass. And your film project—nobody's ever *heard* of Parallax Productions. It's like kids making a home movie. You think I'm going to touch it, you can't be serious."

He expected her to lash back with cold anger, but instead she smiled—slowly and, somehow, disturbingly.

"But I am serious, Gerry," she said, "and I have a feeling that you're going to be happy to help us kids make our little movie. In fact, the price just went up."

Hollywood Insider, **April 28**

Category: Movie Biz (1–10 of 744)

Producer Wainwright announces stunner. He'll head dark horse Parallax deal with rumored $24 mil investment.

PART ONE

ONE

The shrill chirp of my cell phone rousted me out of a dream, a familiar kind that had started in childhood and still came around every so often. I'd be trying to run—whether toward or away from something, I was never sure—but my feet weighed a ton and my body felt like it was struggling through glue. These dreams seemed to last a very long time, and while they weren't exactly nightmares, once or twice a year was plenty.

The clock on my bedside table read 3:17 a.m. I groped in the dark for the phone, already knowing who it was—my younger brother Nick ripped on whatever dope he'd gotten his hands on. These late-night calls were as familiar as the dreams, and about as welcome. But I couldn't ignore them.

Nick and I were close in age, and we'd been tight growing up. In most ways, that was long gone. We were in our midthirties now, and over the years, increasingly, he'd brought little to our family and me except grief. Still, a trace of that bond remained, and I had become the default brother's keeper.

"What's going on, Nick?" I said, careful not to sound annoyed. He usually just wanted money, but there'd been a couple of times when he was in dangerously bad shape, and I'd had to walk a thin line to keep him calm.

"Tommy?" he breathed.

I sat up straighter in bed with the queasy feeling that this was one of those times. He sounded genuinely out of it, much different from his typical brash, cajoling style that stemmed from the beach-boy good looks he'd grown up with. By and large it still worked surprisingly well for him, considering that his body had gone slack, his face was a map of what he'd done to himself, and his once sun-bronzed skin was now glazed with a bar tan.

"Yeah, it's me," I said. "Are you okay?" In the background, I could hear a faint, regular rumbling. It wasn't thunder—there were no storms in the L.A. area now. Surf, maybe.

"Something's fucking with me," he said in that same tense whisper—struggling not to lose control. "It snuck into my head, and I can't get rid of it. It made me come here all alone. Now it's after me."

He wasn't just out of it. He was scared.

"Where are you?" I said. By this time I was across the room, clumsily pulling on the jeans I'd worn yesterday.

"Home. But I can't get in. Somebody nailed boards over everything."

For a second, I didn't know what he was talking about. Then it came—our family's old house near Malibu, where Nick had once lived. That would explain why I was hearing surf.

Except that he'd moved out several months ago—in truth, he'd been kicked out—and now the place was a vacant husk, boarded up and slated for demolition.

"You mean the beach house?" I said.

"Yeah. Home."

"That's not home anymore, Nick. Are you sure it's where you are?" I found a sweatshirt and started working it over my head, managing to keep the phone pressed to one ear or the other.

"Sure. Sure, sure, sure."

"Okay, I'm coming up there right now," I said. "Stay where you are and stay on the phone. We'll make sure nothing hurts you."

"It *is* going to hurt me, Tommy. Hurry."

The connection went dead.

"Son of a *bitch*," I snapped, and called his cell phone number back. No answer—just five rings and then voice mail.

"Pick up, Nick—come on, we've got to keep talking," I said when the message tone came.

Nothing.

I stomped my feet into a pair of running shoes and headed out the door.

TWO

It was mid-May, but the night was chilly and damp with fog rolling in from the Pacific. Even at three o'clock on a Saturday morning, the Santa Monica Freeway was a rushing conveyor belt of electric glare, thousands of mist-blurred headlights. Turning off to the relative quiet of Highway 1 was a relief.

I drove as fast as I could, but my ride was a boxy '84 Land Cruiser that was basically a Jeep, designed for the Australian outback instead of the urban fast lane; I'd bought it used when I was lifeguarding through college, and now it had a quarter million miles on it and looked every one of them. On top of that, the fog kept getting thicker until I felt like I was fighting my way through the swirls dancing like ghosts in my headlight beams. The long glittering arc of the coastline was almost wiped out, blanketed down to flickers that seemed to move.

I tried calling Nick again every couple of minutes, warring with myself over whether to call 911 instead. The sheriffs could get to him sooner, but that would almost certainly mean a drug bust. He'd already had his share of those, to the point where another one was an excellent bet for serious jail time. Then there was the deeper fear that he'd freak out when they showed up, and do something that really *would* get him hurt.

It was a bad choice to have to make. I ended up deciding to keep on going alone. He'd seemed all right physically, and there were explanations for why he wasn't answering—he was too paranoid; he'd wandered away from his phone; he was busy trying to kick through a door and reclaim the home he still thought was his.

I slowed as I passed through the posh enclave of Malibu—traffic was usually so backed up that speeding was impossible, but right now cops might be on the watch—but got on the gas again until I turned off the highway at Point Dume.

Then I started driving into a part of my past that I would have erased if I could have—in a word, money, and a hell of a lot of it. My great-great-grandfather and namesake, the first Thomas Crandall, hadn't technically been a robber baron but was of that stamp. He and his descendants had created one of the private empires in Southern California, rivaling others like the Dohenys, Crockers, and Huntingtons.

I'd started getting uncomfortable with that as soon as I was old enough to understand what it entailed, and the older I got, the less I liked it.

That Thomas Crandall—Tom the First, as he was known in the family—was particularly astute about foreseeing the potential value of real estate and buying it for next to nothing. We still owned a lot of choice turf, and one of the jewels was this place in Malibu—almost four acres of oceanfront headland on the cliffs, sheltered from surrounding development by rows of windswept trees. The only drawback was the ramshackle old house, and that was about to be torn down and a new one built by my other brother, Paul.

That left a real sour taste in my mouth.

The security gate at the driveway entrance was hanging open. As I drove in, my headlights caught the glint of Nick's parked car, a carnival red Jaguar XK8 that he'd bought brand-new, five or six years ago. Now it was dirt-caked and dinged up, the leather interior trashed, and it ran with a sound like there was gravel in the crankcase. In a way, it was like Nick himself—once beautiful and high-powered, but he'd hammered them both into the ground.

At least it meant that he *had* been here, although I couldn't be sure he still was. He might have left with someone else or taken off on foot, making his way across the headlands to the beach or going the other way to the highway.

I parked beside the Jag and stepped out into the misty breeze and the boom of the breakers against the cliffs, a giant slow pulse that I could feel through my feet.

"Nick?" I yelled. "Nick, where are you? It's me, Tom. I'm here." I waited ten seconds, listening hard. The offshore wind was strong enough to muffle my shouting—maybe he just didn't hear me.

Then again, maybe he did.

I got a Maglite from my car and checked his Jaguar first, just in case he was passed out in there. He wasn't, but he'd left tracks. The console was streaked with white powder, and a small paper bindle was lying on the driver's-side floor.

I grimaced at this new bad choice. Just touching the shit would constitute tampering with evidence. But if I left it and had to call for help, sheriff's deputies would spot it right away. I couldn't dump it, either; Nick might need medical attention, and the doctors would want a sample to analyze. But they weren't legally required to inform the police, at least short of a serious crime or autopsy, and I'd learned from experience that if I said the magic words *patient confidentiality*, that would raise the demonic specter of lawsuits and keep hospitals quiet as clams. I found an unused Taco Bell napkin in the litter strewn around, collected the loose powder and bindle into it, wet my sweatshirt sleeve on the car's fog-damp fender and wiped down the console, then stowed the folded napkin in one of my Land Cruiser's storage compartments. I took a quick look around for more dope but didn't see any, and I couldn't take the time to search thoroughly. At least it wouldn't be right in front of the cops.

From there I started with the house, striding around the outside to see if he might have gotten in. But the doors and windows were covered with plywood screwed on tight and undisturbed. As I went I swung the flashlight in arcs to search the surroundings, but came up empty there, too. That left the stretch of headlands out toward the cliffs. If he wasn't there, he was gone, and I didn't see any reason why he would be. Nick was not given to nature walks, day or night.

By now I was coming up against the fear that I'd made a crucial mistake—I should have called 911 right away.

I started zigzagging across the rocky ground, swinging the flashlight beam and shouting his name. Then, finally, I got an answer that cut into me like a razor slash.

A high-pitched keening howl, wild and desperate, came swirling around my ears with the wind. I'd only ever heard anything like it a few times before—back when I was working as a clinician with seriously insane, and often dangerously violent, patients at the state mental hospital in Napa.

I broke into a run.

I still couldn't see him, and the wind made it hard to judge the sound's location—all I could tell was that he was out toward the cliff. But a few seconds later another howl came, and this time I got a better fix.

He wasn't just *at* the cliff—he was on the brink. The drop-off beyond it was almost sheer, sloped like a church steeple, eighty feet down a rock face to the ocean below. I slowed back down to a cautious walk. If a shape suddenly appeared out of the fog charging toward him, he might panic and take off in the wrong direction.

When Nick came into sight, my first instant impression was of a caricature madman in an old black-and-white movie, like Jekyll after drinking the potion that turned him into Hyde—bent forward and pacing with one hand clenched in his tangled hair. His other hand, waving around frantically, was holding something, but I couldn't tell what it was.

I edged closer, hugely relieved that he was alive and at least physically intact—but now facing the problem of how to deal with this. It crossed my mind to tackle him and get him away from that edge, but he was too near it; and for all the damage he'd done to himself, he was still a big, powerful man. We'd been about the same size as we matured, around six-one, one-eighty, but while I'd stayed at that weight, he was well over two hundred by now. It wasn't *good* extra weight, and would make him harder to handle still.

He hadn't seen me yet, and I decided it would be best if he heard me first; he'd recognize my voice instinctively, before he even had time to react, and with any luck, it would start soothing him.

"Nick, it's Tom," I called, trying to sound upbeat and free of the strain I was feeling.

He spun around toward me. His face was pale—he must have been cold, wearing just a T-shirt, below-the-knee shorts, and flip-flops—with staring eyes and bared teeth.

"Stay calm, brother," I said. "I'm here for you, like we talked about a little while ago. Remember?"

His stare stayed riveted on my face.

"There. Are. *Worms.* Eating my brain," he declared in a chilling hoarse croak—the kind of flat-affect certainty I'd seen in psychotics whose inner voices goaded them to sudden assaults, arson, or murdering their infant children.

"Come on, Nick. Let's head to my place, have a beer, and figure this out."

"That's just feeding the worms, Tommy," he said in the same distant but definite tone, like he was explaining something I was too dense to get. "All I *am* now is worm food."

He unclenched his hand from his matted hair and smacked his palm against his temple.

"You just need to smooth out a little," I said. "Hey, how about a Valium? I've got some in my car."

Quick as an eyeblink, he made a stunning change, with his face turning shrewd and snarky.

"Is that the next step on your how-to-deal-with-wackos list, *Doctor* Crandall?" The words sprayed out of his mouth like piss in my face. "I crawl into a cage, pull a lever, and a pill pops into my mouth like an M 'n' M? Don't talk down to me, you mother-fucker."

Worse than the viciousness was his suddenly being very much in control—and very much more the real Nick. I was slammed by the thought that this whole thing was an act, some-thing he'd cooked up to jerk me around or just vent his free-floating rage. It sickened me and brought my own anger flaring up, and I damned near gave in to the urge to walk away and leave him there.

Then, just as fast, the situation took another 180-degree spin. A new sound burst out of nowhere, so abrupt and jarring it made my body jerk—the loud pounding beat of rap music.

It was the ring of Nick's cell phone—*that* was what he was holding in his hand.

I stared in disbelief while he raised it to his ear, as if the reality of what was going on here had stopped dead and we were standing on a golf course. He listened for maybe five seconds.

Then he threw back his head and let out another of those howls. They'd been bad enough from a distance. This close, it was outright terrifying. He flung his hands in the air, flailing wildly around his head like he was trying to fight off a swarm of wasps. I glimpsed the cell phone slip out of his grasp and go sailing over the cliff.

Next thing I knew he was lunging at me, snarling like a pit bull.

From there, everything became a desperate blur. His clawing hands got hold of my shirt, and he rammed his head forward to butt me. I jerked my face aside just in time, brought my knee up into his groin, and stomped on his instep. That slowed him down, but he kept his grip with manic strength. We wrestled around in circles, slipping on the treacherous pebbly soil and gasping for breath.

Every time Nick exhaled, it sounded like he was huffing, "Worms! Worms! Worms!"

Then a chunk of the cliff edge broke loose under my right foot and my foot went with it, kicking helplessly in space. I managed to get my other knee onto solid ground and drag myself back inland, digging my fingers into the earth to pull me along.

"Nick, *no*, we're gonna die!" I yelled, rolling away from him.

And he stopped, just as suddenly as he'd attacked—let his hands fall and stood there inert, as if somebody had jerked his plug.

I scrambled to my feet, sucking air into my aching lungs and trying to think of a way to get on top of this, fast. He could light up again in another eyeblink.

Nothing came to me in those few seconds, but it didn't matter. Without a hint of warning, Nick simply crumpled, like he was falling full length onto a bed.

Right over the edge of the cliff.

THREE

I took off in an all-out sprint to the only place I could climb down after Nick, a narrow switchback trail that we'd played on as kids. The slope was gentler here but still damned steep, and I was no kid anymore. My footholds kept breaking loose, sending me into gut-wrenching slides. Sheets of spray lashed up from the pounding surf, slickening the rocks I clutched at and stinging my eyes. Then my feet found the small ledge we used to jump from.

Close to two minutes had passed since Nick had gone over. If he even survived the fall, he was probably unconscious. In the three summers I'd spent lifeguarding at Newport Beach I'd hauled out a fair number of drowners, revived some by CPR and lost others, and I'd been present at many more such incidents.

Two minutes underwater was a long time.

I jumped, aiming for the clear spot I remembered among the rocks and hoping to Christ that memory was right.

The numbing cold shock of the water washed over me as I hit, landing in a waist-deep trough but the next second swamped by a breaker. The incoming waves clashed with the rebounds off the cliff base, turning the surface into a maelstrom. I dropped down below it, tore off my sneakers, and came up off the sandy bottom in a lunging dive and another and another, each time swimming a few strokes through the roiling surf with my head up to scan for Nick.

Then I spotted his white T-shirt, tossing like a sack of trash that wouldn't quite sink.

By the time I got my hands on his clammy flesh, we were pushing three minutes.

He was facedown, arms and legs hanging limp and hair floating like kelp. With a fall like that there was serious risk of central nervous system damage, and even touching him risked aggravating it, but nothing else was going to matter if I couldn't get him breathing. I rolled him over gently, supporting his neck and trying to shield him from the breakers with my body, and jammed my fingers into his mouth to scoop out anything he might have hacked up. Then I pinched his nostrils shut and clamped my own mouth over his, forcing air into his lungs. Kissing a drowner was another thing I hadn't done for many years, but that taste was something you never forgot. It came from deep within them and right through the salty overlay of brine—fetid, metallic, and hinting at death. Sometimes they were already there.

I started towing him, bucking the surf and blinding spray, digging my toes into the sand for traction when I could, and blowing air into him every few seconds. The only place anywhere nearby where I could get him out of the water was one of the big rocks that jutted above the surface, still splashed by the waves but not as much, and I could do heart massage.

I eased him up onto it and got down to a steady rhythm—thirty presses on his sternum with the heels of my hands, two breaths into his lungs, and then again. He twitched and made croaking sounds every time I shoved down on his chest. When I'd first done CPR, I thought that meant the victim was coming around. It didn't.

But then Nick's lips twisted in a sputtering cough that sounded real. I touched my fingertips to his carotid artery and felt the bump of pulse, thready but definite. I hovered there with my ear close to his mouth and my own heart hammering. Nature usually took charge once the lungs started working, but it was something else you couldn't count on.

The coughs kept coming in spasms, his body fighting to blow out the water he'd inhaled and suck in air. My hands could almost feel him coming back to life as his breathing gradually got less ragged and more regular, his pulse stronger.

Now the problem was getting him out of here, and it was going to be a whole lot trickier because he showed no signs of coming back to consciousness. We couldn't just wait until somebody came along and saw us. The closest accessible beach was a quarter mile away, and especially with the water so rough, I couldn't risk towing him—avoiding spinal damage was top priority now, with internal injury also in the mix. The only choice I could see was to leave him here, call for help—I'd left my own cell phone in my car, thank God—and get back as fast as I could. I wrung out my sodden sweatshirt and covered his torso with it, hoping it might stave off hypothermia a little longer, and stayed with him another half minute to make sure his breathing and pulse were steady. Then I slid back into the ocean and raced for the switchback trail.

With the beating Nick had taken on his fall, it was no surprise that he was still unconscious. Concussion was almost a given, and it might be far worse. But there was another grim possibility I couldn't ignore. Victims who came around after prolonged submersion sometimes suffered brain damage from oxygen deprivation.

Even if he survived his other injuries, I might have resuscitated a living corpse.

FOUR

It took maybe fifteen minutes to run to my car, make the call to 911, and get back to Nick. Help started arriving very soon after that, by land, air, and sea. A team from Malibu Search and Rescue—volunteers who risked their necks for nothing but the satisfaction of saving lives—came rappelling down the cliffs; the Coast Guard sent an MLB, a fast, tough boat designed for dangerous operations in heavy surf; and overhead, the lights of a helicopter from UCLA Medical Center appeared through the fog.

The personnel were just as competent as they were quick. Within another few minutes, they'd hoisted Nick by sling to the hovering copter and gotten me on board the boat, wrapped in blankets with EMTs checking me over. I was a little bruised, but intact; the only things I really felt were my scraped-up bare feet.

The sky was starting to lighten as the MLB pulled up onto Westward Beach, the closest place with vehicle access. I told the crew again how terrific they were and climbed out of the boat. Right away, I saw several media vans and a knot of reporters in the parking area. I hadn't expected that; these kinds of incidents usually didn't attract so much attention. But as soon as I thought about it, the reason was obvious. These kinds of incidents usually didn't involve the bad-boy son of a prominent family.

There were also a couple of L.A. County sheriff's deputies and a man waiting for me who had the look of a plainclothes cop—late forties, solidly built, with a face that seemed friendly but suggested that you wouldn't want to meet him in an interrogation cell.

I should have expected this; of course the police would want my account. I took my time hobbling across the beach to him, trying to get my story together. With the situation turning so serious, my hiding the dope from Nick's car was also more serious, and I wasn't a quick-witted liar.

But another ugly possibility was rising in my mind—that I might be under suspicion for assault or even attempted murder. The scenario was easy to construct. My anger at Nick had grown over the years of trouble he'd given me, and tonight was the last straw. We'd quarreled, and I'd lost my temper and shoved him over the cliff, but then, stricken by fear or remorse, managed to drag him out of the water. It was entirely plausible. Violent incidents where people gave in to bursts of rage, followed by equally sudden changes of heart, were common.

And that would further explain the strong media presence. An implication of foul play would make for an even juicier story.

"Dr. Crandall, I'm Detective Sergeant Drabyak," the waiting man said, flipping open a wallet badge. "Are you sure you don't need medical attention?"

"I'm okay. Thanks."

"You could stand to warm up, I bet. Let's get you in my car."

"That would be great. But I could really use some dry clothes. I've got some in my own car, if you wouldn't mind taking me to it."

"Glad to," he said. "Just out of curiosity, why'd you bring spare clothes?"

Drabyak wasn't wasting any time.

"Just old habit," I said. "If I've been running, swimming, a hike out in the foothills."

Drabyak nodded, apparently satisfied. Apparently.

As we walked toward the parking area, the media cameras started flashing and the reporters closed in, thrusting microphones at me. Their faces loomed forward out of the mist with moving mouths that seemed to have a lot of teeth, and the questions came so fast I only half caught most of them.

"Dr. Crandall, that must have been a harrowing rescue. Can you tell us—"

"Sir, what caused your brother to—"

"Was there a struggle?"

" . . . drugs involved?"

I held up a hand, palm first. "I don't have anything to say right now."

"Come on, people, give him a break," Drabyak called out more forcefully. That stopped the questions, although they still walked along with us, cameras flashing.

We got into his car, a Ford sedan that was unmarked but had door-to-door dashboard electronics, a squawk box emitting bursts of copspeak, and a racked shotgun. Still, the peace and warmth were comforting.

"Ever see that movie *Night of the Living Dead*?" he said wryly, jerking his head toward the figures milling around us.

In spite of it all, I couldn't help smiling.

"How about some coffee?" he said, rummaging under his seat. "Station house crap, but it's hot."

"You bet."

He came up with a battered steel thermos and filled two foam cups with the steaming brew. It was crap, all right, but maybe the most welcome crap I'd ever tasted.

"You've had a hell of a night," he said. "Sure you're feeling all right?"

"I'm sure."

"A lot of people wouldn't be so steady. But I guess it's not the first time you pulled somebody out of the water." He was watching me without seeming to—feeling around.

"It scared the shit out of me every time I did, Detective, and nothing in my life ever scared me like tonight," I said. "But yeah, you get thick-skinned. I'm sure it's the same for you guys, only a lot worse. Nobody was ever shooting at us."

Drabyak exhaled, a sound that seemed both sad and grimly amused.

"There's an upside—we've usually got solid ground under us and air to breathe." He put the car in gear, and we started out. I thought the reporters might follow us, but they didn't; I was sure they weren't done with this, but the immediate high drama was over.

"Dr. Crandall, we might as well get clear right away," Drabyak said. "I need to know what happened between you and your brother. Why don't you give me a rundown while we drive?"

I knew I didn't have to agree—I could have insisted on having a lawyer before I said a word. But that would raise a red flag. I took the gamble that the best way to tamp this down was to talk like I was willing and even eager to. I told him the story, leaving out only the part about the dope in Nick's car.

Drabyak drove slowly, his right wrist hooked over the wheel. Dawn was coming on now, with the early light suffusing the fog.

"Let me confirm a few things," he said. "You and Nick weren't still scuffling when he fell, is that right?"

"Yes. We were a good ten feet apart."

"You never provoked him or tried to harm him? Didn't threaten him in any way? Yell something angry, act like you wanted to keep fighting?"

"Nothing like that. Like I said, I was trying my damnedest

to get him calmed down and safe. I've been annoyed at Nick plenty—no question there. But I'd never do anything to hurt him, and in general, I never blow up. If I couldn't control myself, I'd have dropped out of psychology a long time ago."

Drabyak gave me another of his judicious nods. "Okay, I'm fine with all that. No offense intended, by the way—you don't strike me as the kind of guy who'd throw his brother off a cliff. I just need to cover the turf."

"Understood," I said, relieved that I seemed to be off the hook, at least for now.

"So why did Nick freak out so bad? You said that phone call was what seemed to set him off. Any idea who'd call him at four o'clock in the morning?"

"I haven't had time to think about it," I said. "But right off the top, no, and I don't see how it could figure in. It lasted only a few seconds—what could somebody have said in that short a time that would send him completely ballistic? Besides, everything he said was about the problem being inside his head, not coming from somewhere else."

"Could it have been a suicide attempt?"

I hesitated, but then shook my head. "That's also possible, but Nick's never been suicidal. My personal take is that it doesn't fit with his psychological makeup."

I'd never tried to do an outright clinical assessment on Nick involving tests and such, but it was clear to me that he was somewhere in the hazy area of borderline psychotic—people who tended to be very self-centered and manipulative, thrived on a secret sense of superiority, and by and large liked themselves just fine. They might do plenty of damage to others, but their top priority was taking care of number one.

Finally Drabyak put his finger on the weak point, changing

wrists on the steering wheel and shifting in his seat to face more toward me.

"One more question," he said. "Do you think he was using drugs?"

"I'd rather not speculate on that, Detective." He knew as well as I did that meant yes. "But Nick's had his problems along those lines. Assuming he pulls through this, I guarantee we'll get him a thorough clinical workup and whatever treatment is indicated."

By now our house was coming into sight. Several more L.A. County vehicles were parked in front, patrol cars and investigation units, and the driveway was cordoned off by yellow tape with deputies standing watch. Drabyak stuck his hand out the window, flashing his badge at them, then pulled in among the other vehicles and cut the engine.

"I appreciate your cooperation, Dr. Crandall," he said. "I won't keep you any longer—I know you're anxious to check in on Nick."

"Can you tell me what happens from here?" I said. "Anything else you're going to want me to do?"

He leaned back and hooked a wrist over the wheel again, like he was still driving.

"That depends," he said. "Right now, I don't see any evidence that a crime was committed. No crime, there's usually no reason for us to pursue it. We *could*. Trace that phone call, start looking under rocks, find out what he's been doing and who with. But something could come along to kick this back into gear. And let's face it, the Crandalls being who they are—there's going to be a lot of interest."

FIVE

Ronald Reagan UCLA Medical Center was like a city in itself, but I'd been there a few times before and I knew my way around. I paid eleven bucks for a parking space and went in the emergency room entrance of the huge main hospital. There I spent the next couple of hours absorbing the information about Nick that came along at intervals. While I waited, I finally had time to replay the events in my mind.

What the hell *had* pushed him, literally, over the edge? In the past years he'd had a few episodes of slipping out of reality, but he'd never come close to losing it so wildly, and he'd never been outright violent. The memory of those awful, desperate howls and of him dancing around clutching his hair made me wince. It was like something really had invaded his head and was torturing him.

The best assumption I could make at this point was that two factors had combined—he'd gotten into some really bad dope, and/or way too much of it, and his general mental condition had deteriorated more than I'd realized.

The explanation didn't much satisfy me. The drug part, maybe; who knew what kind of shit was out there on the streets these days? Still, I had trouble believing that an experienced user like Nick would get so sucker punched. I'd turned over the stuff from his car to the hospital, and the analysis might tell us something, but with the lab's backlog, it would be at least a week before the results came back.

I was even less able to convince myself that his mental state had slipped so far. I kept a close eye on him that way, and while he might be slowly losing ground, I'd seen no signs of serious decline that would suggest a complete psychotic meltdown. That sort of thing typically didn't just come out of the blue, but had a long buildup with recognizable kinds of disturbed behavior. Most important, however erratic or unpleasant he might have seemed, he was always still Nick. Last night he was somebody I'd never seen before.

Then there was that phone call. It occurred to me that he might have been having an ongoing argument with whoever it was, and even though the call lasted only a few seconds, that was long enough for him or her to say something that made Nick snap. But I had a hard time buying that, too. As I'd told Drabyak, it didn't fit with Nick's ranting about the terror inside his head, and it just didn't seem plausible that a few words could drive him into such a blind fury.

While I paced, stewing, news kept trickling out of the ER, and it was generally encouraging. Nick had opened his eyes and seemed to be aware of his surroundings. Initial X-rays indicated that his spinal column was intact. Overall, he was physically stable enough to soon be moved to the ICU. But there was still the possibility of brain damage. A CT scan and other tests were in the works; the doctors thought they'd have a more comprehensive picture later today.

I decided to move on. There was no point in hanging around there in the interim, and I had other things to take care of. I'd been teaching at a community college the past couple of years, and right now we were on break, so I didn't have to worry about canceling appointments or formal business matters. But I did have to worry about our mother; that was top priority now.

I'd called her earlier to break the news; she'd wanted to rush to the hospital, but I told her to stay home and I'd come see her soon. She was a strong, intelligent woman, but she had a brittle edge that had gotten more pronounced since my father's death. I wanted to get a sense of how distraught she might be before she walked into this world of hushed urgency, mysterious machines, and tense visitors waiting for word about their loved ones. It seemed too likely to give graphic shape to her fears.

When I walked out of the hospital, it was midmorning. The fog had burned off; it was probably lingering on the coast and up in the canyons, but here the sky was the smog-tinged blue of a typical L.A. day. The parking garage adjoined the main UCLA campus, crowded with bright, good-looking kids eager for summer vacation. I knew that heady feeling, and ordinarily, I'd have been charmed and amused.

I maneuvered my way through the crowded city streets back onto the absolutely jammed Santa Monica Freeway, and headed west to our family home near Arroyo Seco. By now, the adrenaline that had carried me along was gone. I was down to emotional metal on metal, raw nerves and worry. There was the question of what to do with Nick in the long term. If he was seriously impaired, he might require full-time care for the rest of his life. If he recovered, there was a strong risk that he'd go back to his old ways, treatment or not—he'd already been through one rehab program and had started using again the day he got out.

Besides all that, I kept thinking about what Drabyak had implied about the risks of looking under rocks. As far as I knew, Nick's criminal career was limited to small-time dealing. Still, if he owed somebody money or had otherwise crossed them, they might be out for payback.

My other brother and my sister would be no help with any of

that. My mother would try, and she had considerable ability in some spheres, but this wasn't one of them.

The weight was piling on.

As I drove up to my mother's house—the Crandall family's principal homestead, another choice property situated on a cul-de-sac and screened by thick oleander hedges—everything looked pretty much the same as always.

Except for a pair of LAPD motorcycle cops waiting at the driveway entrance—big, stone-jawed guys with Terminator sunglasses, tailored short-sleeved shirts, and knotty biceps that brought the word *steroids* flashing into my mind.

I didn't even have time to wonder what they were doing here. They both came at me fast, the one on the right blocking my way and the other pulling his bike up beside my window.

"Keep your hands where I can see them and get out of your vehicle," he ordered.

I did.

"Put your hands on the hood and spread your feet."

I did that, too, but he stepped up behind me and gave the insides of my ankles each a sharp kick with his boot toe. I spread them a few inches farther.

"You got a driver's license?" he said.

"In my wallet. Left back pocket."

He tugged it out. "How come it's damp?"

"I was swimming earlier."

"Really?" he said, with his tone changed from macho gruff to sardonic. "You always carry your wallet when you go for a dip, Mr.—"

"Crandall." I finished his sentence. "This is my mother's house. My wallet's wet because my brother just almost drowned and I went in after him."

That put a stop to the fun and games, and a long pause told me that he knew he'd stepped in shit and was trying to figure a way out of it. I wasn't inclined to help.

"Okay, you can relax, but wait right here," he said, and this time he added, "sir."

He strode away and handed my license to his partner, who wheeled his bike around and roared off toward the house. Within two minutes, he was back, and the first cop returned my wallet with an air of stiff apology.

"Sorry about that, Dr. Crandall," he said. "The mayor's in there, paying his regards to your mother. We're part of his security escort. Nobody told us you were coming, and, uh, your vehicle doesn't exactly look like it belongs around here."

I nodded curtly. Like Drabyak, they were just doing their job, although he was a class act compared to this smirking schoolyard-bully shit. But I kept my mouth shut. I avoided pissing matches anyway—they were usually pointless, with nothing to gain but a petty ego stroke—and the last thing I wanted right now was to create friction, especially in law enforcement circles.

I got back in the Cruiser and started toward the house. It helped that the mayor—rising political star Joaquin Sandoval—had come to call. That would give my mother a boost.

Much as I loved *her*, coming back to this place where I'd grown up was always a stab to my heart. It was beautiful, even stunning; the long winding drive led through the grounds to an elegant arts and crafts mansion, fronted by a large patio of hand-hewn granite pavestones with a Renaissance-era marble fountain that my great-great-granddad Tom the First had imported from Tuscany. But that was precisely the problem. Like the Malibu property, only more so, it was a monument to wealth and privilege. I couldn't undo my childhood, but I did all I could to distance myself from those aspects of it.

The driveway ended in a parking circle, where two more watchful LAPD cops were waiting beside the mayor's limo. My mother, Audrey, was hurrying across the patio toward me, with Sandoval, my younger sister, Erica, and an old family friend named Hap Rasmussen just behind her. I got out of my car and stepped into Audrey's embrace.

"Oh, Tom," she murmured. The sorrow in her voice said it all. She was close to sixty, her chestnut hair threaded with silver, although her willowy, fine-boned beauty took years off her appearance. She was obviously shaken, but she seemed steadier than I'd feared. Along with the mayor's visit, I was glad that Hap was here. Since my father's death, he was more and more becoming her mainstay.

"Nick's doing okay," I told them. "He's conscious, and his system's strong. They're running tests on him now. With any luck, he'll keep improving."

Audrey let out a long soft breath of pent-up tension, sagging with relief against me. Erica hugged us both, Hap slapped my back, and even Sandoval gave my shoulders a manly clasp.

"What about you?" Audrey said. "It must have been awful."

I kissed her cheek and managed to grin. "It was just like back when I was working the beach, Mama—even made me feel like a young guy again. I could use some decent coffee."

"We've got plenty, dear. Come on inside."

Everybody started toward the house, but Sandoval caught my eye and motioned me to hang back. I knew him only slightly, and only because he was careful to cultivate the acquaintance of big-money families; without doubt, this gesture of concern toward Audrey had the expectation of a campaign check attached.

He'd come up in the barrios, and he was imposing, with a rough-hewn pockmarked face in glaring contrast to the pretty-boy pol look—although he had plenty of that slickness. But he also knew how to turn on a sincere, no-bullshit quality, not that I'd have wanted to depend on it.

"Tom, I've got to get to an appointment—I'm going to sneak out and let you and Audrey catch up," he said. "I'm glad to hear Nick's on the mend."

"Thanks for coming, Your Honor. It means a lot to us."

He glanced around. "I'm not supposed to smoke—it's bad for the image—but I'm dying for one. Bother you?"

"My old man smoked cigars—the house was always full of it," I said. "I know I shouldn't admit this, but I kind of like it."

He shook loose a Marlboro and lit it with a match cupped in one hand.

"Look, this will stay between you and me," he said quietly. "I called the sheriff's department as soon as I heard the news and got hold of that detective you talked to, Drabyak." Sandoval sucked in a deep drag and kept talking through a thin stream of smoke. "I don't see any problem making this disappear. Might be nice if you offered to cover the county and Coast Guard expenses, cut a donation check to Search and Rescue, that sort of thing."

"I'll take care of it ASAP." Along with that check to his campaign coffers.

"Okay. Call me anytime." He ground out the rest of his smoke on a rock ledge, and dropped the butt in the side pocket of his sport coat. "Don't worry. I've got it lined with tinfoil," he said, when he saw my look. "I started getting more careful after I left a spark one time and almost torched myself."

Once burned, twice learned.

As the mayor turned to go, he paused. "By the way, nice work out there, bringing Nick back. It's on the grapevine—cops, search-and-rescue people. You earned yourself a lot of respect."

"It was pure luck," I said.

Mayor Sandoval grinned. "Sure it was."

SIX

On my way into the house I got sidelined again, this time by my sister, waiting inside the door.

"Tommy, I've got this really weird thing I need to tell you," she whispered. Her eyes were flitting around with a deer-in-the-headlights look.

All I could think was, Now what?

Erica, just turned thirty, was the youngest of us four siblings, with me the oldest and Nick and our other brother, Paul, in between. She'd been lucky in inheriting our mother's looks, but she'd come up short on Audrey's grace and canniness; she was good-natured but self-involved, in many ways like an adolescent without much on her mind beyond shopping and partying, although recently she'd gotten engaged to a guy from another wealthy family, and that seemed to be a grounding influence. He was obviously smitten by her looks and probably some quality sack time, but I wondered how much he knew about her otherwise.

Erica had her quirks, including a penchant for inappropriateness, with a case in point being the way she was dressed right now—clingy tank top, a bra that must have been made of gauze, and a very short skirt. Maybe she hadn't known that the mayor and his police escort would be coming by here, but more likely she had. She also liked to sunbathe in the buff around the pool, and she wasn't always careful about it; there'd been a couple of occasions when I'd been here visiting, wandered over that way without realizing she was there, and had to spin an about-face.

"What's going on, Rikki?" I said.

"I'm really, really sorry about Nick. I mean, you know we weren't getting along, but I'd never want anything bad to happen to him."

"Sure, I know that." It was true, although to say the two of them weren't getting along was an understatement. They'd never been close, and the rift had widened over the past years to the point where both of them acted as if the other didn't exist.

"He called me, like, two weeks ago," she said, still whispering. "Then I got this in the mail. The return address is bogus. I checked it." She dug a mailer envelope out of her purse and showed me a DVD disk inside. "It's—" Her hands fluttered like she was trying to catch the right words. "I can't explain. Just look at it—but only like the first minute, okay? And *please* keep it secret." She pushed it at me and hurried away, practically fleeing.

I frowned at it, trying to imagine what this was about. Why would Nick abruptly breach their cold war and contact her? What could make her so upset and furtive? But now wasn't the time to worry about it. I shoved the envelope in a pocket and walked to the dining room with its rosewood banquet table and gaudy chandelier.

My mother was talking on her cell phone, and Hap was at the far end of the room on the house line; no doubt there were calls coming in from well-wishers. Audrey waved me toward the sideboard, spread with fresh pineapple and mangoes, lox and bagels, silver carafes of coffee and hot milk for café au lait. She usually lived a fairly modest lifestyle compared to her peers, but she had no hesitations about amping things up if she felt the need. I'd noticed that she tended to do it when she got anxious, which made perfect sense psychologically. A lot of people found reassurance in spending money, especially if they had plenty of it.

I poured a mug of black coffee and sank into a chair. It felt like the first time I'd stopped moving since this whole thing had started.

"I've left three messages for Paul—nothing back yet," Audrey said to me, putting down her phone with an acerbic look that I was relieved to see. Annoyance meant that her strength was coming to the fore.

Then I set my coffee mug down hard, abruptly remembering that I *did* have an appointment to cancel. I'd spaced it out, but the mention of Paul jarred it loose.

"He's probably at the Lodge," I said.

"He could still return a call from his mother about his brother falling off a cliff and almost dying."

She was right, and it rankled with me, too, but it was just what I'd have expected from Paul. Like Erica, he was on the outs with Nick—the more I thought about it, the more I was realizing that almost everybody was. Like Erica, Paul didn't look far beyond his own pale, and he also had other issues that figured in. He was deeply insecure; it seemed to be in his nature, and it was compounded by a feverish yearning to be a player in the world of L.A. finance and glitz. He was the only one of us kids who'd gravitated toward business. He'd gotten an MBA from Cal Irvine, and since our father's death he'd started managing the family finances. But he didn't quite have whatever it took for the big time, and he never got past the second string. To cover for that, he'd developed a blustery, can't-be-bothered air, always trying to act like he knew exactly what he was doing. But in reality, even small crises threw him and his facade crumbled, which he feared almost pathologically. This situation was a threat in all ways, so he was avoiding it.

I'd long since decided that, what with my three siblings' and my own unadmirable traits—the self-righteous judgments I made about them, for openers—we qualified as a dysfunctional family. But then, I wasn't convinced that there was really any other kind.

"If you get hold of him, tell him to call me, will you?" I said. "I was supposed to go up there and meet him this afternoon, but I'll have to bail."

"Is this about those movie people?"

I nodded.

The family property we called the Lodge—a pristine chunk of near wilderness in the mountains northwest of L.A.—was special to me, the only one of our holdings that I took a strong personal interest in. As a kid I'd spent as much time there as I could maneuver. After Dad's death there'd been some reshuffling of assets, with Paul wanting the Malibu place to build a glossy new house there. I'd much rather have put the land or the proceeds from its sale to some kind of public use. But he was hell-bent, and eventually we'd come up with a compromise I could live with. I would claim the Lodge as a trade-off, then donate that property to a federal or state agency. Paul wasn't any happier about that than I was about his Malibu plans, but I could be stubborn, too. From the time I was young, I'd realized that a surprising number of people had surprisingly firm ideas about who I should be and what I should do—family, teachers, coaches, girlfriends. I'd become quite adept at disappointing them.

Around that same time, Paul had gotten an offer from a film company—an outfit called Parallax Productions—to lease the Lodge as a set. I'd agreed reluctantly, partly to pacify him and boost his ego with a rare business coup, partly because I'd been swamped by our father's passing, the new worries that brought about for Mom, and a few stresses of my own, including breaking up with my girlfriend, moving out of our apartment as a result, and trying to meet the demands of a comparatively new job—in other words, life. It was also true that the Lodge was essentially lying fallow these days, with nobody living there, me being able to visit for only an occasional weekend, and the rest of the family not interested.

A couple of weeks ago, Paul had informed me the set construction was mostly complete and filming about to start; that would take another couple of months. But there was a new wrinkle—Parallax wanted to extend the lease beyond that. Of course Paul had urged me to agree, but I was torn. I didn't want to kick him in the teeth, but I half regretted signing on to the deal in the first place, and I was anxious to get the whole thing out of my hair. I'd come up with another compromise. I hadn't had a chance to get up there since they'd moved in; I'd go look the place over, see how they were treating it and get a general sense of their operation, and make my decision based on that. Paul then invited me to a party there—taking place today.

My mother freshened her coffee and came to sit with me.

"Why don't you just go on up there?" she said. "I'll check in on Nick. There's no need for both of us. I know you—you won't be able to sleep. You'll just prowl around, fretting. Take a nice drive and relax."

She was right again—like most mothers with their children, she usually was. My being gone for a few hours wouldn't make any difference with Nick, my worries about her had backed off, and it would be a relief to get the thing taken care of instead of having it hang over me.

It would also give me a chance to chew Paul's ass about not returning Mom's calls.

"Let me think it over," I said. "I'll check in with you around noon, and if Nick's still doing okay, maybe I will."

"Fine." Then she put her hand on my wrist. "Tom, can you explain what's going on with him?"

I'd been thinking about how to handle this. When I'd first called her earlier, I'd given her an edited version of the story, trying to tone down the immediate shock factor. But she knew the kind of life Nick was living—the problems he'd caused me were nothing compared to her years of heartache—and with Drabyak's hint that there might be deeper trouble in the background, she needed to be on the alert.

"It's pretty much like I told you, Mom, but there are a couple more things you should know," I said.

She sighed. "I was sure there would be. It's such a lose-lose."

I glanced around for Hap; he was off the phone by now, and I wanted him in on this. Hap was clearheaded, shrewd, and essentially one of the family—a lifelong friend of my parents', like an uncle to us kids, and now becoming a sort of surrogate husband to Audrey.

But it wasn't going to blossom into actual romance, since Hap was gay. He kept that part of his life entirely private, and not many people even knew it; on the contrary, women had always drooled over him because of his leonine good looks and broad-shouldered physique. He'd been a terrific swimmer at USC, with a handful of NCAA medals and an Olympic silver for the butterfly leg of the 400-meter medley relay. It was Hap who'd gotten Nick and me into competitive swimming; he'd started coaching us practically as soon as we could walk.

"Hap, why don't you come on over?" I said. "You should hear this, too."

For a second, I was struck by an odd sense of furtiveness in him, almost like he'd been eavesdropping. He was standing at the sideboard with his back turned, but he didn't seem to be doing anything there, and his body jerked slightly when I spoke his name. But that notion was flat-out silly, a product of how wired I was—he'd just been caught up in his own thoughts, and I'd startled him.

"Be right there. I'm looking for my cup," he said. "Ah, what the hell, I'll grab a new one."

But his behavior still seemed odd. When he came to join us, he paced restlessly instead of sitting, and he seemed to avoid eye contact. Of course he was concerned about the situation, but this didn't fit Hap. He usually kept up a calm, genial front that was close to unshakable, and he was guarded about showing deeper emotions, maybe because of his closet life.

Then an explanation occurred to me—he was feeling the guilt that many people get when harm comes to someone they dislike, a sort of reverse schadenfreude. He and Nick were alienated, with a particularly bitter edge that dated back to when Nick and I were in our late teens and Hap was coaching us. Nick had real talent—he'd already far outstripped me—and even Olympic potential. Hap had thrown himself into nurturing it, hoping to relive his own glory days through his protégé.

But Nick pissed all that away, and he'd been a prick about it—the first serious sign that his taking out his anger on safe targets wasn't just childish petulance, but a calculated way of validating himself in his own mind that would become a pattern. Instead of just quitting, which would have been a letdown but acceptable, he'd strung Hap along, pulling stunts like entering important meets, then not showing up, until it became clear that Nick was treating the whole thing—and Hap—as a joke.

The wound went deep.

SEVEN

It didn't take long to give my mother and Hap a more detailed rundown of the events. She handled it calmly; if anything, her take-charge spirit seemed sharpened. Hap remained evasive and didn't say much. Then I left; Audrey wanted to get to the hospital, and I wanted a breather.

With all that had happened, it was still only ten in the morning. If I did go up to the Lodge, I wouldn't leave until early afternoon, so I had a couple of hours. I decided to stop by Nick's place for a look around. Before long I was back on the coast, heading toward Topanga Canyon.

Nick had been simmering with resentment about a number of things, including that our father had cut him off from his trust fund and consigned him to a monthly allowance. The latest sore spot was that the family had evicted him from the Malibu place, which he considered to be his. In fact, he'd been allowed to squat there because the house itself was a worthless albatross, originally built as a beach hangout before the area went so upscale; additions tacked on over time just made it look worse. These days, it fit with the surrounding glitz like the proverbial fish on a bicycle, and it failed to meet modern building codes in just about every way. Our father had resisted mounting pressure from both the city and neighbors to rebuild; he enjoyed those kinds of spats and held out largely just to needle them.

But with our father's death and Paul's takeover of the property, Nick had been forced out, and he was furious about it, especially at Paul. Trying to keep the peace, my mother and I had bought Nick a little 1940s-era bungalow up Topanga Canyon— a compensation that would have made most people weep for joy—with the faint hope that the relative isolation would help keep him out of trouble, or at least make it less noticeable. But he never missed a chance to make it clear that he hated the place, and obviously, our Pollyanna notion fell flat.

I turned off Highway 1 at Topanga and drove the few miles to the bungalow. The area was quiet and private; most of the houses were set back from the road and screened by trees, and the yards and gardens were well tended—except for Nick's. I should have known he'd let things go, but I hadn't been here for a while and hadn't realized how shabby it had gotten. I'd have to arrange for a lawn service. I pulled into the driveway, set the emergency brake, and stepped out to empty his jammed-full mailbox.

Abruptly, the stillness was jarred by the sharp, noisy growl of an engine starting up. It had the distinctive sound of a motorcycle— and it seemed to be coming from behind Nick's bungalow.

I stared in that direction, thinking, What the fuck? The driveway ended in front, with just a pavestone walkway to the rear, and there was nothing back there but a dead end, a small yard that died into a hillside.

Then my gaze was caught by the front door. It was slightly hard to see behind its dark screen—but it looked like it was open.

The motorcycle's noise rose sharply as the rider revved the engine and popped the clutch, and I realized what was going on—the son of a bitch had broken in, heard my car coming, and was now hauling ass out of here.

I dropped Nick's mail and took off running to catch him.

I'd gone maybe only three steps when the bike came into sight, skidding around the rear corner of the house and then springing forward across the weedy front yard. I kept running for a few more steps but didn't even get close; it was already hitting at least thirty miles per hour and cutting away on a diagonal. When it jumped onto the road, the rider opened up into screaming full throttle and blew through the gears.

I spun around toward my car, but then gave it up. He'd be halfway to Highway 1 by the time I could get started. Calling the cops was pointless. I hadn't managed to glimpse the license plate—if it even had one—the rider was wearing a helmet, and all I could tell about the bike was that it was midsize and black.

Not to mention that bringing in the cops was exactly what I wanted to avoid.

I strode on into the house. It had been ransacked, with a window at the back forced open. First guess was that one of Nick's doper buddies had heard about his accident, realized he wouldn't be home for a while, and come to rip off his stash.

There were scumbags, and then there were scumbags.

The house was always a mess anyway, but this was flat-out violent—drawers yanked out and dumped, clothes torn from the closets, the kitchen littered with broken glasses and dishes, the toilet tank lid thrown on the floor. It filled me with helpless anger and deepened the sheer sordidness of the situation.

The intruder probably had gone away empty-handed, since he'd still been looking when I showed up. Nick must have been unusually organized when it came to hiding dope.

Then something occurred to me that I hadn't even thought about until now. As kids, the two of us had been goofing around in our basement, where quite a bit of antique furniture was stored. We'd discovered that one of the pieces, a Queen Anne secretary desk, had secret compartments hidden inside the back panel—a very cool asset for boyish games and contraband. As time went on, and I developed new interests, like girls, I'd pretty much forgotten about it. But not Nick. It was the one item of furniture he laid claim to—no one objected; it was marred and not especially valuable—and he'd moved it first to the Malibu house and then here.

The "why" of that was a no-brainer.

I crouched behind the desk, which had been torn open and rifled like everything else, and slid the panel down a quarter inch to release it. It lifted out to reveal four side-by-side cubbyholes, each a little bigger than a box of checks.

Sure enough, there was his stash—a plastic bag of white powder like the stuff in his car, a few dozen painkillers, and an assortment of other pills I couldn't identify.

Besides the dope, there were two standard plain white envelopes. Neither was sealed, and I could see right off that one was bulging with cash. I pulled the money out, expecting a few hundred bucks in small bills.

Then I rocked back on my heels, with a queasy twisting in my gut. The bills were all hundreds. I made a quick rough count. They totaled close to fifteen thousand dollars.

Nick had never saved a dime in his life; he invariably burned right through his monthly allowance and spent the rest of the month trying to drum up more, cadging from me and probably others. The only immediate explanation I could see was that this was drug money. If so, he was dealing on a much bigger scale than I'd realized. Maybe there was another source, but that didn't make me feel any better—I was sure it wasn't legal.

And maybe *this* was what the intruder had come looking for. If so—especially if Nick owed him the money—he probably wasn't just going to let it go.

The other envelope was thinner; inside were three sheets of

letter-size paper that looked like computer printouts. I stood up and walked to a window for better light to read them by.

This time I was bewildered in an entirely new way.

The top page bore the business logo of a company called GenTell, and started with a heading that read: "Final Certificate of Analysis." After that came boxes labeled "Child" and "Alleged Father," both identified by numbers; a chart of more numbers in columns; and a few paragraphs of explanation. The final line stood out in bold print.

Combined Paternity Index: 99.999%.

It looked like GenTell was a private genetics lab, and this was a paternity test—a DNA analysis confirming the identity of a child's father.

Was *that* what was going on—a woman threatening Nick with a paternity suit? But how would that account for him having so much cash? She'd be demanding money, not giving it to him. Had he amped up his dealing so he could buy her off, and maybe ripped somebody off in the process?

The next two pages made that premise still more confusing. They weren't a continuation of the report, as I'd expected—they were completely separate analyses, almost identical to the first one but with different ID numbers for the children.

I wasn't looking at one paternity test, I was looking at three of them. The kids didn't all seem to have the same father, either—the first two of those ID numbers were the same, but the third was different.

I looked the reports over for another minute or two, but I couldn't glean anything more offhand, let alone guess what Nick was doing with them. Maybe they'd start to make sense when my head was clearer. I pocketed them along with the cash and drugs, replaced the desk panel, then spent a few more minutes walking through the wreckage. I didn't really expect to find any-thing helpful; Nick didn't have a computer or landline phone, and needless to say, he didn't keep any kinds of records. There was some mail scattered around, but it was all junk.

The only item that got my attention was an empty Victoria's Secret shopping bag lying on a closet floor, an almost charming touch amid the gloom. With all of Nick's problems, attracting female company had never been one of them. He liked to drop hints about his studliness; he probably exaggerated, but it was clear that he cultivated a sort of harem, with constant new arriv-als, dropouts, and returns. I'd never met most of his girlfriends or even known who they were, but it also seemed clear that they weren't Suzy Creamcheese types.

A paternity claim or some unsavory spinoff sure wasn't out of the question—and something else to worry about.

I locked up the house and left, figuring I'd come back to-morrow to straighten up and clean out the refrigerator. Outside, I stopped to pick up the mail I'd dropped. Most of it was more junk, flyers, and catalogs—but there was also a statement from Wells Fargo for the debit card he used to draw his allowance.

I took it out and scanned it, just on the chance it might tell me something. Most of the charges were just what I'd have ex-pected—cash withdrawals, merchandise, convenience stores, bars, and restaurants.

But there was one from GenTell, the company that had run the paternity tests, and it was stiff—eighteen hundred and seventy-five bucks.

It looked like the reports were not only legitimate, but Nick had arranged for them himself, and he'd spent a big chunk of his monthly nut doing it. He must have wanted them badly.

EIGHT

I finally made it back full circle to my own place. When I walked in the door I kept right on going to the shower, pulling off my grungy clothes on the way. My outer body had warmed up, but the ocean cold was still in my bones. The hot water felt so good I almost groaned, and I stayed right there while I shaved.

Technically, this was my office. I'd rented it during the interlude after I'd quit my job at Napa State Hospital and before I'd started my current teaching and counseling gig. It wasn't the kind of place you'd expect a psychologist to hang his shingle; it was in the top floor of an old three-story brick warehouse a couple of blocks off Pico north of Culver City. It had gone vacant when the wholesale-furniture business it housed fell victim to outsourcing, and while gentrification was edging close, that hadn't hit here yet. I knew somebody at the company that owned it, and they'd offered me the space with a screaming deal on the rent; they were glad to be getting at least some return, and also just to have somebody there.

Then, about a year ago, my girlfriend and I had parted ways. The breakup itself hadn't been too bad as those things went, but it had slammed me with a realization that had been hard to face. In the course of my training and career, I'd developed an unconscious confidence that I could see into people with an unusual degree of perception. But this time I'd been dense as a rock, and even more about myself than about her.

She'd stayed in our apartment—and I came here to the office to crash until I found another place, sleeping on a foam pad on the floor. Pretty soon, I'd realized that it suited me as well for living as for working. It wasn't zoned residential, so full-time occupancy was technically illegal, but nobody seemed to notice or care, so I figured what the hell and bootlegged in the shower and other basics. I kept a low profile, using the back loading dock entrance in the alley and parking inside. There wasn't much coming and going, just friends occasionally dropping by, and so far, my luck had held.

When I got out of the shower, I was starving. I hadn't felt hungry through most of the day because of my jacked-up nerves, but on my way here from Nick's some internal switch had flipped, and I'd stopped at Barney's in Brentwood to pick up a half-pound bacon-avocado cheeseburger with fries. I tore into them while I was still drying off. By the time I was dressed, they were gone. I spent a minute doctoring up my feet and put on thick cushioned socks; the soles were still a little tender, but now I hardly noticed it.

With the cleanup and food, I was starting to feel like part of the real world again—calmer and not so grim. Nick's situation was worrisome, sure, but I'd been exaggerating the whole thing. His life was permeated with weird elements that I mostly knew nothing about; I'd stumbled onto a few of them that probably weren't even related, and I was weaving that into a sinister tapestry, like a conspiracy theorist. This was sleazy but mundane, and it would all come down to money. If the cash I'd taken from his house belonged to someone else, I'd be glad to hand it over.

I still had a little time left before calling my mother, and I decided to take a look at the DVD that my sister had given me. It had been on my mind all along, feeding my paranoia because she'd been so wrought up and seemed convinced that Nick had something to do with it. But Erica was not a reliable witness, and it would be good to check this off the list. I punched the disk into my player.

The video footage started abruptly and was obviously amateur, shot with a camcorder. A man and woman were frolicking in an indoor Jacuzzi, making out and groping each other. A window behind the tub gave a glimpse outside; it was nighttime, with the lights of nearby houses visible but no indication of where this was. All in all, it looked like a parody of soft porn; the only thing missing was the elevator music.

Except that the woman was Erica, the guy was *not* her prospective fiancé, and although their bodies were mostly submerged, it was clear that they weren't wearing anything but their skins. And it sure didn't look like the action was going to stay soft-core for long.

I clicked off the remote and thought seriously about pouring myself a drink. For most men, confronting a naughty video of their sister would be startling enough, let alone when it was the sister herself who gave it to them.

Well, she had good reason to be alarmed. Other copies could surface; it could even be posted on the Internet—and Erica was about to marry into the kind of old-guard, upper-crust society where people put up an ironclad front of respectability to cover what went on behind it. If this went public, they'd slam the door in her face like she'd come down with the plague.

The obvious questions appeared in my mind like computer pop-ups—but first and foremost was whether Nick was really involved, or Erica was just so freaked-out that she was clutching at somebody to blame.

I picked up a phone and called her. She answered, sounding wary.

"Rikki, that DVD—why didn't you just tell me what was on it?" I said in exasperation.

"I *told* you not to watch more than a minute," she said anxiously. "You didn't, did you?"

"Don't worry. A few seconds were plenty. You didn't know you were being filmed, right?"

"Of course not, are you kidding? I'd never do something like that."

I closed my eyes and rubbed them with my thumb and forefinger, reminding myself that she had an unusual sense of boundaries.

"Okay, give me the story," I said.

The rundown was that she'd gone out clubbing a few weeks ago, ended up at a party with people she didn't know, and met a guy who was cute, persuasive, and happy to share his Ecstasy. That had been enough to tempt her into one last romp before she tied the knot. No one else seemed to notice anything about it; the Jacuzzi was in a private area of the house, and the two of them were alone behind a locked door.

Several days later, the video turned up in her mailbox.

Erica panicked, of course. The obvious first assumption was that she'd been set up for blackmail—maneuvered to the party and lured into the Jacuzzi escapade with the hidden camera placed in advance. But nobody ever contacted her with a demand. She was too scared to go to the police or to confront anyone herself, even if she could have; she didn't know the people who'd hosted the party or anything about the guy except the first name he'd given her, and she had only a vague notion of where the house was. So she'd waited in dread for the bomb to explode, searching her memory for any hint to explain this.

That brought her around to Nick. The day before she'd gotten the DVD, he'd called her—curious timing, especially since he hadn't contacted her in years. It was also strange that he didn't seem to have any real reason for calling; he'd just rambled cryptically until she'd gotten impatient and cut him off. She didn't remember the conversation in detail, but she was sure he hadn't said anything directly connected to the setup.

But he did say something like, "Everybody will get along fine if they stay on their own side of the street," and obliquely hit on that same point a couple of other times.

Erica started wondering if the call was a veiled warning—if Nick was the one who'd set up the video and was letting her know that it would stay secret as long as she didn't cross him. That suspicion got stronger as the days passed without trouble, and while she was still furious and frightened, she felt an odd touch of relief. She had no idea as to what the warning might be *about*, but she hoped it was something she could agree to and head off disaster.

Then came Nick's meltdown, and her panic level shot up again—people would be probing into his activities, and this seamy business might come to light. She finally worked up her nerve and confessed to her eldest brother, imploring me to find a way to keep the lid on.

"It'll be okay, sis," I said, without really meaning it. "Take it easy. I'll be in touch."

I stood there tapping the phone against my thigh and staring at nothing, trying to add this new card to the deck. I wasn't completely convinced about Nick's involvement. A money demand might still come, or maybe someone hated her and intended to publicize the video to damage her life; it could even be a creepy game the party hosts got off on. But that phone call did look bad, and Nick sure seemed to be in full-speed scam mode.

In fact, I'd never known him to be so industrious.

If he was behind the setup, he'd gone to a lot of trouble. Obviously, he expected a payoff. Together with what he'd said to her, that pointed at an ugly new low for him—blackmailing his own sister. I hated to face the thought, but he was probably capable of it. Still, the smoke screen just got thicker. His "Stay on your own side of the street" riff suggested that he wasn't after money—he wanted her not to interfere with something. But she didn't have a clue as to what, and neither did I.

I knew damned well he wouldn't just come out and tell me, and he was an accomplished liar. Prying any reliable information out of him was going to take some doing.

I pushed it all around in my head a little longer but got nowhere except more confused, and I realized I was falling into the rut my mother had predicted—too edgy to sleep but too burned-out to think clearly. I decided to follow through on what she and I had agreed earlier.

If nobody needed me here, I'd drive up to our mountain property this afternoon and meet with the Parallax film people—set this aside for a few hours, then come home to a couple of drinks, a civilized dinner, and a long hard sleep. Tomorrow I'd hit it fresh, figure out how to approach Nick, and try to start putting the pieces together.

But when I called Audrey at the UCLA Medical Center to check on his condition, another wrinkle appeared.

The doctors were cautiously optimistic, she told me. He had a couple of cracked ribs and a fractured elbow, but overall he was still improving and they hadn't found any signs of major damage.

Then she said, "There is one thing. They're not sure, but they think he might have retrograde amnesia. I've never heard of it before—you probably know about it."

I did. Retrograde amnesia was a type of memory loss that sometimes came with brain trauma. Typically, it caused a total blackout about the injury and the time period beforehand, varying from a few hours to much longer.

Nick seemed to fit that pattern. Apparently, he didn't remember anything about what had happened at Malibu—falling over the cliff or even being there—and early indications suggested that his lapse might be on the severe side, extending back for weeks before that.

In itself, retrograde amnesia wasn't usually serious and didn't imply brain damage that would otherwise impair the victim. Often, they recovered some or most of those memories. But not always, and that tended to come slowly over months or even years.

In other words, my chances of getting any useful information out of Nick, at least any time soon, had just taken another dive.

Don't even think about it, I told myself. Time to get out of town.

PART TWO

NINE

Traffic on I-5 north was as thick as this morning's coastal fog, but moving well. Within an hour I was on the gravel Forest Service road that led to our mountain place. I had early memories of making this drive with my parents, back when there was a clear point where the city ended and we'd pass through miles of orange orchards. Now those were mostly gone, eaten up by L.A. sprawl.

But as I got deeper into the forest, that feeling started coming back. The constant urban noise, grinding as a low-level toothache, fell away to silence graced by birdsong. The sky lost its grayish tinge and brightened to a blue that was almost shocking against the green of the mountaintop conifers. Summer's harsh dry heat wasn't yet in full force, and the alpine meadows were sweet with blooms and scent. Above all, you could be alone here in a way that wasn't possible in the city. Of course my head was buzzing about Nick and that situation—there was no way I could stop it—but the peace and quiet were lovely.

That got me thinking about how special the Lodge was and how I wanted to get the Parallax film company out of there—but that would infuriate Paul. Even though he was on my shit list right now, I didn't want another family feud. There was plenty of that going on already.

Beyond all that, I had to admit that I was intrigued by the movie angle—who wouldn't be? I didn't know any specifics about the project itself except a little that I'd gleaned from Paul, but apparently it was a psychological thriller titled *The Velvet Glove*. That added spice, and there was another intriguing kicker.

The head of Parallax Productions—a native Swede named Gunnar Kelso—had been a world-class physicist earlier in his life.

Going from that to filming a thriller seemed like a hell of a career move.

It took another fifteen minutes over the gravel road to reach the turnoff to the Lodge. We kept that unmarked and almost invisible to discourage intruders—just a faint track that seemed to peter out in the pine duff at the nearby tree line. I'd been bracing myself, expecting it to be torn up by the set construction, with constant traffic, heavy equipment, trucks hauling materials and supplies. But I got a pleasant surprise; they'd taken care to groom the terrain and literally cover their tracks. If I hadn't known where to look, I wouldn't even have noticed the extra usage.

Then, as I was making the turn, my gaze jerked upward at a flock of vultures circling overhead. One of them had wheeled sharply and lunged at another, hitting the second bird hard enough to knock it into a dive.

I was so familiar with those vultures, I barely paid attention to them anymore. They were as much a part of the scenery as the cliffs they nested in—ugly snake-necked scavengers with six-foot wingspans, sometimes filling the sky in their search for an easy meal. I'd spent thousands of hours under their hovering presence while I played and daydreamed through long childhood afternoons. Never once had I seen aggressive behavior like that. They might squabble over a carcass on the ground, but in flight they didn't even flap their wings if they could help it. They were gliders, catching rides on the thermal currents until they got where they wanted to go.

I slowed the Cruiser and kept watching them, thinking the

collision must have been a fluke caused by misjudgment or a gust
of wind. But within a minute, I saw another swooping attack. No
doubt about it, the aggression was deliberate.

Maybe this happened with mating or with newcomers trying
to move in on the turf, and I'd just never noticed.

By now I was on the last stretch of the drive, a steep climb up a
ridge with our property lying on the other side—several hundred
acres of cliff-ringed valley that was like a private Shangri-La, a
mix of forest and alpine meadow with a clear granite-lined stream
flowing along the north border. My great-great-grandfather Tom
the First had acquired it under the Homestead Act, a prime example of the rule-bending he excelled at. The government had
expressly designated such land for ranching use, but he'd never
raised a single head of livestock or grown so much as a stalk of
hay there. Instead, he'd promptly built himself a personal hunting lodge, and the place had never been used for anything but
recreation.

When I topped the ridge crest, I stopped and got out to take
a look around, a habit I'd developed long ago. It was an excellent
vantage point, and there'd been a couple of occasions when I'd
gotten forewarning of people down there who didn't belong.

What I saw this time set me back with almost physical force.
The Parallax footprint here was about as subtle as a sonic boom.
The floor of our little valley looked like a FEMA encampment
in the wake of a natural disaster. A security-fenced compound
the size of a football field was crammed with a dozen big trailers,
a couple of semis, boom trucks, cranes, bulldozers, and back-
hoes. The glare of sunlight off all that metal made my eyes smart.
Still, as I looked it over, I had to admit that it was all neat, clean,
and organized—and it *was* what I'd agreed to let them use the
property for.

Beyond the compound, and also surrounded by the security fence, was the set they'd built. It was harder to see, veiled by trees and darkened by the shadow of the cliffs, but it looked at least as big and very bizarre—like a surreal city with clashing architecture and the streets laid out in a twisting maze. The pattern of convolutions seemed to suggest something familiar, and after a few seconds, it came to me—a human brain.

But the single most striking factor was that I was looking at a hell of a lot of money. This was no low-budget project. The construction cost alone must have been staggering, not counting cast and crew, production, and other expenses.

It said a lot about Gunnar Kelso that he was able to put this together, and without major studio backing.

The compound looked deserted; this was Saturday, and filming hadn't yet started. But a dozen expensive vehicles and a few chauffeured limos were parked outside the old log lodge building itself, with several people wandering around nearby. The party was under way.

Then my attention was caught by a man standing alone in the open meadow, a fair-haired, lanky guy wearing a light-colored tunic and loose pants. He seemed to be watching the sky, and while I couldn't quite tell—he was a good quarter mile away— I thought he was holding some kind of small device, maybe a camera. It occurred to me that he might also have noticed the vultures' strange behavior and was filming it.

Even at that distance, just standing there quietly, he gave off a powerful sense of presence. I had a feeling that I was looking at the Parallax head honcho, physicist turned filmmaker Gunnar Kelso.

As if I'd called his name aloud, he swung his gaze in my direction, then raised a hand in greeting. They were expecting me, and he probably realized who I was because Paul would have told them, or more accurately warned them, about the embarrassing old beater I'd be driving.

I raised my hand in return, although it felt a little strange— almost like he was the owner of this place and he was inviting me in.

I climbed back into my ride and started down there. My curiosity about Dr. Kelso and this project was on the rise. I wanted to meet him and try to get a sense of what he was creating here.

TEN

The road dropped down the far side of the ridge and followed the stream through a wooded patch before hooking off to the open meadow where the Lodge stood. This was an especially charming spot, the banks lined with smooth granite boulders and the water dancing along swift and sparkling from spring runoff. Back in the days when you could get away with that sort of thing, Tom the First had built a little stone bridge here that dammed the stream into a deep pond about fifty yards across, an ideal, semi-natural swimming hole.

There was nobody in sight—but a woman's purse of deep red leather was sitting on one of the boulders, standing out like a traffic cone. The raised bank hid my view of the stream along that stretch; probably the purse's owner was nearby, but it made me a little nervous. I decided I'd better make sure nobody had fallen on the slippery granite or had some other kind of mishap.

When I stepped up onto the boulder, I saw that there was no such problem—a man and woman were standing at the water's edge and talking intensely, maybe arguing. They didn't notice me, and my first impulse was to quietly disappear.

But I lingered for a second, captured by the sight of the lady. She looked to be in her early thirties, with long lustrous dark hair, fantastic legs, and tawny skin set off by a lemon yellow sundress.

I knew right away who she was—an actress named Lisa DiFurio. Paul loved to drop names, and she was one of several he'd mentioned as being in the cast, although it hadn't even oc-

curred to me that she'd be here today. Lisa was one of those familiar faces with plenty of celebrity—she'd appeared in several
major movies and played the lead in some smaller releases—but
who'd never quite made it over the edge into big-time stardom.
I didn't know enough about either her or film in general to say
if she was one of those people the camera loved, but right now,
the sunlight and background scenery were definitely calling her
sweetheart.

The man with her didn't exactly shine by comparison; he was
fortyish, unstriking in any apparent way except for an Australian
outback hat that looked straight off the shelf from Orvis. He
seemed to be talking at her more than with her, and his gestures
were impatient. The sound of the rushing water muffled what
he was saying, but I thought I caught the words *symmetry* and
metaphor.

But when Lisa put her fists on her hips and answered, her
voice came across clear as a brick through a window. Her tone
wasn't combative, just exasperated, and laced with humor.

"The audience doesn't *care* about symmetry, Dustin," she
said. "They want to see my tits. *That's* what they care about."

Three was definitely a crowd in this scene, and I was about
to start easing back toward my vehicle. But as Lisa turned away
from the guy, tossing her hair, she saw me. She fixed me with a
cool stare and came walking toward me, stopping about ten feet
away. It looked like she was going to chew me out for eavesdropping, and she wouldn't be any less annoyed if I explained that I
hadn't meant to. I'd still heard what I'd heard.

But instead, she spoke with that same sassy humor. "I thought
I knew all my stalkers. You new on the job?"

Well, well.

"Yeah, first day," I said.

"You better work on your technique. Just walking up in plain sight is pretty pathetic."

"Sorry. I got stage fright and kind of choked."

"Shake it off. It happens to everybody at first," she said. "Just remember what's important. You're obsessed with me, and you love me desperately. The way you prove it is to scare the shit out of me, make my life absolute hell, and maybe try to kill me. And be *creative*—you know, FedEx me a scorpion or something. That's what really turns me on."

Dustin was not amused. He stepped beside her protectively, with a stare at me that was somewhere between challenging and petulant.

"What *are* you doing here?" he said.

I bristled, but this was another pissing match I didn't want to get drawn into.

"I've got a meeting with Gunnar Kelso," I said. "I stopped to make sure somebody was keeping an eye on this purse."

"Oh. You're one of the Crandall people?"

People. I nodded.

"Well, we're going to be shooting a scene on this location, and we need to discuss it in private," he said, still officious but veering away from the bluster where he'd been headed. "Everybody else is over there." He pointed along the road toward the Lodge.

"I can find my way. Thanks."

"Is there anything around here we should worry about?" Lisa said. "I mean, I've heard about mountain lions attacking joggers. It probably sounds silly, but I'm a city girl." Her delivery was a little wide-eyed, over-the-top anxious. Maybe that was just the way she was, but I got the hit that she was having fun with this—more than with the serious discussion I'd interrupted.

There were cougars in this general area, along with bears and rattlesnakes, but they were rare, and by and large they wanted to stay away from humans even more than vice versa. The biggest danger in these woods was ticks, and I seriously doubted that Lisa DiFurio was going to be hiking around in the brush.

"The mosquitoes can get fierce in the evenings," I said. "Otherwise, compared to shopping in L.A., this place is Disneyland."

That was as far as our little sparring match got—Dustin moved in to stake his claim.

"Lisa, can I remind you that we're here for a reason?" he said, exasperated and peremptory. "A very *expensive* reason? Like, making a movie?" He wheeled and walked away.

She rolled her eyes and gave me an apologetic shrug, but she followed him.

ELEVEN

As I parked among the other vehicles, Paul came striding toward me with his brisk, take-charge style. It was an act that tended to fall flat on me anyway, and especially now.

Paul was thirty-three but seemed older, and somehow, he always had; even as a kid, he'd been serious-minded and distant from the goofing off that Nick and I loved. His sandy hair was thinning in a way that his two-hundred-dollar haircut couldn't cover, and the lines in his face were getting deeper. I suspected that his studied self-importance was taking on a life of its own and weighing him down.

He leaned in the Cruiser's window while the engine was still running, looking really uncomfortable and beaded with the kind of sweat that suggested he'd started the day with bourbon on his cornflakes.

"I got the messages about Nick," was the first thing he said, in a raspy whisper. "Nobody here seems to know about it—I'd like to keep it that way, okay?"

"Jesus, Paul." It wasn't hard to believe that would be his immediate worry—just depressing. "Have you called Mom back yet?"

"I haven't had a second, Tom. This is very important business, and these are very important people. I'm busting my ass to stay on top of it."

"That's just bullshit, and you know it. She's eating her heart out over this, so act like a fucking grown-up and spend a couple of your precious minutes telling her you love her and you're there for her."

His face took on a nasty look, like he was about to get into it with me. But then he deflated and shifted his gaze away.

"Sorry—I really am wired," he muttered.

"We all are," I said, a little more kindly. "Just make it right, okay? Now, how about letting me out of the car?"

He stepped back so I could open the door. "So how's Nick doing?" he asked.

"He seems to be in pretty good shape, considering." Given Paul's level of concern, I wasn't about to volunteer any details.

"What the hell *happened*?" he said. "He just flipped out?"

"More or less."

"Has he told you anything?"

"Not yet," I said. "It looks like he might have some memory loss."

"What do you mean?"

"It's a kind of amnesia. He's blank about the accident and awhile before that."

Paul's nervous, shifting eyes seemed to freeze in place for a second or two. He looked stunned, giving an odd impression of a man who'd just been told he'd won the lottery and was trying to believe it. Then this gaze flicked past me, over my shoulder.

"Great—I mean, I'm glad to hear he's doing good," Paul said hastily. "I'll call Mom, I promise. But here comes Gunnar."

I turned. I'd guessed right—the man who'd been standing alone in the meadow was walking toward us.

Gunnar Kelso seemed to be around sixty, but that might have been off by years either way; he was one of those men who'd probably looked about the same for decades and would for the rest of his life. He was handsome in a rugged Viking way, lean-jawed and glacial-eyed. But most striking was that presence. It was hard to describe, but it was something I'd first started becoming aware of with a few of my professors at Stanford. They clearly thought well of themselves, with good reason; groundbreaking research was the norm, and if they didn't already have a Nobel or Templeton or other such accolade, they were in the running. But they never wore it on their sleeves—they had no interest in that. Their minds operated on a different plane, and that was where they focused.

Still, Kelso wasn't short on down-to-earth charm. He gave me a craggy smile and a firm handshake.

"A pleasure to meet you, Tom," he said. "I hope you're not too appalled at what we've done to your beautiful property. I assure you we'll restore everything carefully." His English was excellent, with just a trace of Nordic accent and the slightly formal usage of an educated European.

"No, it looks to me like you've got that under control," I said. "Although I admit, there's a lot more—stuff—than I'd imagined."

"Quite so. I've discovered that making a film is a journey that requires a great deal of baggage. If you do see anything you don't approve of, by all means tell me and I'll do my best to set it right. If you're interested, I'd be glad to give you a quick tour of our set. And I confess to an ulterior motive—Paul has told me that you're a psychologist, and I'd value your opinion on a question regarding our project. It's better shown than described."

Was I interested? You bet. Of course this was another dose of Kelso's calculated charm; he wanted my agreement on the lease extension and was courting me by offering a gesture of respect. But that was fine; I was long past any illusions that people would like me just for myself. He was handling it gracefully, and at least he'd taken the trouble to make it more than just a sop—it implied engagement and even challenge. I wasn't much of a gamesman in the usual ways, but I was already sure that I'd enjoy a round with this fascinating man; no doubt I'd come out humbled but entertained, and maybe learn something in the process.

"I don't know that I can be much help with your question," I said. "But sure, I'd like that."

Paul had stayed quiet through all this; he seemed to be somewhat awed by Kelso. But he also seemed to have turned antsy, and when he did speak up it wasn't in his usual pushy way, but to extricate himself.

"I'm going to let you guys get acquainted," Paul said, with a glance at Kelso as if asking permission. "There's a bar and buffet inside, Tom—come on in when you're ready." He hurried toward the Lodge, back on task again, whatever the task was.

"Yes, why don't you go relax?" Kelso said to me. "I've lunched already, and I have a few minor things to take care of. Shall we meet here again in half an hour?"

I told him that sounded fine; he headed off and I walked to the Lodge, a dignified old building that was expertly built of massive fir logs squared off and precisely dovetailed at the corners. It had half a dozen bedrooms and a spacious main den with a high vaulted ceiling, huge stone fireplace, and trophy big game heads mounted on the walls. As I climbed the porch steps, I saw through the windows that there were a dozen people inside, chatting or cruising the buffet tables.

Then, just as I was reaching for the doorknob, I glimpsed Paul. He was off in a corner apart from the group, talking intently with a woman. Presumably, that was what he'd been in a hurry to do.

But wondering about the why of it blew right out of my mind, because his hand was resting on her rump.

I made an abrupt turn aside from the door, walked to the far end of the porch, and stood there, trying to get my mind around this new development.

Paul was married, with a three-year-old daughter.

TWELVE

After a minute or so, I walked back to the door and on into the room. The first thing that hit me was how goddamned attractive these people were. They must have been cast members; the men were hunky in that slightly bratty young-actor way, the women like icons of sheer beauty, all of them glowing with health and confidence. It drove home the point that I was in movieland, a world as alien to me as another galaxy.

Paul was still talking with his female friend, although he'd removed his hand from her behind, and he waved at me to come join them. She had more of a cool businesslike look than the other guests, and she was older—probably a couple of years older than Paul. But she was very attractive, with auburn hair cut to her jawline and a trim, almost boyish figure that she obviously took care to keep that way.

"Tom, Cynthia Trask," Paul said. "CFO of Parallax Productions. Believe me, you don't want to play poker with her."

She laughed disarmingly and said, "Oh, he's just a sore loser." But her eyes never changed, and they were eyes that measured things carefully. She knew how to get what she wanted. Apparently, what she wanted was Paul, and what she was measuring was me.

"I have to trust him on that one, Cynthia," I said. "He's a good cardplayer."

"I think she hides an ace in her bra." Paul gave me a hammy wink.

She rolled her eyes. "As if I'd need to."

"Next time, I'm going to check," he said, and slipped his hand around her waist.

That settled one question. I'd thought maybe my earlier glimpse had caught them in an unguarded moment, and the affair was secret. But this was an unmistakable signal. Paul wanted me to know.

They both watched me closely, probably expecting me to react with shock or disapproval. It was damned awkward, for sure.

I said nothing. They were consenting adults.

But privately, I was more concerned than I let on. I admitted that my take was cold, but also realistic, steering clear of moral judgments. I felt vaguely bad for Paul's wife, but I didn't have any loyalty issues there. I'd never cared for her—she was snobby and uninteresting—and the feeling was more than mutual; she had a near phobia about me and my offbeat lifestyle, and she'd done her best to widen the gulf between Paul and me. Cynthia Trask was a sharp contrast, and I even felt a touch of wishing him well. For all his worldly airs, he hadn't dated much before he'd gotten married, and I was sure he'd never tied in to anything like her. It looked like he was in for a head-spinning ride.

If this was just a fling, that was that. But if it turned out to be more—especially if they intended to get married—the situation changed dramatically. Besides all the emotional upheaval—including his little girl, who I *would* feel bad about—a divorce would be very expensive. The bulk of the Crandall fortune was in stable long-term holdings, but Paul still controlled tens of millions in more liquid assets that might be vulnerable to transfer of ownership or litigation. If Cynthia was digging for gold, it could get a whole lot more expensive still.

I wasn't going to make such an assumption about her so hastily and with no evidence, and things could even turn out the other way around—that she'd be a shrewd partner in the family business and rein in Paul's often-questionable judgment. But I decided I'd have a private word with our lawyer to get him thinking about potential consequences.

"By the way, Tom, nobody else knows about us outside this circle," Cynthia said, indicating the room with a turn of her head. Presumably, that meant people associated with Parallax—and she was also including me. That gave me a hint as to why they were telling me at all. It was a sort of preemptive strike. They, or more probably Cynthia, figured that trying to draw me in was a better bet than having me stunned and angry when the news dropped on me from some other source.

Then Paul threw me another curve, a first inkling that he had another new passion besides Cynthia—that his involvement with Parallax went much deeper than straight business. He leaned toward me confidingly, with the air of someone passing on weighty and privileged information.

"See, Tom—awhile ago I started feeling like I had to do something with my life besides just make money," he said. I managed not to wince. "Then I met Cynthia, and she'd been in the same place. She introduced me to Gunnar, and—well, the work he's doing is really important. Parallax is about a lot more than making movies."

"How so?"

"I'll let her explain. She's been with Parallax a lot longer."

Cynthia didn't show the same recent-convert fervor as Paul; she'd probably made this same pitch many times, and it was more like, *This is how it is—take it or leave it.*

"It's impossible to really explain," she said. "You have to spend time around Gunnar—then it just starts to come to you. But basically, when he was at the Planck Institute years ago, he started trying to integrate philosophy with his research—not just theoretically, but in terms of real life. The mainstream scientific community didn't like it, and they hounded him out. But he kept going on his own, and he finally made a breakthrough. Do you know quantum mechanics, Tom?"

"I took some physics a long time ago, and I wasn't much good at it. I remember a few basics, but that's all."

"Atoms and molecules have electrons orbiting around the nucleus, right? They're constantly bombarded by quanta, tiny bundles of energy. If an electron absorbs enough of them, it jumps to another orbit—a quantum leap. Gunnar realized that it's the same in our lives, except the energy is personal power. We can learn to accumulate it and make our own quantum leaps."

"It's *science*," Paul interrupted emphatically. "That's the key."

Huh.

My first hit was an obvious one—that this had a cultlike ring. I was reasonably familiar with cult mentality in general and with several specific variations. I'd encountered all that fairly often both in clinical work and with the college kids I counseled, and it tied in to one of my major interests, the strange psychology of cognitive dissonance. Quasi-scientific spins weren't unusual in cults, especially in the more sophisticated ones. My own take on that tended toward cynical; by my lights, the object was precisely what Paul seemed so enraptured by—to give members a sense of superiority because they weren't buying into not just unfounded and often outlandish beliefs, but an intellectual system.

But the quantum physics angle was new to me, and at first glance it did seem to have some logic, backed by Kelso's impressive credentials. He sure didn't come across as the kind of messianic raver that tended to crop up in that field.

Then again, first glance also brought up a string of questions, starting with just what this "personal power" was, along with how you were supposed to acquire and apply it.

But before I could ask anything, Cynthia ended the conversation, nudging Paul with her elbow.

"Let's quit babbling—Tom's supposed to be enjoying himself," she said.

"Right, right," Paul agreed. "How about a drink, Tom? *I'm* ready."

"Not just yet. Thanks."

"Dig into the buffet, then. It's a choice spread."

It was certainly that—caviar, pâté de foie gras, prosciutto, iced bowls of giant prawns, a dozen exotic side dishes; a steam table with grilled salmon, prime rib, and coq au vin; and a full bar with a wine selection that looked like it came from the Palms.

Tempting as it was, the burger I'd wolfed a couple of hours ago was holding me fine. I wasn't about to have a drink, either. Paul's involvement with Cynthia was troubling enough, but the double whammy of that and Parallax, with the two deeply intertwined, raised a serious red flag. I wanted my radar as sharp and clear as I could keep it.

Well, coming here had accomplished what I'd hoped for— taking my mind off Nick and Erica.

THIRTEEN

I poured myself a glass of sparkling water and stayed at the fringes, in the kind of fly-on-the-wall observer role I'd often found useful in my work. What I gleaned was oddly comforting. None of the usual cult signs showed in any obvious way—no sense of passiveness, constraint to obedience, or a rigid moral code. Nobody approached me in that phony friendly way that was a lead-in to proselytizing. The conversations were bright-toned, the behavior energetic; alcohol flowed freely, and I suspected there were other party drugs around; and there was plenty of openly sexual flirting.

If Parallax *was* a cult, there was probably a waiting list to get in.

Then, after a few minutes, Lisa DiFurio came stalking through the door.

Dustin, the outback-hatted man she'd been with, walked in behind her, but it was clear that they weren't together; he had a sulky expression, and she was pointedly keeping her back to him. Apparently, the tone of their conversation had not improved. She didn't waste any time getting to the bar and grabbing a glass of Pouilly-Fuissé.

She wasn't the prettiest face in the room—mouth a little wide, nose thin and aquiline, cheekbones almost harsh—but she had a sensuous quality that glowed like a fire in a roomful of fluorescent lamps. The other women knew it; I caught several cool sidelong glances at her as she passed. That was oddly comforting, too. The Parallax philosophy wasn't putting any damper on plain old jealousy.

Then Lisa did the last thing in the world I'd have expected—walked over to me.

"I'm hoping you're the one person here who won't talk about film or art," she said. "Or God forbid, film *as* art. Deal?"

"That's easy. I don't know anything about either one."

"*I* do—he's been lecturing me about it all morning. I feel like a torture victim. Every time he said the word *nuance*, it was like needles under my fingernails, and he said it a lot."

"I couldn't help noticing that the two of you seemed to have a difference of opinion," I said.

"We sure do. He thinks he's going to get laid." She sipped her wine, looking as nonchalant as if she'd just mentioned that she enjoyed sailing.

Dustin had been watching us all this time; he was clear across the room, and he couldn't have heard, but from his glowering face, he might as well have.

"Who is he?" I said.

"Dustin Sperry—the director. I'm Lisa."

"I know. Tom Crandall."

"Nice to meet you, but let's go back to the 'I know.' Is it a good 'I know' or a bad 'I know'?"

"It's just from seeing your movies, and I confess I haven't seen them all," I said. "What I have seen, I liked a lot."

"Then you definitely haven't seen them all—I believe you there. But we're not going to talk about film, right?"

"Sorry. Short attention span."

"So what did you like? About the ones you saw?"

I grinned. "Mostly the nuances."

"Prick. I was just starting to trust you, and you twist the

knife." Then her gaze darted off to the side. "Heads up," she whispered. "Here comes Chris, high as the moon on mushrooms and ego."

The guy she was talking about was a real hunk, with shaggy blond hair, teeth so white they could blind you, and a suntanned, chiseled physique. He was the one other face in the room that had seemed most familiar to me, and now I made the connection—he was Chris Breen, a hot young action-adventure star. Several of the babes were hovering around him with their body language saying it all; he seemed not just used to that, but oblivious to any other possibility. He was also obviously stoned out of his skull. As he walked toward Lisa and me, he actually gave the impression of floating, and I was sure that his wide, dancing eyes were seeing things I wasn't.

He managed to focus on us, looking mysterious and a little perturbed. "I'm starting to feel the *nahngs*—I've got to chill out," he said. Then, to me, "Dude, somebody said this is your place. Anywhere good to go swimming?"

"Go out to the road you came in on and head back a quarter mile, just past that little bridge," I said. "There's a pool in the creek—where you were earlier, Lisa."

"Excellent. How about it, Leese?"

"Sorry, Chris. Swimming's not my thing. But I'm sure you'll have plenty of company."

His eyes went back to that glitter of seeing into another dimension. "Hey, yeah, like—water nymphs!" He returned to his harem, this time moving more purposefully.

"Water nymphs," Lisa murmured wryly. "It'll be more like the beach at Rio—Brazilians everywhere you look."

I smiled again. "His riff about—what did he call them, *nahngs*? Did that actually mean anything?"

"Sort of. It's *Nhangs*, capital N-h. They're in the movie. The part about him *feeling* them's in the mushrooms. Hey, are you leaving here anytime soon—like back to L.A.?"

"As soon as I can. I'm supposed to have a talk with Dr. Kelso, but I wouldn't think it'll take too long."

"Could I follow you to the freeway? When I was coming in, I saw one of the limos ahead and just tagged along the last few miles—I wasn't really paying attention, and I'm afraid I'll get lost."

"Of course," I said. "You really want to miss the rest of the party?"

"I'm not much of a party girl these days. I did my share of it, back when. And Dustin's just waiting to corner me again."

"I've got a feeling you can handle him. But yeah, sure—I'll come look for you when I'm done."

"I'll be right around here. Unless I kill him first."

"I'll hurry. I wouldn't want that on my conscience."

That wry look came back onto her face, but with more of an edge this time—like a beautiful cat with a glossy coat that you yearn to touch, even though you know there are fangs and claws attached.

"Not much conscience in this business, honey," she said.

FOURTEEN

By now a half hour had passed; it was time to meet up with Kelso. I found him outside chatting with Chris Breen's swimming party. They were loading a couple of car trunks with iced coolers of drinks and urging Kelso to come along. He had the amused look of a parent dealing with a bunch of kids who were up to harmless mischief. There did seem to be a summer-camp element about it.

"Not just now—I'll wander by later," I heard him say. He didn't seem inclined to bask in the adulation that came his way, although he clearly didn't mind it, either.

When he saw me, he split away from the group, and the two of us started walking. I followed his lead; it looked like he was taking us toward the bizarre city set.

"Does our party seem bacchanalian to you?" Kelso said.

"No, it actually strikes me as pretty tame, at least from what I've seen so far."

"It will get livelier, I assure you. I don't care to drink much or use drugs myself—they impair my thinking. But I don't see it as my role to play nursemaid to my associates, and it would be futile to try. I insist only that they stay within safe limits."

"Associates" was an interesting choice of words. He'd also tacitly confirmed his authority in a way that went far beyond the mechanics of making a movie.

"I don't want to play nursemaid either, but I hope nobody's going to get hammered and drive back to L.A.," I said.

He shook his head. "We're very careful about that sort of thing. Some of them will stay here for the night; there are chauffeurs and designated drivers for the others."

We reached the security fence that surrounded the set—eight-foot-high chain-link angled out at the top and monitored at intervals by cameras on stalks. There was a kiosk for a guard outside the main gate, but it was vacant, presumably considered unnecessary today with all the people around. Kelso opened the gate, a complicated procedure that required inserting an electronic key card and punching a numbered code. Parallax didn't want anybody inside that fence who didn't belong there. The gate closed behind us automatically, and I got a memory flash of places like the Napa state hospital. There was a sense of finality—once you were in, you were in.

"I'll activate some of the features," he said, stepping into a trailer. "When we film we'll use auxiliary lighting and other effects, but this will give you an idea."

While I waited, I scanned what I could see of the actual set, which started a hundred feet ahead. Besides the clashing architecture and deliberately seamy construction, it was darkened to twilight by the shade of the cliffs.

The effect was striking and a little eerie—then, abruptly, it got eerier still. The ground started to exude a soft luminescent glow, enhancing the surreal hues. Dim lights appeared in windows and along the narrow streets; inside toward the center, I glimpsed the flash of a neon sign. Indistinct shapes seemed to be moving in the shadows.

The sense was that the city had its own subtle life.

Kelso came back a minute later, and we started toward it, crossing from sunlight into the darker, cooler artificial dusk.

"We've tried to bring together several elements in this

project," he said. "One is the detective-noir genre—I'm a great fan. Yourself?"

Well, here was another intriguing facet to the scientist-philosopher-filmmaker.

"I don't know a lot about it, but some," I said, with the feeling that I'd already said that a lot today and I probably wasn't done yet.

"What interests me most about it are the true-to-life ambiguities. No one is all good or bad, nothing can be trusted, the hero must battle his own weaknesses, and so on. That's the overall context we're working in."

As we entered the grounds of the city's first major structure, a faux-marble ancient temple, I tried to get a fix on the noir aspect. The general ambience fit the bill and even went over the top—but how did the temple, with neighbors like a jungle village and a street with a futuristic sci-fi look, fit in?

"The design doesn't seem exactly traditional," I said.

"It reflects the nature of this place," he said. "It's like our own world in many ways, but also merges into otherworld and the realm of dreams. The unexpected is everywhere; it's dangerous, but exciting and alluring. Shall I give you a sketch of the story?"

"Please."

"It begins with a young soldier on a reconnaissance patrol," Kelso said. "He falls into an ambush, an explosion knocks him unconscious, and he awakens in this place. Right away, he encounters a ravishing woman."

That would be Lisa DiFurio, with gallant Chris Breen as the soldier.

"But then she's suddenly abducted by a band of creatures called *Nhangs*—treacherous, vicious shape-shifters," Kelso went on. "He tries to save her, but he's overpowered. From there he's thrown into the role of the detective-noir figure, searching for her through a series of adventures, continually finding her and losing her again. He comes to realize that he's in a sort of maze, and the adventures are tests where he wins or loses power. Each time, he ends up back at the center, with the bartender dispensing advice."

Kelso pointed ahead at the flashing neon sign I'd noticed. Now I could see that the place was a tawdry tavern, and the sign read THE VELVET GLOVE—the film's title. Along with it was a logo of a black-gloved hand raising a martini glass. At first glance, this seemed as traditionally noir as it got, right out of Chandler and Hammett.

Then I realized that the bit of wrist protruding from the glove had a metallic gleam—the proverbial iron fist—and that the glass stem it held between thumb and forefinger was actually a long, slender human neck, which it appeared to be toying with, perhaps about to snap. The upper part of the glass wasn't exactly a face, but it was skillfully twisted in a way that suggested a sense of angst.

Wow.

I metaphorically scratched my head at this curious blend—a familiar quest-type story line, a structure that suggested certain board and video games, an alternative universe setting imbued with Freudian-Jungian concepts of underlying consciousness, all with noir overtones, including a bartender making sage remarks while he polished the glasses.

Whether that would fly at the box office, I couldn't begin to guess.

Now we were coming to the tall columned entrance of the temple itself. The interior was dark, flickering with low firelight at several places—and as my eyes adjusted, I realized that fine white mist was swirling in the air.

"This is another important site in our story," Kelso said, stepping inside. "The home of an oracle like at ancient Delphi—a priestess who foretells destinies. It's our single most lavish set."

I followed him in. The mist, rising from a ragged narrow chasm in the stone floor, gave the sense of being in a sauna; it wasn't that hot, but warm enough to bead my face with sweat, and it had a pleasantly pungent aroma like eucalyptus.

I recalled once reading somewhere that the vapor at Delphi was believed to have mystical properties that gave the sibyl her visions, and that she induced them by straddling the chasm to absorb the vapors vaginally. I'd never run into any evidence to back that up, and this mist, of course, was artificial. But it definitely had penetrating power—I could feel the sharp aromatic tingle reaching deep up into my sinuses like a menthol cold medicine.

Then Kelso gave the conversation a twist that had an eerie feel to it, as if we were edging into this world ourselves.

FIFTEEN

"I mentioned a question I'd like to ask you—it has to do with the story's outcome," Kelso said. "You're experienced in how people think, and you're not bound by the conventions of the film world."

I shrugged. "Sure." I seriously doubted he was really looking for advice—so what was this about?

"The script is essentially settled—we'll probably make minor changes as we film. But I'm not satisfied with the ending. As it stands, we've gone with the opinion of experts who agree that a feel-good triumph would be best for marketing purposes. But I'm a stubborn Swede, and I'd prefer the two-edged approach of noir—the victory has tragic overtones.

"In my view, the hero is faced with a final dilemma. He can leave this hazardous existence and go on to a safe and pleasant future. Or he can stay, but no longer as a pawn. He'll become a master, one of those who battle to control this world. His power will be greatly heightened; he may be able to accomplish much good. But he also may be forced to do harm, and his danger continues—including defeat that could cost him everything."

Kelso paused, apparently waiting for a response.

"What happens with the woman?" I said.

His head moved in a slight nod, as if that was what he'd expected me to ask.

"That adds to the tension," he said. "She must make the same choice. But they're separated, with no chance to talk about it—

each can guess only what the other will do. To me, the most intriguing resolution would be for the man to choose safety because he thinks that will be *her* choice—but instead she does just the opposite, and they lose each other forever." He gave me another glance like he was gauging my reaction, but this time he went on talking.

"So, my question," he said. "In your opinion, would that also intrigue viewers, or would they be repelled by it?"

I needed a moment to think about that, and the heat and pungent mist weren't helping; I was almost starting to feel dizzy.

"I'm going to step outside and cool off, Dr. Kelso," I said.

"Oh, yes, sorry. The vapor is a bit stifling—we're trying to make the set appear authentic."

A pretty, steamed-up priestess in a clingy gown probably wouldn't hurt in terms of audience appeal, either.

I walked out into the courtyard and stayed in the shade of the columned portico. As the light breeze cooled my skin and the eucalyptus fragrance faded, my mental gears started to mesh again.

The scenario that Kelso described was similar to a classic type of psychology experiment known as the prisoner's dilemma; there were numerous variations, including more complex ones called *n*-dilemmas. The basic premise was along the lines that subjects could achieve a mutual goal—like escape—by cooperating, but they forfeited any personal rewards. If they acted in their own self-interest instead, they might gain personally, but everybody stayed in the slammer—which made the rewards less enjoyable or even worthless.

Kelso had to know I'd recognize that, and now it seemed that his "question" was a byzantine way of putting me to that test. I started wondering if this was really about Parallax—if he was sizing me up to see if I'd be suitable material for them.

"Well, I'm sure you've already heard this opinion," I said. "Most people want to identify with heroes, and feel that they'd do the brave thing—go for the risk and power."

"So if our hero backed away, he'd be seen as cowardly and let the audience down?"

"A lot might depend on how you handled it. But if he doesn't do what a hero's supposed to do, then yes, I'd say it's a hard sell—no matter how smart and noble his reasons might be. A factor you'd have to overcome, anyway."

"And yet we have the great noir examples that end with similar disappointment. *The Maltese Falcon*. The incomparable *Chinatown*."

I shook my head slowly, reaching back into my memory. "That takes me even farther out of my league. But as I recall, those guys don't exactly back off. They give it their best shot, but at the end they realize they've been *had*, and there's just nothing more they can do."

Kelso gave me his approving, raised-eyebrow look. "I think I was right in judging you as a professional, Tom." Cryptic as that seemed, he didn't elaborate. "I'll be glad to show you around more if you'd like, but I don't want to keep you."

"I'd love to, Dr. Kelso, but I think I'd better get back to L.A."

We recrossed the temple grounds in silence, with Kelso apparently ruminating. My gaze wandered skyward, and I glimpsed a couple of the vultures. They were circling lower and tighter now, like they were zeroing in on a carcass; I couldn't tell if they were still fighting. I thought about asking Kelso if that was why he'd been watching them, but then he spoke.

"There is another option for the ending, of course," he said.

"Not as noir, but not entirely feel-good, either. Hero and heroine do stay together—because they both take the risk."

"I'd guess that would be a better crowd pleaser," I said.

With plenty of room for ambiguity—and somewhere in the mix, the treacherous, shape-shifting *Nhangs*. Whatever the hell *that* was all about.

SIXTEEN

When we got to the security gate, Kelso said he hoped I wouldn't think he was being rude, but he needed to stay there and take care of some work. We wrapped up our meeting with cordial good-byes. He'd never mentioned the lease; maybe he figured that his job was to impress me, and he'd leave the business dealings to Paul. That was fine with me—I wanted time to digest all this.

I walked on alone to the Lodge. When it came into sight, I got a pleasant little jolt—Lisa was sitting on the porch steps, reading a bound sheaf of papers that I assumed was a script. Her bright yellow dress stood out like the sun.

But as I got close I could tell that she seemed subdued, without her earlier sparkle. Her shoulders were hunched, her overall posture tense; she didn't glance up until I was right in front of her, and when she did, her smile looked forced.

I wondered if she'd gotten into it again with Dustin Sperry. I'd half expected him to still be hanging around her, but I didn't see him.

"What happened to your admirer?" I said.

"I convinced him he'd have more fun with the water nymphs than with me."

"It didn't take him long to get over you."

"Oh, he'll be back. He's one of those guys who can't stand dealing with a woman until he's fucked her."

It seemed clear that she'd already told him to go fuck him*self*, maybe not in quite those words but still in ways that would make most men's testicles shrivel.

"Why do you put up with it?" I said.

She held up the script and gave it a fierce shake. "This. I've got a lot riding on it. Like my career and the rest of my life."

"It's that important?"

"Where I'm at in the game, yeah."

I finally caught the drift of what she was getting at.

"Are you saying he could fire you?" I said.

"Not straight-out fire. But he's a good director, and he's got a lot of clout. He could put on pressure to get me replaced—tell people I was hard to work with, I wasn't turning out right for the part, all that." She tucked the script into her purse. "I'm feeling kind of bitchy, in case you haven't noticed."

"Maybe just worn down?"

"Maybe. Are we ready?"

"Anytime," I said.

She slung the purse over her shoulder and came down the steps. I walked with her to her car, a surprisingly modest bronze Lexus with smoked windows—she probably figured she was highly visible enough without driving something flashier—and opened the door for her, rewarded by a warm glance and a glimpse of tawny thigh.

Then, as I turned toward the Cruiser, I was hit by a ripple of euphoria so intense it made my scalp tingle. It came on suddenly out of nowhere, lasted ten or fifteen seconds, and then receded.

But came from where? I hadn't touched a drop of liquor since my usual couple of after-work drinks last evening; when I was younger I'd sampled some recreational drugs, but never much and not for years; and this wasn't like any of that, anyway. It didn't disturb my mental clarity in the slightest and left no other effects. True, it was pleasant to meet a woman who was both beautiful and interesting, and to spend even a few minutes in her company. But this was much more than pleasant and much more an actual sensation—a rush of pure pleasure.

The only explanation that occurred was that it was a sort of reverse-stress reaction—I'd gotten worn down, running on minimal sleep with the strain of Nick's situation and my new worries about Paul, and my system was compensating in this odd way instead of a more typical slippage. I didn't know if that made sense, but considering the result, who cared?

I got into the Cruiser, lit it up, and started away with Lisa following. Nobody seemed to be paying any attention to us.

Except, I realized abruptly, for Paul's girlfriend—Cynthia Trask.

I hadn't noticed her until now. She was sitting in the property's gazebo, built around the same time as the Lodge and sited on a small rise that gave a good view all around. Paul wasn't with her, and no one else was anywhere nearby. There was no doubt that she saw Lisa and me leaving together; she was looking right at us.

But what struck me most was her posture—leaning back, relaxed, with her legs crossed and her forearms resting on the chair arms, like a queen on her throne. As we passed, she smiled and raised one hand, a gesture that didn't seem so much a wave as a benediction, acknowledging her subjects and allowing them to go on their way.

I recalled that I'd had a similar feeling about Kelso when I'd first seen him as I came in. It was something else going on in my subconscious, I decided; I was feeling defensive about the property, unhappy with myself about the way I'd handled this arrangement, and I was childishly casting around for someone else to blame.

Lisa and I drove on, reaching the stretch of road that ran close to the pool where the swimming party had headed. A dozen or more of them were sunbathing on the granite rocks or frolicking in the water, and like she'd said, there was plenty of skin on display. It did look like not entirely innocent fun, and I had to admit there'd been a time when I'd have hankered to join in. But that sort of thing didn't interest me anymore. Much, anyway.

Then I spotted Dustin Sperry, which was easy because he was still wearing that hat, about the only article of clothing in the mix. He was sprawled on the bank, flanked by a pair of lounging beauties.

The strife between him and Lisa was none of my damn business, but I sure didn't like what she'd told me, and this irritated me further; it somehow seemed to underline the contemptuous way he was treating her and the general arrogance I'd sensed in him.

Then, quick as an explosion, my annoyance flared up into violent anger. It was so intense, so focused on him, that I lost track of driving and the Cruiser started to swerve off the road. I had to hit the brakes hard, and so did Lisa; mercifully, we weren't going fast and she was following at a safe distance.

I sat there shaking my head hard, trying to clear it. The surge washed away as suddenly as it came, but it still left me with a strange feeling like a lingering, unpleasant mental aftertaste.

My glance caught my side rearview mirror, and I saw that Lisa was leaning out of her window, looking at me warily.

Well, *that* was a classy way to impress a lady.

I let out my breath and made the best I could of it, waving back at her, then circling my thumb and forefinger for *all okay*. She nodded cautiously.

Physician, heal thyself, I thought as we drove on. With the sudden onslaught of all the bullshit, I hadn't been paying attention to my own head, and it was playing tricks on me in a way that was brand-new. I must have been considerably more stressed-out than I'd realized. I'd have to put my internal watchdog on alert, although that was easier said than done.

SEVENTEEN

Lisa stayed behind me for a while after we got on the highways, but before long we were separated by traffic; the closer to L.A. we were, the more it increased, like a rain-swollen stream turning into a raging river. When I realized she was gone, I felt a stab of loss. Every time I'd glanced in my rearview mirror and seen her there, I'd gotten a sweet little kick. I liked her—she seemed smart, witty, tough but good-humored, and her brassy way of calling things the way she saw them was delightful.

I assumed she was in with Parallax, but she obviously had an independent streak and didn't feel constrained by group pressure; she'd shot down Chris Breen without batting an eye, besides driving up there by herself and leaving when she damn well pleased.

But the only way I was ever likely to see her again was on-screen. It had crossed my mind to ask for her phone number—she wasn't wearing a ring, she didn't give the sense of being seriously involved with anyone, and I even imagined that she'd felt a little spark herself. Then again, our worlds were far apart, and no doubt mine would quickly bore her. I already had plenty on my mind without chasing a pipe dream, anyway.

That downer brought back the grinding reality of Nick's situation. Despite my intentions to shine it on for the rest of today, it wasn't going to leave me alone. I was on I-405 now, not all that far from UCLA. I decided to stop in at the hospital and see how he was doing.

The upper-level ICU was a secured area, and getting in required clearance via intercom. When I checked in at the nurses' station, they assured me that Nick was maintaining well—and gave me a note, a message from the clinical lab, asking me to call Dr. Ivy Shin. I hadn't met her, and there was no other information, but it was probably related to Nick's toxicology. That brought back my worry about the dope I'd hidden from the cops—that the lab might have found out something about it that they'd be legally required to pass on.

I called Dr. Shin's extension on a hospital phone but got her voice mail. For the time being, I let it go. I was listed as Nick's primary contact, the ER and ICU had my phone numbers, and if it was really urgent, they'd have called me. I walked on down the hall to Nick's room.

I could see him before I got there; the ICU rooms had a lot of glass so the nurses could keep steady watch, and the beds were right in the middle—with surgical booms mounted ominously above them so the docs could get right to work if a serious problem arose. Nick was still obviously damaged goods—hooked to an IV and monitors, with breathing tubes in his nostrils, elbow in a cast, calves encased in knee-high blood-pressure socks, and his exposed flesh dark with bruising—but he looked like a human being again instead of a helpless, battered shape. As I walked to his bedside, his head rolled toward me, eyes vague from the morphine drip,

"How you feeling, brother?" I said, as cheerfully as I could.

He didn't answer, although he was obviously able to talk by now; he'd told the doctors enough for them to suspect retrograde amnesia. Maybe it was because of the sedative, maybe because of me. I hadn't expected an in-depth coherent talk, but I'd hoped I might get a few hints of information. That would have to go on the back burner, too.

"Anything I can get you?" I said.

"How about a shot of Demerol?" His speech was labored, the words mumbled.

"The morphine's not taking care of the pain?"

"No. I hurt all over."

"Well, I'll ask if they'll strengthen the drip, but I don't think they're going to give you Demerol on top of that."

"Why not? Long as I'm stuck here, I might as well enjoy it."

I had to bite off my annoyance—keep from pointing out that the only person who'd gotten him stuck here was him, and the single major thing he needed was to get off drugs, not use this as an opportunity to grasp for more.

But his quick focus on it told me he wasn't as out of it as he seemed—or wanted to seem.

"Do you know what happened to you, Nick?" I said.

"Some." He reached for a plastic cup of water and took a slurp.

"What's the last thing you remember?"

"I don't know. Just hanging around my place, I guess. It's all mixed up."

"How about something specific you did? When, where, who you were with?"

This time he paused briefly before he answered. "Why does that matter?"

"It'll help the doctors gauge your progress."

"Fuck the doctors," he muttered.

I bristled again, more sharply. I'd been trying to maintain sympathy for him—he *was* badly beat up and looking at a long, no-fun recovery—but his attitude was wearing thin fast.

"They saved your life, Nick," I said.

His shoulders rose in a slight shrug. "They'll get their money."

No thanks to you, I thought. "Okay, rest up—I'll be around."

I started toward the door—then decided to try a quick reality check.

"Everybody's thinking about you and wishing you well," I said, pausing. "Oh, yeah—Erica told me you called her. I was glad to hear it."

His head rolled toward me again—this time more quickly, with a hint of wariness cutting through the glaze in his eyes.

"I did?" he said. "When?"

"A couple of weeks ago. You don't remember?"

"No. Why would I call her?"

"She didn't really say. I assumed just to break the ice. I mean, you guys hadn't talked in quite awhile, right?"

He made a scornful little *phhh* sound. "Break the ice? With her? No way."

"You're saying you *didn't* call her?"

"What I'm saying is, you can't trust her." Then he kept talking, his voice more animated and with a familiar cajoling tone—very different from his flat, few-word statements of a moment ago. "She always pulled weird shit and acted like she didn't know it. She's a nympho, for Christ's sake. The way she used to parade around bare-ass."

I could almost hear the click in my head. Of all the things to pick out of the blue, Nick had come up with a sexual reference.

"It was weird, yeah," I said. "But how does that figure into whether you talked to her?"

"Just that I could see her pulling something sleazy and trying to blame it on me. Probably figures I'm too fucked-up to call her on it."

Now he seemed guarded, so I backed off. This was already a lot to think about.

"No, I'm sure it's nothing like that," I said. "She was yakking, being spacey, and I must have misunderstood her. Forget it."

Nick closed his eyes and turned his face away. My visit was over.

I walked out into the hospital corridor, its bright sanitized look a glaring contrast to my bleak mood.

Nick might have some genuine memory loss, but he wasn't only exaggerating it—he was flat-out lying. Worse—far worse—was the reason. He did know about that sex video of Erica, and he was trying to cover it up. He'd immediately branded her an untrustworthy slut, although I hadn't said anything remotely along those lines. I hadn't suggested anything accusing, either, but he'd jumped to deflect blame from himself and toward her.

All of which left me right where I'd been before. Nowhere.

EIGHTEEN

I still wanted to talk to Dr. Shin. The lab was in the next building, just across the way; this time, instead of calling, I walked over there. An attendant at the main desk said he thought she was still around, and paged her. She answered right away and told me to come on back to her office. After another quick clearance procedure, I was allowed to enter the inner precinct.

When I tapped on the half-open door, she was sitting inside, working intently at a computer monitor. She stood to greet me; she couldn't have been more than five feet tall, and she seemed shy, even fragile. But her eyes showed calm, steady competence, with the framed diplomas on her wall, from Occidental and UCSF medical school, backing that up. And I found out right off that she had her own way of getting things done.

The first thing she did was close the office door.

"I took an unofficial look at the drug sample you brought in," she said. "Technically, that's a breach of protocol, and I'd be in an awkward spot if it came out. But there's such a long waiting list, we can't do an official workup for another couple of weeks, and I thought I could at least give you an idea of what's involved."

"I won't say a word. Trust me—we're on the same page there," I said, relieved, "and I really appreciate your concern. But, you know, why?"

"Your family paid for my college, Dr. Crandall. My parents came from South Korea. I grew up in the back room of our laundry. But I got a Crandall Foundation scholarship, and I was able to go to college instead of pressing clothes. I'm glad to be able to pay back a little."

Well, son of a bitch. I blinked in astonishment, pleased and touched.

"That's a real nice thing to hear," I said.

"Much more than nice for us. My parents have a house now, and no more laundry."

The Crandall Foundation was a trust started in the 1950s; it dispensed several hundred thousand dollars per year in grants and scholarships, and to charities. For all that I disliked about wealth, the foundation brought home the truth that sometimes money could accomplish a lot that good intentions alone couldn't touch.

"By the way, please call me Tom," I said.

She smiled, looking shy again. "Thank you. Same for me." Then she sat at her computer, back to business.

"The drug is just cocaine, cut with lidocaine but reasonably pure," she said. "None of the additives like meth or PCP that we'd typically associate with a violent loss of control. But there is one odd thing." After some fast-fingered keyboard magic, she brought up a photograph.

"This is TEM imaging, from an electron microscope," she said. "These are the cocaine crystals"—she pointed at cross-hatched structures of white and gold lines that looked something like lie detector readouts—"and here's what's unusual."

Her fingertips moved to clusters of other shapes scattered among the crystals. These were less distinct, but they appeared to be cylindrical and of uniform size, as if a superthin wire had been neatly chopped into bits.

She swiveled around in her chair to face me. "They look like nanoparticles. Metal would show up better, so I'd guess they're something like carbon or silicone."

"Does that tell you anything?" I said.

"Not in itself—it's just that I've never seen nanos in a street-drug sample before. But they're getting very common these days, used in all kinds of products. Most likely they just got into this mix by accident, somewhere along the way."

"And Nick inhaled them along with the coke?"

"He would have, yes. I don't see how that would affect his behavior—as far as I know they'd be inert, not causing a chemical reaction in the brain like a drug. But I'm no expert in that field, and I wanted to let you know in case something turns up that might seem related."

I thanked her and headed for home again, remembering Nick's chilling words when I'd first found him on the cliff.

There are worms eating my brain.

PART THREE

NINETEEN

When I made it back to my place, I finally poured the drink I'd been promising myself all day, a healthy splash of Bombay Sapphire on ice with a lemon wedge. Then I started looking for possible pathways to information.

The nano information was intriguing, but I couldn't see that it shed any light. For now, at least, I decided to go along with Ivy's guess that the particles had gotten into the dope accidentally and weren't involved in Nick's meltdown. God only knows there were plenty of other reasons why he'd feel a meat grinder in his head.

But one thing that did bear looking into was his recent phone calls. His cell phone itself was lost, but I could check the records online. The account, like his allowance and utilities, was paid by the family through automatic debits, and—as his de facto guardian and occasional bail bondsman—I had access to all that information.

I savored the sharp bite of the gin while I pulled up his account on my computer, jumped through the user ID and password hoops, and found the current bill. The calls were listed right up to date, with the final one—when we'd been on the cliff early this morning, just before he attacked me—at 4:20 a.m.

I blinked in surprise when I saw that it had come from an 800 number.

A toll-free call, made to a cell phone, at four in the morning? What the hell was *that* all about?

I started scanning the other numbers on the bill. There were five or six pages of them; Nick had kept that phone working hard.

And at least two dozen other calls from 800 or 888 exchanges had come during the previous several days. Every one of the numbers was different, so this didn't seem to be an ongoing transaction with a particular retailer or anything like that; moreover and stranger still, the calls were all incoming and lasted less than a minute, and many were after midnight.

The smell of scam was getting thicker all the time.

A little more online maneuvering got me a couple of toll-free directories with reverse searches to identify the caller. But as I typed in the numbers from Nick's bill, the results came up blank again and again.

I realized that they must be ghost numbers operating via VoIP, Voice over Internet Protocol—virtually impossible to trace, often used for suspect or outright illegal purposes like information phishing, solicitations from phony organizations, and sleazy robocalls.

So the callers had been careful to stay anonymous; the calls might all be from a single source after all, since VoIP systems could easily manipulate caller ID; and I could probably assume that the final one he'd gotten on the cliff was part of the same chain. All that added to the disturbing sense, but didn't tell me anything specifically useful.

I spent a minute looking up the call Erica said Nick had made to her. Sure enough, there it was—twelve days ago, lasting eight minutes. That left me more convinced than ever that he knew about the video, and that he remembered the call perfectly well.

I got up and poured another drink.

Nothing else in the bill stood out except the glaring absence of toll-free calls earlier in the month; they'd started suddenly in the last week. I decided to make one more pass before calling it a day and rustling up some dinner. I printed out the pages and started going through them with a pen, noting numbers that were frequently repeated. As Detective Drabyak had mentioned, I might be able to track down some of them and get an idea of who Nick had been hanging around with.

Then I noticed that one of them seemed vaguely familiar—an 813 exchange with quite a few calls both incoming and outgoing, and the most recent one yesterday. I was puzzled as to why it rang a bell. I didn't think it could be a mutual friend—Nick and I hadn't had any of those for close to fifteen years—and there weren't any businesses or restaurants we both frequented. The only other information listed besides the number was the place of origin, Los Angeles, which didn't exactly narrow it down. I sat back in my chair and took a sip of gin, mentally groping for the connection.

When it came, I almost choked.

Hap Rasmussen.

I set my glass down hard on the desk, pulled open the top drawer, and got out my address book to make sure. I was right.

Hap, our ex-swimming coach, old family friend, and—I had thought—Nick's venomous enemy.

It was astonishing enough that the two of them were even in contact. But far beyond that, Hap had been at my mother's house this morning, through all her shock, agonizing, and the struggle to make sense of this—and he'd never said a fucking word about it. No wonder he'd seemed uncomfortable.

I'd been coping all right with my annoyance so far—at Nick jerking me around, Paul's callousness, and the antics of my hot-pants sister—but this jacked me up to real anger. For Hap to treat my mother like that was despicable, and personally, being burned by somebody I trusted left me bitter like nothing else I knew.

On top of that, it was deeply disturbing in itself. Until now, I'd always thought of Hap as the epitome of a stand-up guy, with deep affection and respect for Audrey. Well-grounded people like that rarely veered radically out of character; when they did, they had a serious reason. Whatever Hap's reason was, it meant hiding his contact with Nick.

Christ, was Hap tied in with Nick's current troubles? There was no obvious connection, but it seemed like a hell of a coincidence otherwise.

I tried calling Hap but got no answer. I wondered if he was screening—avoiding me because he figured the conversation would be about Nick, and he'd have to keep up his lie and maybe get entangled in it.

But I wanted to talk to him—now.

There was no guarantee he'd be home, but his condo in Century City wasn't far away, a straight no-freeways shot along Pico.

At least I'd be doing something instead of sitting here fuming.

TWENTY

Hap lived in one of L.A.'s older high-rises, a classy twenty-story tower with full amenities—doormen and maid service, gardens, tennis courts, and an Olympic-size swimming pool, where he still kept up his daily workouts. These were nice digs if you could afford them; he owned a lucrative business, importing high-end Asian merchandise like jewelry and rugs.

A parking valet came to meet me as I pulled up in front. The old Cruiser sometimes got the fish eye at places like this, with their fleets of gleaming luxury vehicles. But this guy, a middle-aged Latino with a sweet, wise face, looked it over with obvious *afición* for my rough workhorse jewel. I handed him a ten-dollar bill along with the keys and asked him to hold off on garaging it—I might be right back.

When I got to the lobby entrance, the doorman stepped forward smartly and ushered me in.

"Good evening, sir. How may I help you?" He was much slicker than the valet, with a sharply pressed uniform and the kind of polished manners that suggested he'd had professional training.

I'd decided that the best way to handle this was to have the desk phone Hap. My caller ID wouldn't be in the mix, and if he answered, he'd have a hard time turning me away.

"I have an appointment with Mr. Rasmussen in 14C," I said. "If you'd just tell him Dr. Crandall's here."

The doorman's bland politeness turned hesitant. "I'm sorry, sir—Mr. Rasmussen was called away on business. He left earlier this afternoon."

"Away? You mean on a trip?"

"I believe so. He asked me to call him a cab to the airport."

What? Not only did the son of a bitch stonewall us about Nick, but he was leaving town without a word? I was starting to think that Hap wasn't veering out of character at all—that he was accomplished at deceit, and I'd just never picked up on it.

Another gold star for my acute psychological perception.

The doorman either couldn't or wouldn't tell me where Hap had gone or for how long—Hap had probably instructed him not to—and I didn't think he'd go for a bribe; he had a good job to protect. But another idea came to me as I walked back outside to my car, still at the curb with the valet standing beside it. The parking crew might be hungrier for cash, and this guy seemed friendly anyway. This time as he gave me the keys, I slipped him a twenty.

"Is no need, sir—you already take care of me," he said, but he didn't resist palming the bill.

"I could use a little help," I said quietly. "You know Mr. Rasmussen?"

"Sure. Peach color 280-SL."

"I'm an old friend of his. We had a misunderstanding and I need to work it out. The doorman said he went to the airport. Any idea where he was headed?"

He scratched his furrowed cheek. "All I know is I hear him tell the cabdriver, Singapore Airlines."

I exhaled wearily. Singapore was where the other end of Hap's business was located; he spent a lot of time there and even owned a villa. He could stay for months.

The valet's gaze turned sympathetic. "Long way from here, huh?"

"A long way in *all* the ways. Did he ever have a visitor who drove a red Jag XK8? Guy about my age, looks something like me?"

The valet nodded slowly. "When I first see you tonight, I think you are him with a haircut. But he's bigger around and he don't take care of his ride."

So Nick wasn't only in phone contact with Hap—they'd been meeting each other.

"Yeah, that's him," I said. "Was he here a lot?"

"He start showing up a few months ago. Once, twice a week."

"Any idea what was going on?"

"Not for sure, but they don't look like they're having fun. People say Mr. Rasmussen got money trouble. Maybe something about that."

This was the first I'd heard of Hap's financial troubles—his business had probably taken a hit from the weak economy, like so many others. But if he needed money, Nick was scheming to *get* money, and the two of them had suddenly started seeing each other, it fit way too close for comfort that Hap might be in on Nick's scheme. It would also explain his furtiveness this morning and his abrupt departure. He knew that we'd be looking into things, and he was afraid that it would come to light.

Which would mean that whatever it was, it was serious.

The valet put a kindly hand on my shoulder. *"Lo siento, amigo,"* he said. "You don't like to hear that."

"Sabe Dios. But I needed to. *Gracias."*

I groped for my wallet and started to pull out another twenty, but this time he waved it away firmly.

"Suerta," he said.

I got back in my car and I was just about to turn out of the condo parking lot onto the street when my cell phone rang. I hesitated. I was in no mood for chatting, but it might be my mother or the hospital, so I pulled over and looked at the caller ID.

The screen read DIFURIO LISA.

I stared at it through another ring, wondering if my brain was playing tricks on me again. But her name stayed right there.

I clicked the talk button. "Lisa?"

"Tom, I hope I'm not interrupting you at a bad time."

"No, it's fine—I'm glad to hear from you."

In fact, I was much more than glad—I was touched by that same kind of euphoria as when we were leaving the Lodge, a rush that seemed to pulse through my nerves. What *was* it with this woman I'd met only a few hours ago and spent only a few minutes with?

"I feel like such an idiot," she said. "I finally got around to reading today's *Times* and saw about your brother's accident. I had no *idea* you were coming from something like that. Believe me, I'd never have been such a smart-ass."

"Your brand of smart-ass was just right—helped me get it off my mind for a while. He's doing well, by the way."

"Thank God—the poor guy. Poor *you*. I can't imagine diving into that freezing water."

"Hush. You'll make me cold all over again."

She laughed. "I've been accused of a lot of things, but never that."

I smiled, too. "I don't have any trouble believing it."

Neither of us spoke for the next few seconds—one of those knotty pauses where the conversation has to take a turn, but it's not clear who's going to make it or in what direction.

Then Lisa said, "Look, I'm not shy. It goes with the actress turf. Are you, like, involved with anybody?"

"Well, no. Between relationships, as the saying goes."

"Me, too. So how about I come to your place and bring dinner? You're probably wiped out, and I'm a good Italian girl. Okay, not so good, but still Italian. Steak, pasta, vino?"

All I could think of to say was, "Really?"

Talk about a day ending up better than it started.

TWENTY-ONE

I had a hibachi on my rooftop and used it fairly often, usually just for burgers. But tonight two thick filet mignons were sizzling on it, while Ms. DiFurio—looking sexy-tough in tight jeans and a black pullover—and I sipped Chianti with a wonderful jaw-puckering edge. She'd also brought the makings for angel-hair pasta in parmesan sauce, an avocado salad with vinaigrette dressing, and a melt-in-your-mouth fresh sourdough baguette.

Lisa wandered to the roof edge while I sliced into the filets to check them. They were close to done—two, three more minutes.

"This is nice up here," she said. "Right in the middle of all the bullshit, but out of it."

"It was your idea, remember?"

"Lucky guess."

"Yeah, it's sort of a third-world penthouse," I said. "The roof's perfect for hanging out and not doing what I should."

"Who wouldn't?"

I picked up my wineglass and walked over to join her. The evening was crisp and, by L.A. standards, clear. The sun had set, with the fading daylight giving windows a glow and softening the city's grimy sprawl. Then again, maybe the glow was only in my eyes. I was still in a state of mild disbelief that she was here.

"I'm trying to pick out the studios," she said. "I have a lousy sense of direction, so I use them kind of like landmarks to find my way around. Paramount's easy, you head toward the sign and then off to the right." She pointed north toward the huge white

HOLLYWOOD sign on what was arguably the world's most famous hill. "So MGM—whoops, it's Sony now—should be on the other side of us?" Her hand swung in an arc to point southward.

"Very good," I said. "Have you worked there much?"

She sighed theatrically. "Honey, I've done 'em all."

That seemed like a good lead-in, and maybe an invitation, to get back to where we'd left off talking at the Lodge—that she saw the Parallax film as a make-or-break career move, and the director might try to get her replaced.

"But now you're worried about Dustin Sperry," I said.

"Some. If it happens, it's not the end of the world—I'll still get work. But this is a good part, and it's a lead. I mean, we're not talking Ingrid Bergman in *Casablanca*—I'm playing a bimbo— but it's my first real chance to prove I'm a looker who can *act*."

Her gaze was steady, sincere, and while that brassy wit was still there, she was somehow softer—even pained. It was the first time I'd been this close to her, and I saw that her hazel eyes were flecked with gold.

"If it flies, I get more of those chances," she went on. "But if I get fired, I go the other way." She shrugged. "I honest to God don't care about being a superstar or making huge money. I just don't want to fade off into a has-been who's never really even *been*."

"That's a tough spot to be in."

"In a way, but let's face it—it's a problem most people would kill for." Then she paused. "But that's all I've talked about, isn't it? And I've talked about it a lot. Come on, your turn."

"Well," I said, trying to think of how to put it. "I guess I've got something vaguely like that going on, too. Except you're try- ing to move forward and I'm not. I've been drifting along like I'm trying to figure out what I want to be when I grow up."

"The *Times* piece about your brother said you're a psychologist."

"I've got the papers, yeah. I'm teaching now, and I like it, but somehow I can't see myself settling in for the long term. Before that I was doing clinical work, but I'm pretty sure I'm out of that for good."

"Some kind of a blow-up there?"

"More like I lost faith in myself, or lost my nerve, or both," I said. "I was working with violent patients. Getting worn down by it anyway, and then there was this evil son of a bitch who conned his way to an insanity plea and then a release. My gut told me it was all wrong, but I didn't have any tangible evidence. He'd gone through his treatment with flying colors—*supposed* treatment, guys like that just play the game.

"I 'expressed my concerns,' to use the official terminology, and maybe I could have stopped it if I'd really thrown my weight behind it. Probably not—I was junior, and I didn't have much weight to throw. Anyway, I left it at that and went along. Within a month, he raped and murdered an eight-year-old girl. When the blame started flying, I got my share of it, and rightly so. I still could have stayed on there, but . . . " I shook my head.

In fact, it was the only time in my life I'd ever seriously considered suicide.

Lisa's eyes had changed while I was talking—like maybe she was thinking that between the drama with Nick and what I'd just told her, I was more trouble-prone than the harmless, somewhat nerdy guy she'd taken me for, and she'd just remembered that she had to go home and wash her hair. I wouldn't have blamed her a bit.

But she murmured, "That's a *real* tough spot."

I raised my wineglass. "Enough gloom and doom. Would you please go back to being a smart-ass?"

She grinned and touched my glass with her own. "I never stop for long. Drink up. I'll get us a refill."

I'd let the steaks get a little too done, but they tasted grand and so did everything else. Lisa insisted on helping with the dishes, and at some point we were both at the sink and she sort of leaned back against me and my hand moved of its own accord to rest lightly on her hip, just as naturally as if this was the thousandth time instead of the first. It lasted only a couple of seconds before we moved apart, but it was one of those electric moments you're blessed to ever get, when you know that this is happening both ways.

TWENTY-TWO

Lisa wore a lot of gold that went with her skin tone and added to her exotic look—big hoop earrings, several bangles, and a cuff bracelet inlaid with a jade oval. She'd taken it off to wash dishes, and as she clasped it back on I admired it aloud.

"Gunnar gave it to me," she said.

I was impressed. I didn't know much about jewelry prices, but I could tell this wasn't cheap.

And I confess, I felt a touch of jealousy—wondering if she and Gunnar Kelso might have a past involvement, or even a present one.

She glanced at me, probably realizing that I might. "It doesn't mean anything romantic," she said. "He just does things like that, with other people, too. It's more like he sees something in you he wants to bring out, and it's a symbol."

"What is it he wants to bring out in you?"

"He never says. It's up to you to figure it out. I know how that sounds, but—things do change. In your head, in your life."

"Cynthia Trask was talking about that earlier today," I said. "What's your take on her, by the way?"

Lisa shrugged. "We get along okay—we're not around each other much. She comes on chilly, although I hear she leaves scorch marks on the guys."

"Seems like 'guys' includes my brother."

"You upset about it?"

"Not exactly upset. But he *is* married, and there are other issues. I'd like to know what I'm dealing with."

"Well, Cynthia can take care of herself, no doubt about that. But I really don't know anything about what they've got going— I barely know Paul at all."

More and more, I was feeling the same way.

"How about if we go sit awhile?" I said. "I'd like to hear more about Kelso and Parallax."

Lisa smiled. "You want to know what you're dealing with there, too?"

"It figures in, yes. And I admit I'm skeptical about that kind of thing—but not entirely." In fact, I was less so than I let on.

"Sure, I'll tell you what I can," she said. "It's not like there're any big secrets."

I dug out a bottle of Rémy Martin that had been gathering dust for a while, and we settled down with it in what passed for my living room. The last daylight had faded from the windows, replaced by the electric blaze of nighttime L.A.

I was a rapt audience as Lisa started talking, with the sweetener of the little things I kept noticing about her, like the delicate veins of her forearms or the arch of a sandaled foot.

She'd been involved with Parallax for about two years, she said. Its organization was very loose, with no formal rules, codes, or even membership. Kelso was very hands-off, approachable but never pushy. He spent a lot of time in private pursuing theoretical work; only another mind like his could comprehend it, but it involved trying to quantify his ideas through mathematics. Lisa had glimpsed computer graphics that she described as so complex they'd give you an instant headache.

Then she gave me a sketch of the philosophy itself. Like Kelso's movie world in *The Velvet Glove*, it was a curious blend of elements, some traditional but modernized, and given a gloss of science that walked the edge of science fiction.

It was easy to see how this had put Kelso in the crosshairs of mainstream science.

For openers, he held that the universe was inhabited by unseen intelligences—he called them the Gatekeepers—that were engaged in perpetual struggle with each other and used human beings like pawns.

This much was an echo of an age-old theme—war in heaven, a battle for human souls. But then Kelso gave it an interesting twist. The reason for this war wasn't nearly so lofty.

It was for possession of energy—specifically, a mysterious form of it, a sort of cosmic life force, which Kelso called Pneuma; the word had connotations of both breath and soul. This energy was unrecognized by science and so far he'd been unable to quantify it himself, although his theoretical work focused heavily on that. But he believed that it was like electricity or water in that it could be measured, harnessed, directed—even stolen.

Human beings innately possessed the Pneuma. It flowed through channels, a sort of vast cosmic wiring harness to which we were all attached. The Gatekeepers did *not* innately possess it, but it was their source of power, so they competed for it. The mechanics of this process were byzantine; essentially, the Gatekeepers tapped into the energy channels and then tried to exert subliminal mind control over humans. The more people they controlled and the more completely, the more energy they got.

Some of the Gatekeepers were benign and used the energy in positive ways. But others clouded human minds by barraging them with distracting thoughts, then drained off the Pneuma life force, insidiously weakening their victims, who had no idea it was even going on.

From here, Kelso's thinking took a more practical turn. The

energy theft could be stopped by awakening a dormant mental faculty—another idea that had a familiar ring, although also with a twist. His term for this was the Sentry; it was something like a computer security system. Arousing it didn't require any rigorous discipline or formal stages, just continually nudging it and reminding it what it was. The increased flow of Pneuma would renew strength and lead to the "quantum leaps" that Cynthia and Paul had talked about, and the entire process would continue to mushroom, bringing the individual to enhanced states of mental clarity and personal power.

At this point, Lisa paused. "So, does that all sound completely wacko?"

I shook my head slowly. "No—not in context, compared to other belief systems. It actually seems well thought out and logically consistent, and the beliefs themselves don't strike me as any farther out than a lot of what's in established religions. But they *are* beliefs, and they are pretty far-out, and I'd personally have a real hard time accepting them."

There was also the fact that it somehow seemed a little too good to be true.

"It takes some getting used to, and I admit I've still got my problems with it all," she said, "but Gunnar's fine with that. He just lays it down like, this is how it is, take it or leave it, and if you give it a chance, you might be surprised. Kind of like driving a car—you don't have to know how the engine works to get where you want to go."

Little as I knew Lisa, she sure didn't seem unbalanced in any way, let alone naive or gullible. Ditto for Kelso, and it was hard to believe he was just a charlatan. Maybe there was some other explanation that was eluding me completely.

Or was there really something to this—that he'd managed to

identify a hidden universe, just as earlier scientists had discovered the invisible worlds of atoms, microorganisms, forces like gravity and magnetism—and someday, this would be just as much an accepted scientific reality?

I genuinely did try to keep an open mind, but that notion was a very tough sell.

Well, the acid test of any theory was, Did it work?

"So what happens as this change comes over you?" I said. "Are there tangible results?"

"There can be. But this isn't about wishing for *things*, like one of those pop-psychology visualization deals. Gunnar doesn't want people thinking like that—he's real clear about it." She sipped her brandy, watching me over the rim of the glass.

"I'm playing devil's advocate now, but it does sound like that," I said. "How's it different?"

"The idea is that as you bring in more energy, you get better at what you do. If you're better at your work, you make more money. And so on."

I grinned. "Sorry, but *that* sounds kind of mundane—like a diet or exercise program. I thought there was something more mysterious involved."

Lisa smiled back, but her gaze shifted away; she looked like she was trying to make up her mind about something.

"Maybe there is," she finally said, "but I'm afraid this *will* sound too far-out."

"Try me." I stood up to add another splash of Rémy to our glasses.

"Well—when the energy channels open up, it's like that can light up parts of your mind that were always dark before. And that don't ever light up for most people. Gunnar says it'll start with something that's buried in you and spread from there. So for me, I loved to play gypsy when I was little. Let's face it, in a way, I still do." She shook her forearm, clinking her bangles musically. "I'd pretend I could see things in a crystal ball, all that. But there was never anything *real* about it. Then, awhile ago—some things happened." She shrugged, looking at me like she expected me to laugh out loud.

I was far from doing that, but my hands did pause as I opened the bottle.

"You mean you *could* start telling the future?" I said.

"It's not clear-cut—no crystal ball stuff. More like something would flash through my mind just out of the blue, and it would turn out to be true."

I finished refreshing both brandy glasses and took a healthy swig out of mine. Psychic ability was at the top of every skeptic's list, and another explanation came readily to mind—she might not expect any tangible payoffs from Kelso's mental gymnastics, but subconsciously she still wanted validation, and this was the form it took, a wish fulfillment that went back to childhood. Even very sincere people are susceptible to that sort of thing.

But goddammit, I just didn't get that sense from her. And I wasn't entirely skeptical about psychic phenomena, either. There was a lot of well-attested evidence for those, and the "scientific" explanations offered to debunk them often seemed more preposterous than the claims of their advocates.

"Can you control this at all?" I said.

"Not *control* it—I played around with it some and realized I could kind of *invite* it. But I haven't done it for a while—it's a little spooky when I'm alone."

Then she leaned forward with her elbows on her knees and both hands cupped around her glass, and her gaze turned shy.

"I could try right now if you want," she said.

It was another moment like our brief brush-up in the kitchen—both an offer and a test of trust.

"I'd be fascinated," I said.

"I can't promise anything."

"You don't need to. So what do we do?"

"I just think of whatever it is I want to find out about, and, you know, open up. It helps if there's something related to it that I can hold in my hands." She hesitated, then said, "Look, I know you're torn up about your brother Nick. But I've got a feeling it's not just about what happened—there's something else really eating at you. I could try there and see if anything comes."

That raised my eyebrows. Maybe it was just an intuitive guess, but I was quite sure I hadn't said anything about it.

I went to the small safe box where I kept important records, and where I'd stashed the things I'd taken from Nick's house. I got out the envelope with the DNA paternity tests and took it back to Lisa.

"Do you need to know what this is? Any other information?" I said.

"No. Just give me a few seconds to concentrate." She closed her eyes and took several deep slow breaths, with the envelope resting on her upturned palms.

"Is there a motorcycle involved?" she said.

I stared at her. There were a lot of motorcycles in L.A.—but this was really pushing the bounds of coincidence.

"Yes," I said. "Can you tell who's riding it?"

She shook her head hesitantly. "I can't really *see* these things—it's more like I'm feeling them. But I do get the feeling—this is weird, but I'm almost sure it's a woman. She's running from something, and she's furious about it."

I kept on staring, trying to process this.

Lisa stayed quiet and still for another half minute, then opened her eyes and sagged slightly.

"Sorry, that's all," she said. She looked shaken, like this had drained her, and I quickly sat beside her.

"Lisa, *I'm* sorry—I didn't realize it would rough you up like that."

"I'm fine, but that's why I don't like doing it alone," she said. "Did I call it right?"

"So right it's scary, from what I can tell," I said. "I went to Nick's house this morning. Somebody on a motorcycle had broken in, and took off when I showed up. I never even thought about it being a woman, but I guess it could have been."

"Good. You can still think I'm an airhead, but at least I didn't prove it."

I raised my hands to gently grip her shoulders. "That's bullshit and I hope you know it," I said. "It makes *me* feel like a fool. Which has been going on all day."

She settled in against me, and our bodies rearranged themselves, with my arm finding its way around her.

"Somebody who was a fool in the right ways might be kind of nice," she murmured. "Most of the guys I know are smart in the wrong ones."

I wasn't so dumb that I didn't know when a woman wanted to be kissed.

Neither of us saw any reason to stop there. If there was any way to describe something like that, I didn't know it.

Lisa left around one in the morning, telling me firmly that we both needed sleep, and if she stayed, we'd just keep each other awake. I walked her downstairs to her car, parked beside mine in the garage, and watched her drive away, already fearing that her half of the brief trance we'd shared would quickly dissolve—that she had come over here on impulse and taken me to bed because she felt sorry for me, and that would be the end of it.

Then I fell back into bed, finally giving in to exhaustion. At first I crashed like a dead man. But within an hour I was restless, drifting in and out of sleep and waking up in sudden starts—not from anything tangible like bad dreams, but something that didn't seem to have any cause and yet gnawed at me in a way that amounted almost to dread.

When the gray light of morning brought me around, I got to my feet with the kind of grogginess you feel after a sleep like that, and the kind of loneliness you feel when the musk of a woman's perfume lingers on the pillows, but she is gone.

TWENTY-THREE

A shower and some strong coffee helped to clear my head, and I figured that the best way to stave off my moping was to get busy. First stop of the day was another trip to Nick's place. This time I had a few specific notions of what to look for that I could easily have missed yesterday—anything that might relate to the VoIP phone calls, or to Hap, or to the video of Erica.

Before I could get out the door, my own phone rang. It was the detective I'd talked to yesterday, Drabyak. I answered nervously, afraid that the lid had popped off that dreaded can of worms after all.

"I don't have any news about your brother, Dr. Crandall, and it looks like the case isn't going any further," he said.

"I appreciate knowing that, Detective," I said, relieved.

He didn't speak again for several seconds. I could picture him slouched in his car, one wrist hooked over the steering wheel, staring out the window at nothing while his mind worked busily at whatever was on it.

Then he said, "I've got another reason for calling. I could maybe use your help down the line."

"How so?"

"I've done some nosing around since we talked. Sort of on the cop grapevine, putting some pieces together. There've been other incidents in the past few months that all have this kind of feel. They seem random because they're spread out over different times and areas, but it's the same stuff. People just coming unhinged. Assaults, tearing up their own homes and themselves. Some suicides, some comas, survivors who say that out of no-where, they'd get a killer pain in their head and they'd go bat shit. Didn't know what they were doing or care." He didn't have to add, "Like your brother."

My first thought was, Nick's cocaine—the nanoparticle ad-ditive that Ivy Shin had found in it *was* somehow causing this, and the stuff was getting into drugs on a widespread basis. But I wasn't about to say so. I'd try to help Drabyak if I could, but not at the price of admitting that Nick had possessed the coke and I had hidden it.

Drabyak's next words undercut that, anyway.

"The strangest thing is, we're not talking druggies or people on the edge," he said. "These are very high-*powered* people. A glitzy lawyer—you'd recognize his name. A big-shot movie exec. Somebody who's top level in county government. Like that."

"Is there anything that seems to tie in with Nick?"

"Not yet—but that's what I'm getting at. I have a hard time believing this is just happening by itself. My gut feeling is, there's something starting up that we're going to see more of, and we might be looking at a real problem. So if you do turn up some-thing, Dr. Crandall—you know, that your brother tells you, or whatever—keep my phone number handy, will you?"

I assured him that I would.

TWENTY-FOUR

When I got to Nick's house, it looked the same as when I'd left. I spent a couple of minutes clearing the refrigerator of perishables, to get that over with—there wasn't much, Nick lived mainly on fast food—and took the garbage out to the bin. I decided to leave the cleanup at that for now; there was no hurry on the rest, and no point in disturbing things more than I had to.

Then I started prowling again, with my eyes open for anything, including more dope, but with DVDs at the top of my list. It had occurred to me that Nick might have a copy of the Erica video that wasn't stashed in the secretary desk simply because it was too big for the cubbyhole; and it would hide in plain sight—just an apparent blank, probably the same kind of Sony disk she'd given me, that an intruder looking for drugs or money wouldn't even notice.

Nick liked movies, and there were plenty of them lying around, probably a hundred or more, but no blanks that I could see—no signs that he'd ever done any camcorder filming or even copied anything. They were all commercially produced, mostly action flicks and comedies, with a fair sampling of porn. I figured I'd better look inside the cases, so I started picking my way through the wreckage and checking them out.

I worked my way over to a pile of the triple X's, a jumble of flesh tones and alluring female shapes. A few were old standbys like *Deep Throat* with stars who'd practically become household names, but most were more recent and I'd never heard of either the films or the actors.

The fifth or sixth one of those I opened, titled *Pink Panther-ettes*, stood out—not because the disk inside was the blank I was looking for, but because there was a bright red, life-size imprint of a woman's lips on it. Below that was a handwritten inscription:

To Nick—can you feel these, baby? Love, D.

I touched the imprint carefully. The lip gloss was dried and faded but real, not part of the packaging—the result of a sultry wet kiss.

The video appeared to be a collection of vignettes, with several female stars posed on the cover. They all had obvious porn names, but none of them began with *D*. The film was also five years old. No immediate help there, but it did point to Nick having a direct connection with that world—and it was a good bet that "D" was one of these actresses, using the initial of her real name. I set the disk aside and went through the rest of them, now thinking that if she and Nick had been an item, he might have more samples of her work; maybe that would help me identify her.

Nothing definite turned up, no more personal seals like the lipstick—but one of the ladies did appear in three more videos. She was billed as Kandi Kane, a somewhat hard-edged blonde who seemed to be a backup player rather than a lead.

And damned if she didn't start looking vaguely familiar, although I was reasonably sure I'd never seen her in action. I set the four DVD cases on a table and studied her photos, trolling for the memory. After a minute, I started to hook into it.

One night last year, Nick had stopped by my place to hit me up for some cash, and she'd been with him. Her name was Denise. Her hair, longish in the DVD cover pix, was cut short in a shag, and there was no sign of that taunting fuck-me smile; she'd seemed wary, worn down, and she was in her midthirties, past her prime in an industry that was endlessly flooded with fresh young talent.

She and Nick had stayed only a few minutes. She hadn't talked much; she'd mentioned that she worked in a shop at Venice Beach, but not surprisingly, said nothing about her porn career, which was probably over.

But she would still know people in that world. And if I were Nick, looking for somebody to set up that video of Erica—who had the know-how or connections to do it and who wouldn't be overly scrupulous about the legality—a girlfriend like Denise, aka Kandi Kane, would be a logical place to start.

It would sure be worth having a talk with her. But how to find her? I didn't know her last name; there were a lot of shops on Venice Beach, and I had no idea which one she worked at, if she even still did; and I could be sure that Nick would dodge any questions that angled in that direction.

I chewed it over in my mind as I went through the rest of his stuff, including all the old mail, receipts, and other papers I could find, drawing a blank all around. But at some point, for no conscious reason, I started thinking about how I'd stumbled into Hap Rasmussen and Nick being in contact. It was via phone records—and I wondered if those might help here, too. It stood to reason that Nick would have been talking to whoever else was involved with the Erica video, around the time that it was made.

I hustled back home and went straight to my computer, calling up Nick's phone records and concentrating on the period when Erica's video would have been made.

Right away, I spotted a number with several calls both ways. The incoming ones listed its city of origin as Venice, California. I didn't have any trouble tracing this one; it was neither a cell phone nor VoIP, but commercial.

Blossom's Beachwear and Specialties, on Ocean Front Walk in Venice Beach.

TWENTY-FIVE

For sheer energy, along with a liberal dose of insanity, Venice Beach was tough to beat, and on this warm Sunday it was packed. Making my way through the whizzing roller skaters and bicyclists, I felt like a duck in a shooting gallery, and in long pants and a shirt, I was way overdressed; a lot of the outfits on parade could have been measured in square inches, and the tattoos would have covered the beachfront. The boardwalk bristled with every kind of carnival hustle, with a predatory world below the surface. There were a lot of cops around, for good reason. Tourists, in particular, tended not to realize that a walk up an innocent-looking side street could part them from their money, and if they were uncooperative or unlucky, their lives.

Blossom's Beachwear was a narrow storefront shoehorned into a row of shops toward the south end of the boardwalk; the window displayed items like T-shirts reading IF YOU WANT SAFE SEX, GO FUCK YOURSELF, microscopic thong bikinis, and a rack of off-color joke postcards.

And inside behind the counter stood Denise, dressed to match the merchandise in a tube top and cutoffs. She was attractive enough to make the outfit work, but age-wise, she was pushing the envelope.

She was busy ringing up a customer and barely gave me a glance at first. But then she looked again quickly, and I could tell that she recognized me—and that she was already not happy about my being there.

I pretended to poke around through the merchandise as if I was interested. When the customer left, she came over to me—smiling, but with her tense body language screaming *nervous*.

"Hi, Denise," I said. "You remember who I am?"

"Nick's brother, right?"

"Tom, yeah. You heard what happened to him?"

She nodded, her smile fading a little. "How's he doing?"

"Pretty fair. You can visit him if you want. He's at UCLA."

"Sure, I'll do that," she said. Her gaze flicked past me toward the steady stream of passersby on the boardwalk; people were pausing to check out the merchandise and starting to drift into the store. "Look, thanks for the heads-up, but I'm getting busy. So if you don't mind—"

"I didn't come here to give you a heads-up," I said. "We need to talk."

"Maybe *you* need to talk. I don't see why I do."

"I think we have a common interest—a lot to lose."

The smile was all gone now, with her eyes both hostile and a little scared. This kind of acting was not in her repertoire.

"I'll have to get someone to take over the counter for me," she said. "Give me a couple of minutes."

I waited on the boardwalk, trying to stay out of the way of the gawking crowd and blitz of speeding wheels, until she came out.

"Let's go around back," she said. "You can't smoke on the beach anymore. Fucking rules about everything." I followed her into the small cul-de-sac beside the shop. She took a cigarette from her purse and lit up. She had her own share of body art, but it was fairly restrained—a heart on her left breast, a slave bracelet around an ankle, and something just visible at the base of her spine, maybe a rose.

"So what's this about?" she said, and added defensively, "I haven't really been seeing Nick for a while."

She'd damned sure been talking to him on the phone, but I let it go for the moment. I didn't have any proof of what I suspected, and she obviously wasn't just going to come out and admit anything. Best bet was to make it clear that she'd damned well *better* be scared.

"It's about how Nick was into something that could seriously damage people's lives," I said. "I'm trying to keep that from happening. I need some information."

"What's it got to do with me?"

"Let's say a video was made that shouldn't have been."

By now she'd had time to prepare herself, and she answered with a shrug. But it was too casual and came too late.

"I don't even know where you're coming from," she said. "I don't make videos."

"I'm glad to hear that. Because if this one ever turns up in public, if there's ever even a whisper about it, the people who did make it are going to prison. Slam dunk."

I could tell that one hit harder, but she kept it up, shaking her head, dragging on the cigarette and exhaling a thin curl of smoke.

"Sorry. Can't help," she said. "Is that it?"

"Not quite." I was carrying a plastic shopping bag, like I'd bought something on my way here. But what was in it was the lipstick-imprinted Kandi Kane video that I'd taken from Nick's house.

I pulled out the DVD and held it up for a couple of seconds, just long enough for her to register what it was.

Her pissed-off look vaporized, swept away by alarm. Then her eyes narrowed and she tried another bluff, but it was feeble.

"Did you get off on watching it?" she said.

"Haven't had the pleasure yet."

"So what does it have to do with anything?"

"I know about the phone calls between you and Nick, too," I said. "That's how I found you here. Come on, Denise. If the cops get into this, you'll be the first bug to hit the windshield."

She turned away, tapping her cigarette ash and grinding it under her sandaled, crimson-nailed foot.

"Look, I wasn't really in on it, okay?" she said. "Nick told me he wanted a sneak video and asked if I knew somebody who could do it. I gave him a name. That's all. I don't know *why* he wanted it, or who he was going to film."

"No idea why, huh?"

She shook her head again, this time emphatically. "Not a clue. Nick usually ran his mouth a lot, but not about this. He acted like it was a nuclear secret."

I was inclined to believe her about that much, given how out-of-character careful Nick seemed to have been overall.

"Who made the video?" I said.

"Just a guy."

"I need to have a talk with him, too."

"All he did was set it up and burn the disk," she said, now looking worried and with a hint of pleading in her voice. "Nick didn't tell him what was going on with it, either. We didn't *want* to know more. You understand about that?"

I spent a few seconds deciding whether to keep pushing, but then opted to back off. She obviously did not want to give up "just a guy's" name; he was probably not a very *nice* guy, who might decide to take out his rage on her. And a good cop–bad cop routine right now might disarm her into talking more. I could come at her again if I needed to.

"All right, let's cut a deal," I said. "You tell him what I told you, and make sure the word gets to anybody else who knows about it. Not one fucking ripple about this better surface, ever. I'll put it on hold and hope it stays there. But if something goes wrong—they're up against the power structure that owns the bones of this city." I didn't like saying things like that, but it was true.

"I'll tell him, and he'll hear it, believe me."

"There's still no guarantee I can keep this under wraps, Denise," I said. Her eyes got wary again. "There's a lot more involved, I'm just starting to find out how much. I don't expect you to like me, but if you've got anything else that might help me out—it might help you, too."

She leaned back against a wall, cupping one elbow with her other hand and finishing off the smoke with a final fierce drag.

"Me and Nick got together once in a while, usually when he felt like it," she said. "I could tell he was into something—like he was expecting some kind of big payoff. I don't know what it was about—that's the honest to God truth. But there was one weird thing I've been thinking about.

"I was over at his place one night last week, and he got a phone call and I could hear enough to know somebody was coming by. Then he told me I had to leave—wouldn't say why, got kind of nasty about it. Pissed me off, man—I've done a lot for Nick, and all of a sudden he's tossing me away. I wanted to see what this was, you know? So I went along with it, took off in my car, but I parked down the road and snuck back. Pretty soon, this motorcycle comes rolling in."

That got my attention. "What did it look like?"

"Medium-size, black, kind of fancy. Not a *biker* bike like a Harley. Anyway, I didn't know who this was, but I just assume it's a guy, right? But then she takes off her helmet."

TWENTY-SIX

I walked back to my car, feeling almost light-headed about what I'd learned from Denise. The motorcycle and the female rider—slim, smallish, with a leather jacket and silver helmet—were a spot-on match for the ones I'd seen at Nick's yesterday.

And also for Lisa's eerie glimpse into the ether last night. *Is there a motorcycle involved? I think the person riding it is a woman.*

Denise had peeked in through a window at Nick's house—now suspecting that he'd sent her away so he could tryst with another girlfriend. But the encounter didn't seem romantic. Instead, the woman, although attractive, had a cold edge, and this appeared to be strictly business—she gave Nick an envelope stuffed with cash, along with a bag of white powder that was obviously drugs.

"That's what I can't figure out," Denise had said. "Why's she bringing him money *and* dope? You either buy it or sell it."

Good question.

The woman was fair-skinned and in her midthirties; Denise wasn't able to see her hair, hidden by a do-rag bandanna she wore under her helmet. When it looked like she was about to leave, Denise slipped away. The coldness that she sensed in the other woman had her spooked, and considering that Denise was not exactly a Sunday school teacher, that was saying something.

That was the end of the story, and of the information I could get from her. She claimed that she hadn't seen or spoken with Nick since that night. She was angry about his making her leave, angrier that he didn't call to smooth things over, and nervous about what she'd seen. Then she'd heard about his accident and realized the same thing that Hap had, along with God knew who else—Nick's recent activities were likely to come under scrutiny. But unlike Hap, she couldn't afford to pick up and leave town; she was just hoping to stay under the radar.

The situation made for a strange dynamic between her and me. In one way I was an enemy, with the power to cause her serious grief—in another way, an ally, with my own reasons for wanting to quell the trouble. I couldn't overlook the fact that she'd helped set up the video of Erica—even if she didn't know the who or why of it, she knew it was slimy. But it was a safe guess that Denise hadn't had much in the way of life choices, had gotten too used to men pushing her around—with Nick a prime example—and now she was getting older and doing what she could to get by. And tawdry though it all was, I got the odd sense that she really did care for him.

I didn't see any clear direction to go next. But the parking space I'd rented had a decent view of the beach and was even in the shade, so I decided to spend a few more minutes there trying to put things together. I rolled down the Cruiser's windows, got a notepad and pen, and started on a list of the major points that had turned up so far.

Nick's meltdown and his fall off the cliff. Was it a psychotic episode, or was there an outside cause? The dope he'd been do-ing was the first obvious possibility, and Dr. Shin at UCLA had found an additive she'd never seen before; she thought it was nanoparticles. Thousands of them would have gotten lodged in his brain via inhalation. But they weren't chemically active, and she didn't see how that would have affected his behavior; prob-ably they'd just gotten in the mix somehow during the manufac-turing process.

Nick had gotten a VoIP cell phone call just before he went completely berserk and attacked me, and quite a few similar calls during the previous days, many at odd times. I didn't see how those could have contributed directly to his breakdown, either, but maybe they had indirectly. I suspected that they figured into whatever scam he was running, and the calls might have been threats or some other tightening vise. But I had no idea what the scam was, and tracing the calls was next to impossible.

He was sitting on a lot of cash. It seemed likely that had come—along with the cocaine—from the woman on the motorcycle. She'd later returned and broken in, probably to try to recover it. But as Denise had pointed out, why had she delivered *both* drugs and money to him in the first place? There was no exchange of one for the other—it was more like she was paying him for something, using both as forms of currency. But paying him for what?

The next couple of factors were, if anything, more puzzling still. Nick had arranged and paid for DNA paternity tests for three unknown individuals and hidden them carefully. Clearly, they were important to him.

Then there was the sex video of Erica, which I now knew for sure he'd also arranged. It was tough to believe that he was capable of doing that to his own sister, but I had to admit that he was. It would have required an elaborate setup and another chunk of cash—like the DNA tests, this was important to him—which would have made sense if the object was blackmail. But while the phone call he'd made to her smacked of that, he hadn't demanded money or anything else tangible—he'd warned her not to interfere with something unspecified.

Finally, Nick had a scheme going with Hap Rasmussen. This might be unrelated, although the timing and the sudden about-face after their years of antagonism were suspect—especially if Hap was in money trouble.

I sat there a couple of minutes longer, watching the Venice Beach show and pushing it all around in my head. Nick going berserk. Coke laced with nanoparticles. VoIP phone calls. A pile of cash. Paternity tests. Sleazy video of our sister. Hap. Christ, how could Hap and Erica both even fit into this? They were worlds apart, with no connection except the casual family acquaintance. What could the paternity tests have to do with either of them, or with any of the rest of it? And on and on.

Well, at least I had a better handle on what I didn't know.

Now I had to face the bitter task of bringing my mother up to speed. It was going to give another twist to her already ravaged heart. But if I tried to keep it from her, she'd find out anyway, and that would only make it worse. I decided to get it over with. I took out my phone and called her.

With her unerring maternal prescience, she put her finger right on a sore spot as soon as I said hello.

"I've been trying to get hold of Hap, but he doesn't answer," she said. "I'm starting to get worried—thinking maybe I should go check on him."

"Stay put, Mom. I'm going to come over. I've got some news that figures in."

TWENTY-SEVEN

When I got to her house, she was sitting out on the porch with a pitcher of martinis that was a drink or two down. I didn't blame her a bit, and with any luck, it would help to cushion the blow. In fact, I'd have loved to join her, but I didn't feel I could afford to start letting down right now.

"What can I get you, dear?" she said.

"I'm okay—you relax." I sat across the table from her. She sipped her drink, with her eyebrows raised inquiringly. *Well?*

"I lied to you," I said. "This isn't just more of the same. I'd rather not tell you this—I'd rather not know it myself."

"That sounds ominous."

"The reason Hap's not answering is that he flew to Indonesia yesterday."

Her mouth opened in dismay. "He did *what*? Just like that, without saying anything?"

"I'm afraid he might have a good reason. Did he ever say anything to you about money problems?"

"Well—nothing in detail, but I did get that sense. He'd been borrowing from me, a few thousand here and there. But he made it sound like it was just to tide him over through a shortfall."

I exhaled, then went ahead and laid it down.

"Nick was running some kind of money scam," I said. "I don't know what, but not his usual nickel-dime stuff. I think it's big and ugly—and I've got a feeling Hap's in on it."

If I ever had to invent a curse along the lines of, *May you live in interesting times,* it would go, *May you someday have to tell your mother what I just told mine.* She stared at me, then lowered her face into her hands. I got up and stepped over to her. But I was finding out that Audrey was made of sterner stuff than I'd realized. She came back up dry-eyed, even managing a shaky smile.

"I'm trying to decide which one of them to kill first," she said.

I sagged a little with relief, then leaned down and kissed the top of her head.

"Take your pick—but leave the other one for me, okay?" I sat again and filled her glass from the martini pitcher.

"How could that happen?" she said. "They loathe each other. They haven't talked in years."

"They've been talking plenty these last few weeks. Nick called Erica, too, and lied to me about it."

My mother took another measured sip of her drink. "All right, tell me the rest," she said. "I know you've been trying to shield me, Tom, and it's sweet. Funny how that works—when kids are young, it's the parents who do it. Then it turns the other way around. But now, 'sweet' is off the table."

I did, picking up the thread from the time I'd left here yesterday, gone to Nick's house, and found the drugs and cash—along with the DNA paternity tests.

"I need to get an expert to look at them," I said. "The only thing I could tell was that two of them seemed to have the same father, but the third was different."

But then I paused. Audrey's face had started taking on a peculiar expression that wasn't worry or anger or puzzlement. It was more like slow, spreading shock.

"*What*, Mom?" I said.

She turned her head to the side, gazing past me.

"I'm hearing the rattle of a skeleton," she murmured.

Jesus wept—my mother? The one person in all this whom I'd assumed was pristine?

"Okay, enough," I said. "Time for *you* to come clean with *me*."

She rose a little unsteadily to her feet. I got up again to brace her, but she waved me away.

"Just give me a minute." She went to the porch railing, grasping it with both hands and leaning forward like an old-time sailor's wife on a widow's walk, watching the sea for his returning ship.

I stayed where I was, waiting.

"Things do catch up with us, don't they?" she said. "I always thought it would. But my God, what a bizarre way for it to happen."

"Then it should fit right in with everything else," I said.

"I'm getting there, hon. I'm not trying to be dramatic. It's just hard to say." She shook her head almost dreamily. "I had an affair, Tom. After you and Nick were born. The two of you have the same father, just like you always thought. So does Erica. But not Paul."

When that one hit home, my feet just about left the floor.

"I have to think that's what those tests are about," my mother said. "Nick must have found out and wanted proof." She was still standing there gripping the rail and looking forlorn. I recovered enough to step over to her and put my arm around her shoulders. She leaned her head against me gratefully.

"Who was the man?" I said.

She turned her face toward me, and I thought I saw in her

eyes, along with the sorrow of all that this meant, a great relief at finally laying the burden down.

"That's what made this fall into place for me," she said. "He's the only other person who ever knew—the only one who could have told Nick. It was Hap, darling. Paul's real father is Hap."

TWENTY-EIGHT

I stayed with Audrey for another hour, coaxing the rest of the story out of her while she downed another couple of drinks. Now I *really* wanted to climb into the martini pitcher myself, but staying clear-minded was that much more important. Eventually, she started to wind down, and I convinced her that she needed to rest. I walked her inside, got her settled on a couch, and covered her with a blanket. Then I went back out into the sunlight and just stood there, soaking it up as if it could reach deep into me and brighten my heart.

Well, there it was, the key to the puzzle—a secret hidden in my mother's demure bosom all these years, that I'd grown up right beside and never had the faintest hint of. Now the pieces were snapping together with almost dizzying speed—and it was a grim little picture emerging.

The roots went back more than thirty years, to early in my parents' marriage. My father was a powerful man who believed that as long as he supported his family well, he had the right to a private life away from us, including other women. My mother knew but had no choice except to suffer it quietly or leave him. And with Nick and me to care for, both of us still tykes, that wasn't in the cards.

But the old man's infidelities made her feel justified in thinking about a private life of her own—there was an element of revenge, she admitted—and her eye started focusing on Hap. At first glance he seemed like an odd choice; but they'd been close,

affectionate friends for years, he was gorgeous, and even his being gay added to the intrigue.

"It was a challenge," she had told me. "I think a lot of women
feel that draw at some point—am I attractive enough to turn
him around?"

Hap was willing to experiment, but no real chemistry ever
developed, and the affair didn't last long. They managed to come
out of it with their affection intact.

And with Paul on the way.

Audrey was still sleeping with my father through that time,
and no one, including him, ever suspected that the child wasn't
his. No one ever would have—except Hap.

There was no telling yet how he and Nick had hooked up.
I could envision a scenario where they'd run into each other by
chance. Nick was always on the lookout for money, and he knew
that Hap's hatred for him was really love-hate still smoldering under the bitterness. He'd homed in on that, thinking he could use
it to bilk Hap. It turned out to be a bust because Hap was on thin
ice himself. But it gave them a common interest, and the Crandall
fortune, maddeningly close to them both, was an obvious target.

Somehow in the mix, Hap confessed the secret about Paul.
That was when things turned ugly. My guess was that Hap was
essentially a dupe, lured in by Nick's manipulation, with Nick
using him like he used everyone else. Hap was implicated, no
doubt—already nervous and more so as things got more serious,
and finally scared enough to leave town. It was almost more sad-
dening than angering that he would sink so low, and right now
he was probably feeling about as miserable as a human being
could get.

But the driving force behind the scheme was Nick; it had his
stamp all over it.

And what it came down to was blackmail.

Paul was illegitimate. If that became known, his claim to any inheritance—any share or control of family assets, money, property—would be in jeopardy or even entirely void. There'd be long and tangled court battles where the only winners were the lawyers, with spin-off litigation from business partners, relatives who felt that *they* now had a claim, and so on. Paul would be devastated financially, and almost worse, he'd lose the cachet he'd been riding on all his life, of being the scion of the Crandall family and fortune. All in all, he'd be shattered.

Nick had decided that this was his ticket back into the family money—to approach Paul and threaten to take him down unless Paul opened the coffers. Without doubt, Nick's rage at being thrown out of the Malibu house added a vicious edge, and I wondered if he'd demanded its return as part of the deal. It might be why he'd made that addled claim to me that he still lived there.

First, Nick made impressively careful preparations. He got the paternity tests done to prove Paul's illegitimacy. He'd easily have pilfered DNA samples from Dad, Paul, and me—a few strands of hair, one of the old man's sweat-soaked golf hats, even a licked envelope would do.

Of course Nick had intended for the dealings and the payoffs to be secret, but he was canny enough to realize that this might come to the family's attention. Paul would have to come up with a lot of money, and while he'd try to conceal it, he was not the sharpest knife in the drawer. Nick figured that if Audrey or I found out—enraged though we'd be—he could handle us. We might make him back off, but we wouldn't take it public or send him to prison. To him, that was a risk worth taking.

But Erica was a different story. If she copped, she was guaranteed to go ballistic, and the whole thing would blow up with her. So Nick had set up the sleazy video and given her a warning. She didn't understand it, but she would have if push had come to shove—cross him, and personal disaster for her was only a few clicks of a mouse away.

Then he'd made his pitch to Paul. It wasn't clear how far things had gone, but my guess was that Paul had caved and made at least one payment to Nick, the cash and drugs I'd found at his house.

Well, if I looked at it gimlet-eyed, I had to say that Nick's bad luck was the family's good luck—his breakdown had saved us a lot of damage. I felt sorry as hell for Paul, although he was not the soul of sensitivity and his worries about losing money and status would outweigh any emotional shock. I recalled his stunned look of relief when I'd told him about Nick's amnesia, and now I understood that, too; he was off the hook, or at least so he thought.

The best course I could see from here was to clamp the lid on tight. Audrey would take the secret to her grave, and so would I. The last thing in the world Paul wanted was exposure, and the same was true of Hap. Erica had no inkling about any of it, and with luck, she never would.

As for Nick, I had no hesitations about how to handle him— tell him flat out that I knew what he'd done, and I knew he remembered a lot more about it than he was letting on, but he'd *better* fucking forget that it ever happened. If I ever heard another whisper about it or anything like it, I would personally turn him in to the police.

But there was still plenty to worry about, starting with the possibility that other people knew about this and might try to exploit it for their own profit. The female motorcycle rider, for instance. She might not know what the payment was for, but then again, she had to be someone Paul knew and trusted reasonably well, and he was a big talker, particularly when he was nervous. It seemed clear that she was at home with crime; besides the drug delivery angle, she'd pulled a B and E. Another troubling wrinkle was the thought that she might have been double-crossing Paul—that she wasn't trying to recover the stuff for him, but he didn't even know about the break-in and she intended to keep it herself.

The other candidate at the top of that list was Paul's new squeeze, Cynthia Trask.

And as that thought crossed my mind, the connection came like a lightning flash.

The motorcycle babe *was* Cynthia Trask.

Everything fit to a T—her relationship with Paul, her physical appearance, even the chill factor that Denise had described. That meant she damned well did know what was going on—and that brought me another sudden near certainty. When she'd ransacked Nick's house, she wasn't looking for the money and dope. At that time, only a few hours after his fall, it still looked like he might die or be seriously brain-damaged—and Cynthia wanted to destroy those paternity tests before somebody else might stumble across them. Then the threat to Paul would have disappeared.

For all the bad bullshit involved, I'd had a lot of luck, too—Nick's taking unusual care to hide the DNA charts, my thinking to look for them in the old desk, then finding the further links that helped me make sense of this—and now I realized that in a backhanded way, here was another touch of it. If Cynthia got troublesome, I just might be able to cause her some trouble, too.

Before I left my mother's place, I went back inside to check on her. She looked like she was resting comfortably; she didn't open her eyes, but she must have heard me.

"I'm all right—you run along," she murmured. "I know you have a lot on your mind."

No argument there. But I felt that I was starting to close my fist on something besides thin air.

I'd had my cell phone turned off since I got here, not wanting any interruptions while she and I talked; as I walked to my car, I checked the voice mail.

There was only one message, and it stopped me cold.

"Dr. Crandall, this is Marilyn at UCLA Medical Center," a woman's voice said, with a tone of controlled urgency. "Please contact us as soon as you can."

I remembered Marilyn from yesterday—one of the nurses in the ICU, a fiftyish woman with the generous face of a professional caregiver. I punched the callback number she left and got her on the phone.

"I'm very sorry to have to tell you this," she said. "There's been a change in your brother's condition."

I listened numbly to her brief explanation. Nick had suffered a cerebral aneurysm and had been rushed into emergency surgery. It seemed that his blood pressure had risen suddenly and sharply. There was no apparent reason for the spike, but it had burst a blood vessel possibly already weakened by his concussion.

I drove straight to the hospital, and events took another strange twist. Right away, I found Marilyn to get an update on Nick; she told me his condition was basically unchanged, and he was still in surgery.

Then she said, "This isn't directly related, Dr. Crandall, but I thought you might like to know. A detective came by this morning to talk to your brother—a man named Drabyak. Nick was resting, so we asked him to come back later. He said he would, but he hasn't yet."

At the moment, I was too worried about Nick to be more than vaguely surprised. But after I settled down some, with nothing to do but wait around, I decided to give Drabyak a call and find out what had sparked his renewed interest in Nick. I got his voice mail, left a message, and went back to waiting.

Within another two hours, Nick was physically stable again, but he was still in a coma. This time, nobody was offering assurances that he'd ever come out of it.

I didn't hear from Drabyak for the rest of that day. When I tried him again the next morning, I just got his voice mail again.

But early in the afternoon, I got a call from a woman named Susan Brownlee, an assistant to Mayor Sandoval. She was very polite, but I had the feeling she knew how not to be. She started off with the usual formalities—the mayor sent his sympathy about Nick, and so on.

Then the conversation took an unsettling twist.

"Dr. Crandall, I should tell you that the detective you spoke with, Sergeant Drabyak, won't be available for a while," she said. "He had a family emergency, and he had to take an unexpected leave of absence. If you have any questions for him, please call me directly, and I'll see to it that you get the help you need."

Family emergency? That was a hell of a coincidence, and so was the timing. I couldn't help wondering if Drabyak had been shoved out of the picture by someone who had a lot of juice— maybe connected to those prominent people he was investigating—and this was a way of letting me know it.

If I needed help, I wasn't going to be turning to my erstwhile pal Joaquin Sandoval or anyone else in those circles, that was for sure.

TWENTY-NINE

The next Friday morning, I headed north on Highway 1 to Malibu again, getting ready for what was going to be a really unpleasant encounter with Paul. I'd had to call him several times before I finally got hold of him last night and told him I had news that I had to deliver in person. He didn't like the sound of that and tried to put me off, saying that he was going to spend today at the Malibu house; he was starting to move forward with his plans to build his new house. I said I'd drive on up and meet him there midmorning.

I'd spent most of the past week dealing with Nick's medical situation and trying to get a fix on the future in general. His looked bleak, with no signs of recovering consciousness, and I had to keep myself on a tight leash. To have him almost die, start making a miraculous recovery, and then suddenly plunge back was crushing. The ugly cloud around him made it close to unbearable. And the grim decision of how long to keep him on life support was starting to appear on the horizon.

So I concentrated on practicalities in order to stave off my emotions—with Paul being the other major issue.

My mother and I had talked the situation over, then brought in our longtime chief legal counsel, Lou Monroe—the man I'd intended to talk to anyway about Paul's affair with Cynthia Trask.

Lou's grasp of the situation was quick and steely. He was very smart and the essence of professional integrity—we could trust him absolutely with the paternity secret. He was also very tough, and he'd gun down anybody who threatened the family interests, even a member. The three of us had come to a decision.

Paul's involvement in the family business was over.

He didn't yet know anything about this, or even that we'd uncovered the blackmail scheme. I'd volunteered to tell him. Although he was going to be furious, I was actually looking forward to it—partly just to get it over with, but partly because the more I'd thought about it, the angrier at him I'd gotten. He knew damned well that he was putting the family at risk to cover his own greedy ass, and his callousness was underscored by his worrying about his goddamned glossy house project only days after Nick fell into the coma.

I still felt sorry for him in a way, but I'd hardened my heart about that, too.

The morning was sunny and the town of Malibu was getting into summery mode as I drove through, with plenty of tourists and the beaches getting crowded. I crawled along with the traffic to Point Dume, then turned off toward the headlands. I wouldn't have been surprised if Paul had stood me up, but when I got to our boarded-up old house, his BMW was parked in the driveway. I walked around to the back and found him on the patio, standing over a thick sheaf of blueprints and talking on his cell phone.

As he looked up at me, I got an eerie little hit. With his sandy brown hair and wide, square-jawed face, I could see hints of resemblance between him and Hap.

"Okay, baby, I've got to go—Tom's here," Paul said into the phone. "I'll call you again in a little while." He clicked it off and gave me his executive smile. "Cynthia says hi."

"I'm sure." I was feeling a little easier about her by now because I'd gotten another piece of information that pretty much nailed her as the woman who'd delivered the cocaine to Nick and then broke into his house. Lou Monroe knew a lot of people, and he'd had no problem discreetly tapping into California DMV registration records. Cynthia owned a black 2006 MV F4CC— a very rare Italian racing motorcycle that retailed for a modest $120,000. I didn't see any reason to tip my hand about it, but if I got one, I was going to let her know that I could put a serious kink in her glossy life.

Paul was nervous, and that led him into his usual evasive bluster.

"Hey, have you seen these plans yet?" he said. "Take a look."

I feigned polite interest as he showed me the architectural renderings of the new house, then flipped through the blueprints pointing out features and luxuries. The place was eleven thousand square feet and probably close to that many million dollars, with a high-ceilinged ocean exposure that was mostly glass and every other bell and whistle you could dream of—in other words, a monument to arrogance and poor taste. Most rankling of all was my certainty that he wasn't even building it for his wife and child, but for himself and Cynthia.

"Very impressive," I said. "You ready to talk?"

He gave me an irritated shrug. "Sure." Then he rolled up the prints and tucked them under his arm officiously—an unsubtle hint that he was busy, and the sooner I got out of here, the better.

"Paul, you're my brother and I love you," I said. "I'm sorry about this, but I've got to do it. I know what happened with you and Nick—the blackmail, the whole deal. I found those paternity tests at his place. I told Mom about them, she told me about Hap, and the rest came together."

I'd never before seen the blood literally drain from somebody's face. For a few seconds I thought he was actually going to pass out, and I tensed myself to jump forward and grab him. But he stayed on his feet, turning his back and slowly walking away a few steps.

"Don't even think about trying to bullshit me," I said. "I'll cut to the chase. I'm here to tell you you're fired."

He swung back around to stare at me. "You can't *do* that," he stammered.

"You left us no choice, Paul. If you'd been up-front with us as soon as Nick hit on you, we'd have stuck with you—tried to work through the legal issues, all that. But hiding it destroyed our faith in your judgment. We also suspect that you intended to commit fraud with the finances—maybe already did, and maybe other crimes, too. And above all, you betrayed our trust. If you want to take it to court, go ahead. You'll get skinned alive, and you know it."

I was expecting his shock to erupt into rage any second. But instead, incredibly, a slow smile spread across his face—the kind of patronizing look that goes along with the line, "You brought a knife to a gunfight." It was as startling as when he'd turned pale, and much more unsettling.

"Tom, you think you're so fucking smart. But you have no idea what you're saying."

"I don't think I'm smart, Paul—I've been around too many people who *are* smart, and I know the difference. I know real well what I'm saying, too, so let me finish. You're going to come out of this just fine." *A hell of a lot better than you deserve,* I was sorely tempted to add. "Nobody else knows about it except Mom and Lou, and we'll do our best to keep it that way. You'll stay a full family member same as ever, and so will your kids. You'll keep your own inheritance, including this property. But no more access to family funds or business."

He went on as if he hadn't even heard me.

"No, you *don't* know what you're saying. Cynthia and I tried to help you—to open a door. But you ignored us."

"Open a door? What the fuck are *you* saying?"

"That you're making a really serious mistake."

I bristled. "If you're getting into threat turf, Paul, you're the one making the serious mistake. Yet another one."

"It's not a threat—it's for your own good," he said. "See, there's somebody behind that door. Except it's not a door like that"—he pointed at the slider that led from the patio into the house—"and they're not people. And this is really going to piss them off."

I was struck by the thought that with all the worrying I'd done about Nick's mental condition, I'd failed to realize that Paul was doing a space walk of his own—no doubt thanks to the influence of his new squeeze and Parallax.

"In that case, thanks for the warning," I said. "By the way, I made up my mind about that lease extension at the Lodge. I'll give Parallax time to finish the movie—call it four months. After that, I want them out."

He shook his head almost pityingly. "You better back off all this, Tom."

"Believe me, I wish none of it had happened. Give me a call if you want to talk." I turned and walked to my car.

For outright strange, that was tough to beat.

The riff about him and Cynthia trying to open a door must have meant the pep talk they'd given me at the Lodge last week, obviously aimed at getting me interested in Parallax; at a guess, the nonpeople behind the door alluded to the otherworldly Gate-keepers that Lisa had mentioned. But them being angry at me about this? Even a hint that they intended to punish me somehow?

I put it down to bluster, psychobabble—the Parallax equivalent of any religious fanatic threatening divine retribution against unbelievers. Paul would rant and sulk for a while, but then reality would settle in—including that he was still a rich man about to build a glitzy new house in Malibu, for Christ's sake. He'd probably find other ways to squander his inheritance, but maybe hardnosed Cynthia would keep him in check. Then again, maybe she would help him burn right through it. But that was no longer my problem; I just hoped they stayed off my radar.

With that unhappy encounter taken care of and the overall situation seeming more under control, I let my thoughts relax in a much happier direction—Lisa. We'd seen each other twice more since that first dinner, and we had a date this evening. I felt a touch guilty about embarking on a romance under these circumstances, especially because of Nick. But what good would it do him or anyone else if I held back? Besides, she was the one oasis in all this; when I was with her, I could almost literally feel myself coming more to life, and leaving her brought that same chilly anxiety I'd felt the first time.

THIRTY

It was time to start drifting back toward a normal routine. I had plenty to catch up on, that was for sure; I'd been letting everything else slide, including work. Above all, I wanted to shake off that miserable, near-panicky feeling that there was always something more important I *should* be doing.

I'd never had migraines, thank God, but for the first time in my life I'd been getting headaches that seemed in that ballpark—not terribly severe but still damned unpleasant, impairing my concentration and amping up that hollow anxiety. They were like a stealthy enemy that attacked when I was alone, invading my dreams and tearing up my sleep. I put it down to stress, figuring I'd racked up a fair amount of that.

So I deliberately took things slow as the day moved on—drove home by a circuitous route, dawdled over grocery shopping on the way, spent some quality time shredding a bushel of accumulated junk mail, and so on. My place was looking pretty shabby, too, but since I was going to Lisa's later instead of her coming here, cleaning could wait for tomorrow.

Toward midafternoon I headed out again, this time for Waterton College, where I'd been making a slender living as a faculty adjunct. I needed to check in at my office there; summer session would be starting in early June. I also needed exercise. I usually worked out three or four times a week on the campus—a half hour in the weight room and a couple-mile run in the surrounding foothills—but I'd been letting that go like everything else, and I was starting to feel slack.

I had another reason for going there, too—dependents. There was a clan of feral cats that hung out in a grove of trees and shrubs near my office. They'd correctly figured me for a soft touch as soon as I moved in, and they started putting the paw on me. Before long we were doing lunch together—mine—and by now I'd gotten in the habit of bringing them a sack of food when I started my run, sort of like paying a toll. I knew it wasn't politically correct, it would encourage more breeding, and all that. But the sight of the scrawny little beasts with their matted fur, mewing hungrily, was too much for me. They still wouldn't let me touch them, but they were always there waiting when I came walking by, darting between my feet and yelling at me to surrender the goods. Just now I was behind on the vig, and I had no doubt that they were keeping careful score.

Waterton was toward the west end of the Valley; the afternoon was sunny, the temperature just right, and the drive pleasant, if not very interesting.

Which was probably why, even though I didn't want to think about Paul anymore, my mind kept going back to him just like had happened with Nick when all this first blew up.

I hadn't had time to give much thought to the potential cultlike aspects of Parallax, but with Paul's strange pronouncement, that was back on my radar and I had to start sorting things out. Lisa's involvement, for instance, seemed benign; she was interested and inclined to accept the thinking—and I had to admit, no way could I explain her psychic glimpse of a woman on a motorcycle—but that was as far as it went. She maintained a healthy awareness that it was in the nature of an experiment, something she was trying out that might fall through. There was no psychological *dependence* on it.

But Paul had the fervor of the convert, which suggested to me that he was a prime candidate for the trap of cognitive dissonance, a sort of convoluted form of denial. Strictly speaking, this wasn't my field, but I encountered it a lot, and to me it was one of the strangest and most intriguing threads that wove through the human psyche. There was much speculation and much disagreement as to the *why* of it, but vastly oversimplified, it went something like this.

It is no secret that emotions often, even most often, overpower reason. If people come to believe in or care for something strongly—a religion, a political stance, a prejudice, a family member or close friend—there is a tendency to cling to that belief even if it is proved to them beyond doubt that they are getting ripped off, emotionally and often enough, financially. Just about everyone has experienced it with a loved one at one time or another; I certainly had with Nick.

With most people, reason will prevail sooner or later and they'll back off. But a surprising number of others are especially susceptible—particular personality types figure in, although they might be as intelligent, competent, and "normal" as anyone else—and here is where it gets both fascinating and frightening. In these cases, nothing can convince them to give up the belief; on the contrary, the more blatantly false and damaging it gets, the more doggedly they'll hang on. They will buy into increasingly absurd rationales to justify it—rather than admit they've been chumps, they become bigger ones. There are well-documented examples of perpetrators essentially laughing in their victims' faces without that changing a thing.

In other words, a great many people will fight ferociously *against* their own best interests, and *for* interests that are out to use them and even ruin them, if the right strings are pulled.

Needless to say, demagogues, power brokers, and con artists have understood this from time immemorial and figured out a lot of ways to pull those strings; by and large, old tried-and-true techniques still work just fine. The baseline premise, driven home to the subjects over and over, is that they are *superior*. The reasons might include their race, their beliefs, or just their good taste in buying a particular product; often, they advance through stages of gaining more insider knowledge and privilege. All troubles are blamed on enemies, who are belittled, even dehumanized and persecuted; if there are no real enemies, they are created, with scapegoats common and dirty tactics blamed on them which actually are used by the blamers themselves. Disagreement and even questioning are not tolerated, education is disparaged or forbidden, accurate information suppressed or distorted, and so on.

Modern psychology has given a huge boost to refining all that, and it has mushroomed into an industry, largely covert, that reaches into political spin-doctoring and propaganda, indoctrination of all forms—particularly effective with young kids—many applications in industry and the military, advertising, and damned near every other area where someone is trying to influence someone else on a large scale.

I'd gotten very interested in all that as a student, but set it aside to pursue what seemed like a more sensible career. But over the past couple of years that interest had reawakened, and now, what with Parallax an influence both in my family and with Lisa, it had taken a personal turn.

I didn't see any clear direction in which it might go. But I did have the sense that my life was turning a page, and that somehow that would figure into what came next.

THIRTY-ONE

I parked in the Waterton College faculty lot and started walking, with the cat food in my day pack. I figured that feeding them was probably breaking some kind of rule, so I tried to do it on the sly and kept the stuff out of sight.

The campus was pleasantly quiet during break. This was a two-year community college, but a big and very pretty one—built in the 1940s, with Spanish architecture, several hundred acres of wooded grounds, gardens, and even a redwood grove. Attendance was upward of 20,000 students per semester, with a high percentage transferring on to full four-year institutions; an excellent use of taxpayer money, by my lights, and I felt lucky to be working there. It had been a good home for the past few years, what with my washout from clinical work, my father's death, the breakup with my ex-girlfriend, and trying to keep tabs on Nick. The job was enough but not too much, with a real reward in feeling that I could genuinely get an important concept across to a class, or counsel sullen, suspicious kids who'd come from unbelievably fucked-up backgrounds—dope, sex, and abuse, sometimes from infancy—and maybe start them seeing that they weren't to blame and they had a chance to pull themselves out.

I walked on to the gym, changed, and went to the weight room to get the more onerous part of the workout over with first—nothing serious, just a few sets of bench presses, pull-downs, sit-ups on an incline board, and such, to keep the muscle tone from turning to soup. I didn't swim much anymore. I'd spent so many thousands of hours when I was younger following that black line on the bottom or chasing a water polo ball or bucking surf at the beach that I'd lost my taste for it; and while the weights seemed heavier as I aged, and so did my feet when I ran, I liked being out in the open air and working up a sweat I could feel.

Later today, however, I was going to hit the water again. Lisa had a pool at her home, but she'd never learned much beyond dog-paddling, and she'd asked me to give her a few pointers.

You bet.

When I was done in the weight room, I got the cat food from my locker and headed out to the running path, expecting my furry little buddies to come out and start yelling at me about why the hell I'd been gone so long.

But this time, there was no sign of them.

I was worried. In the trees and thick bushes they could probably get away from dogs, but they'd be at risk from more dangerous predators—coyotes, raccoons, bobcats, or even a cougar.

As I looked around, I noticed a fair amount of whitish dust sprinkled on the ground and foliage. Christ, had the maintenance department decided the cats were too much of a nuisance and deliberately poisoned them? But it was probably a pesticide or fertilizer, and they'd been living with all that stuff for years.

I walked to the edge of the thicket, shaking the food sack. "Hey, you guys, it's just me," I called. "Come on out, let me see you so I know you're okay." I took another couple of steps forward on the narrow little path where I usually dumped the food.

That was when the poison theory crashed hard. A throaty yowl came rising up from ahead—the kind of hair-raising, ululating sound that cats make when they're warning off an enemy or about to attack. A couple of others joined in, like a chorus of banshees.

I stopped. Now I was starting to see them, sinuous shapes darting through the rustling bushes.

It honest to God felt like they were surrounding me.

Abruptly, one of them lunged out on a tree limb above my head and swiped at my face, hissing and spitting. I jerked away just in time to avoid the slash and caught a glimpse of the creature's yellow eyes, filled with fury that seemed almost demonic.

I got out of there a lot faster than I'd gone in and kept backing away for several more steps, nervous that they might follow. Instead, they went quiet again, which was far eerier still—like knowing that you were looking straight at something lying in wait to rip you apart.

What—the—*fuck*?

Could somebody have scared or harmed them so badly that they were all suddenly terrified of humans? I doubted it; there were quite a few of them, probably a couple of dozen, and it was hard to imagine what could cause such a sweeping and radical behavior change. A disease outbreak—maybe rabies? That seemed more within the realm of possibility, although I still had a hard time buying that so many animals could get infected so quickly and turn from feral but friendly to uniformly vicious, in just one week. But it was a possibility I had to take seriously—if they were dangerous, much as I hated the thought, they'd have to be put down. I decided to give it a couple of days; over the weekend, especially during break, there'd hardly be anyone around. If I got the same kind of reception on Monday, I'd have to inform the administration. I dumped out my sack of food in a new spot—they'd find it if they wanted it—and took off on my run.

After the workout and a shower, I stopped by my cubbyhole office to check mail and messages, and to gather a few materials I wanted to work on at home. I wasn't in any rush, and after

going through e-mails I decided to further my own education
a little.

The issue of the nanoparticles in Nick's cocaine hadn't
come up again since my talk with Dr. Ivy Shin at UCLA, and
I'd hardly thought about it while I dealt with the other pressing
matters. But I was curious, and I figured it couldn't hurt to have
a nodding acquaintance with this hot new technology.

The word *nano* itself was hot, I discovered; when I typed it
into Google, it brought up about 130 million matches. Most of
them seemed to be for gadgets like Apple iPods and even a brand
of cars, so I tried "nanotechnology." The result was still a respect-
able ten million, and more along the lines of what I was looking
for. I winnowed out a few of the less technical ones and tried to
get an overview.

It was a relatively new branch of science; the famously eccentric physicist Richard Feynman was credited with first proposing
the existence of the ultratiny particles in the late 1950s. Just *how*
tiny they were was mind-boggling. Medieval theologians may
have debated about how many angels could dance on the head of
a pin, but modern science gave a concrete estimate of the number of nanos that could fit—several million. A human hair was
100,000 nanos thick.

Over the next decades, research accelerated explosively. By
now, as Ivy had said, the particles were everywhere—in socks
to make them drier, tennis balls to make them smoother, razor blades to make them sharper, as fillers in food and additives in pharmaceuticals and cosmetics. New applications
were hitting the market literally every week, with possibilities touted that ranged from new cancer treatments to fuel
sources. There were also some red flags about safety issues,
including fears that they could be used for virulent WMD,

and of course there were potential consequences that nobody could yet imagine.

Public awareness of all this was not high, and as near as I could tell, no form of regulation was poised to step in. On the contrary, the industry seemed to be a wide-open gold rush with a lot of interests wanting to keep it that way. We were all going to spend our lives surrounded by increasing trillions of the little motes.

I locked up the office and headed to my car, on my way to my swim date with Ms. DiFurio.

THIRTY-TWO

The drive to Lisa's place in the Hollywood Hills was only about ten miles from the college as the crow flies, but it still took me a good half hour. I knew it was just the same old everyday traffic, but it somehow seemed even more frantic than usual, with drivers appearing out of nowhere in my rearview mirror just inches from my bumper, then lunging around to cut me off. It was like everybody's life depended on beating somebody else to the next red light.

I decided that I was just more jangled than I'd realized from my encounter with those cats. I'd put it out of my mind while I was in my office, but I'd started reliving it again during the drive, and I could tell that it was going to keep nagging at me. It was simply so *wrong*—not in the sense that it was their fault, but having the rug jerked out from under me, a pleasant little ritual suddenly turned into an ugly, baffling slap in the face. Maybe the really bothersome thing was that it had come right as I thought I was getting back on track.

I made it to the gated community where Lisa lived a little after five. The place wasn't wildly upscale, and her own house was fairly modest, but a female celeb like her, living alone, needed the security. I'd been here once before, and the same guard was at the kiosk today; he clearly wasn't impressed by my vehicle, but he probably remembered it. Still, he took his time checking my license plates against the guest list before waving me through.

I parked in Lisa's driveway and rang the bell. She came to the door wearing a terry-cloth wrapper over a turquoise bikini—ready for her swimming lesson. But as soon as she saw me, her smile changed to a worried look and she raised her hand to touch my face like a mother with a fevered child.

"What's going on with you?" she said.

"I'm fine. Just hectic traffic."

She nodded, although she didn't seem convinced. Then her eyes widened and her hand went to her mouth.

"Oh, God, I'm so stupid—I never even thought about this," she said. "I hope it's not because of Nick. You know, the swimming thing."

"No, no, that doesn't have anything to do with it. I'm pretty much bulletproof about pulling people out of the water, even my brother." I pulled a bathing suit out of my backpack. "Is there a designated changing room?"

"Right here's fine, honey. I hate it that we even have to wear the fucking things, but you never know when there's some creep up in a tree with a camera."

"I hate it, too, but it'll help me stay on task."

I put on the suit and followed her downstairs to the pool. The house wasn't either big or fancy, but comfortable and tastefully furnished. A few features did set it apart from the norm—a big comfortable screening room for viewing daily rushes and other professional needs, a hardwood-floored dance and exercise studio, and a *lot* of closets, all of them packed.

The lower level of the house was set back into a hillside and surrounded the swimming pool patio on three sides, with the fourth side an open view west to the ocean. It was nicely private except, as she'd pointed out, for the possibility of paparazzi or stalkers. She loved to paddle around, but she was afraid to go deeper than her waist, which, I assured her, was very wise. I probably sounded pompous, but it was something I felt strongly about, for good reason.

"When something goes wrong, you're talking seconds, and it can happen in a little pool just like this one within a couple of feet of the edge," I said. "Usually people panic, start thrashing around, and wear themselves out."

That was also a prime way for would-be rescuers to get drowned. Victims would cling to them with desperate strength and pin their arms, or try to climb up on them and submerge their heads, until both went down. Lifeguards who had to make that kind of a jump were trained to surface dive several feet in front of the victims, grab their ankles, turn them facing away, then get them in a kind of sleeper hold.

"You're supposed to try to float, right?" Lisa said. "Like on your back? I've tried it, but I can't make it work very well. Maybe if I had bigger boobs."

"Well, they did call those old lifejackets Mae Wests."

She rolled her eyes. "So now am I going to have to listen to breaststroke jokes?"

"Not unless you start them. Okay, there's the back float and the dead man's float, and they're both good to know, especially if you're stuck out in open water for a long time—your boat capsizes, something like that. But first line of defense is to thrash *efficiently.*"

I hopped into the pool's shallow end and took her hand as she came down the ladder, then led her out a little ways and had her wait there while I went on out shoulder deep.

"This is called the eggbeater kick," I said, demonstrating. "It's sort of like pedaling a bicycle except more side to side, and you're shaking your ass. Use your hands, too—palms down flat, back and forth like you're doing the Charleston." The eggbeater was natural once you got the hang of it and also very powerful, the mainstay of water polo players; a good goalie could lunge up above the surface to midthighs. Strong swimmers could keep it up indefinitely, and just about anyone in reasonably good physical condition could do it for the critical couple of minutes that might separate rescue from death.

Lisa came out toward me, a little timidly as the water deepened, then turned around and gave it a try while I held her waist.

"It *is* kind of like dancing," she said after a minute. "Good workout, too. *Monster* thighs."

"You'll pick it up in no time. It's tiring at first, but you learn to slow down and let the water carry you."

"I'll keep practicing."

"Stay where you can touch bottom."

"Don't worry. So let me catch my breath a minute, and why don't you go ahead and swim? I can probably learn some things just by watching."

We moved back into shallower water; then I took off for a leisurely freestyle lap. I felt a little shameless about showing off, but what the hey. I glided into the deep end wall and rolled, swinging my legs up over in a flip turn. My feet touched the side, and I shoved back out.

And *Lord*—in that instant, out of nowhere, my head got jolted by a violent shock. It was like nothing I'd ever felt or imagined—not exactly painful, but creepy, nasty, like every cell in my brain was suddenly writhing.

I let out a yell, or what would have been a yell except that I was underwater, and came within a heartbeat of doing just what I'd been preaching about—panicking and inhaling a mouthful.

I completely lost my bearings and my sense of up and down; it took me several seconds of twisting around before I found the surface. I grabbed the pool edge and clung there, sucking in air.

By then the sensation was ebbing. I realized that Lisa had gotten out of the pool and was hurrying toward me anxiously.

"I'm okay," I managed to say, and tried to believe it.

THIRTY-THREE

A few minutes later, I was dressed again and sitting on the upstairs deck watching the sun make its slow dive to the Pacific
horizon—and trying to figure out what the hell was going on
with me. I tried to find a feasible explanation—that while I was
twisting around in the flip turn, I'd sharply pinched a nerve. But
that was bullshit, and I didn't believe either that it was evidence
of a brain tumor or ministroke or any such thing. It crossed my
mind that I could have caught a disease from Nick when I was
giving him mouth-to-mouth, like a rare virus that attacked the
meninges and caused hallucinations or agony. "Worms eating my
brain" was a damned good description of what I'd felt, and goddamned savage worms. But I'd never heard of any such condition, and with all the tests the hospital had run on him, there'd
been no suggestion like that.

Lisa came out of the house and handed me a brimming glass
of Bombay gin on the rocks with a lemon wedge.

"I canceled our dinner rez and ordered a pizza," she said.

I nodded with relief. I didn't want to face the world right now
anyway, and if I had another episode like that in public, it would
not be a pretty scene.

"Now tell me what's going on with you," she insisted. "Have
other things like this been happening?"

"Nothing like this, no. There *was* something weird earlier
today." I told her about the incident with the cats, and finished,
"I know that had me on edge, and there's still all the fallout from

Nick bouncing around in my head. It all must have made some-thing slip for a second. But you can't help wondering if it's going to keep on slipping."

Lisa's face had taken on a look I hadn't seen before—like something was dawning on her that she found very unsettling.

"Has anything happened that involved Parallax?" she said.

Parallax? What could that have to do with this? But she had to have a reason for asking. I thought back over the past week, shaking my head—then stopped.

"Not directly," I said. "I did have a run-in with Paul this morning where Parallax seemed to figure in, or at least he seemed to think so. There's nothing mysterious about why it happened, although it was pretty strange how he handled it."

"Tell me."

I hated holding out on her, but the blackmail story had to stay secret, so I hedged about that.

"The family lost confidence in his business judgment, so we cut him loose," I said. "It was a righteous bust—he'd been screw-ing up. We treated him well money-wise, but of course he was steamed. I'm sure Cynthia's not happy, either. Anyway, he half-assed threatened me—told me it would piss off the Gatekeepers."

Lisa's face was getting more somber—with a touch of alarm in her eyes.

"Maybe it did," she said.

That came as almost as much of a shock as the jolt in the pool.

"Are you serious?" I said incredulously. "Why? How?"

Her shoulders lifted in a slow shrug. "I can't really explain it. But there's this vague sort of feeling—it's not really even a rumor—that if you interfere with Parallax, it can come back on you."

Leaving aside how preposterous that sounded, I hadn't interfered with them, and I started to say so.

Although I *had* refused to extend their lease.

Then it occurred to me that there might be another level to this. Had Paul been covertly funneling money to Parallax, and I'd cut off that supply? With Cynthia Trask involved, I sure wouldn't have a hard time believing that.

And *then* came a thought that was far more hair-raising still. Threatening Paul's money was exactly what Nick had done. Soon afterward, he'd suffered the mental torment that nearly killed him, followed by the unexplained brain aneurysm that had pretty much finished the job.

But that was beyond preposterous—it was flat insane.

"Lisa, I'm sorry, but that sounds like voodoo," I said.

She came over to me and put her cool hands on my shoulders, massaging them soothingly.

"I know exactly what you mean, and I'm not saying I'm right," she said. "Look, I think you should talk to Gunnar. If there's anybody who might understand about this, it's him. I could call him right now."

I didn't want to talk to Kelso. I didn't want to admit the faintest shred of possibility that there might be something to this. But I didn't want Lisa to feel that I was just dismissing her. And I didn't see how it could hurt.

After a minute, I nodded. "Okay. And thanks, darlin'."

"It'll probably take me a minute to get him. You relax."

That was not in the cards. It was a toss-up as to which was worse—the worry that I was slipping into serious mental impairment, or feeling like an utter fool for even agreeing to discuss this thing.

Talk about cognitive dissonance.

Lisa was gone maybe five minutes before she came back and handed me a phone.

"Hello, Tom," Kelso said in his calm voice. "I'm sorry you're having difficulties. I'll gladly try to help."

"That's very kind of you, Dr. Kelso. But right off the top, I have to admit I'm very skeptical about the Gatekeepers and all that."

"Understood. But perhaps it gives you some insight into my own feelings as a young physicist at the Planck Institute, when I first started looking into these matters."

"I can hardly imagine," I said. That much was true.

"Let me put the situation in a slightly different light. It is not like a personal vendetta. The Gatekeepers channel energy in particular patterns for particular purposes. If that flow gets disrupted, it hampers them in achieving their aims. These particular powers don't wish us harm—quite the contrary. But the stakes are high, and if they must be ruthless to solve a problem, so be it."

Well, that did sound a *little* less wacko—but all the more disturbing.

"Ruthless, like—getting rid of the problem's cause?" I said.

"That would be a last resort—only if that cause was unreasonably stubborn. I don't know the details of your situation, Tom, just the little that Lisa told me. But my sense is that it could be smoothed over quite easily—and, in the long run, to your advantage."

"What would you advise me to do?"

"Have you thought about our conversation last week?"

I hesitated. Where was this going?

"Sorry, not as much as I've wanted to," I said. "Things have been really hectic."

"I'd suggest you find the time without delay, and examine closely what was said. Then let's talk again."

The phone clicked off, leaving me standing there in disbelief. Last week's conversation with Kelso had seemed pretty far-out at the time. But it was nothing compared to the one I'd had just now.

THIRTY-FOUR

I spent the rest of the evening warily braced for another of those searing blasts to my head. It was like knowing there was somebody right behind you who might clobber you with a blackjack at any second. Lisa and I talked about the situation and about Parallax in general, but everything about both seemed hazy; there wasn't much tangible to get hold of to try to approach this logically. We gave up on it and went to bed early, and for a while, everything left my mind except her.

But by 2:00 a.m. I was wide-awake, and I could tell I was going to stay that way. There was no point in tossing around and disturbing her, so I eased out of bed, got my clothes, and made coffee in the kitchen. Then I went to sit outside on the deck again.

L.A. looked just the same at this hour of the night as it did in the evenings, an endless spread of lights with the freeways like shooting streams of lava. Rome might be the Eternal City, but this was the one that never slowed down.

Again, I thought back through my talk with Kelso at the Lodge last week.

The crux was that the male lead in his movie—a soldier who'd fallen into a bizarre, dangerous alternative universe where he adventured trying to rescue an elusive woman—ended up facing a major choice. He could leave and move on to a place of safety and comfort. Or he could stay, with greatly enhanced power—as one of the masters who fought for control of that world—but also greatly enhanced risk.

Was he pointing at a parallel between my situation and the soldier's? The risky path of power would be to accept his teachings and get drawn into Parallax. Instead, I'd done nothing—a tacit retreat into my familiar world and ideas.

Now the message seemed to be that I needed to reconsider and make a definite move one way or the other. Except that if my place of supposed safety and comfort was going to be haunted by ugly brain shocks and vicious hostility from anyone I might encounter, even animals, it wasn't much of a choice.

With his offer of help, was he implying that he could actually contact the Gatekeepers—intercede like a saint or prophet, call them off? Could it conceivably be true—and even explain why I'd been left in peace this evening? Had he arranged a sort of cease-fire while I thought it over?

But that was only looking at it within the context of Kelso's paradigm. I hadn't completely given up on skepticism and reason. As I turned it all around now, alone and more clear-minded than I'd been earlier, my thoughts kept stopping at Nick. There were two similarities between our situations. The first one, tenuous, was his description of worms in his brain. The second was much more definite, and it came down to one of the oldest adages in the book.

Follow the money trail. Nick and I had both threatened Paul's wealth, and it was a damned easy jump to think that the Gatekeepers' energy patterns we'd disrupted involved cash flow into Parallax coffers.

Was the almighty dollar really that almighty? The masterful powers that controlled human destiny so venal that they would pitilessly hound and destroy somebody who threatened their earthly bank accounts?

Or was there something at work on a less cosmic scale?

I still couldn't begin to explain all the weirdness, but it was a place to start.

I made a decision then, although not the one that Kelso was angling for—to drive up to the Lodge, right now, and do some covert surveillance. I'd get there long before anyone else was stirring, and I could easily hide my vehicle and look around without being spotted. I didn't have any particular object in mind—no actual reason even to think there might be anything suspicious going on. But on Saturday, there wouldn't be any filming; the only people around would probably be Parallax insiders, and it would be interesting to see who they were and what they did. And if nothing else, just spending some time looking things over would help me order my thoughts.

I hesitated about waking Lisa, but I couldn't see just leaving her a note, and I selfishly wanted to inhale her warmth again. I knelt down by her side of the bed and stroked her hair.

"Sweetie, I'm going to take off," I said.

"Oh, sure, just fuck me and leave me," she murmured drowsily. Then her eyes opened. "You're what?"

"I'm restless, and I've got something in my head. I'm better off dealing with it than just bouncing off the walls here."

The room was dim, but I could see anxiety come into her face. "You sure you know what you're doing?" she said.

"No."

There was a long pause. "Okay, but give me a good-night kiss," she said.

Forty minutes later, I got dressed once more and made my way out into the bright L.A. darkness.

PART FOUR

THIRTY-FIVE

The sky was getting light as I drove the last stretch of gravel road to the Lodge, although this mountain terrain would stay in shadow for another good hour. I took it slow with my headlights out, stopping every couple of minutes to listen. The only sounds were the forest waking up—the sweet liquid trill of meadowlarks, the raucous croak of crows and scolding squirrels.

When I got to the cutoff point, I put the Cruiser in four-wheel drive and left the road, jouncing carefully overland for another half mile and parking behind a screen of pines. I loaded a small knapsack with the basics—bottled water and some convenience-store food I'd bought along the way, and my father's Bausch & Lomb Zephyr hunting binoculars.

Then I took off on foot, hiking up the mountainside behind the cliffs to the north of our land. It was about a two-mile walk; I'd been all over this turf as a kid and knew the way precisely. But it was mostly steep, and there was no real trail, so I had to pick my way through patches of thick brush and deadfall; even in the early-morning cool, I was sweating long before I got to the top. From there the going was easy—mostly flat, open granite. I brushed off my clothes carefully in case of ticks, helped myself to a generous drink of water, and walked the last quarter mile to the cliff edge.

I hadn't shaken off that feeling that there was something behind my back—that at any second I might get hit with another brain shock that would run me off the road while I was driving or poleax me in this back country where no one would find me; or even that the mysterious influence would provoke some genuinely dangerous wild critter and I'd become the target of its fury. But I'd been fine since the episode in Lisa's pool.

The thought that maybe Kelso really *had* put in the fix with the Gatekeepers was almost more unsettling than the attacks themselves.

I found a good vantage point where I could see without being seen, and hunkered down prone. Everything of interest was within a half mile, and with the fine old binoculars, I could read a license plate at that distance.

The place looked about the same as last time I'd been here, except that it mostly seemed dead. The chain-link-fenced movie set with its bizarre minicity was empty and locked up tight, with no employee vehicles parked there. The security kiosk was also empty, and I recalled that there hadn't been a guard here last Saturday either. Then, it was understandable—there were plenty of people around. But now it seemed odd; even out here in the boonies, the set was vulnerable to theft and vandalism.

But then I saw that there were two vehicles parked outside the log Lodge building—a black Hummer and a vintage Porsche. It looked like somebody had spent the night, which suggested that they were high up in the Parallax food chain.

The Lodge was as still as the film set; it was just past 6:00 a.m., so probably nobody would be stirring for a while. I settled in to wait.

But within a few minutes I saw movement, and not just stirring but purposeful action. A third vehicle came driving out from behind the Lodge—a big Chevy Yukon SUV, with the driver's craggy profile clear through the open window.

Gunnar Kelso.

I got the sense that he had a relaxed air of anticipation, like a man heading off for a day of fishing. But he only went as far as the film set's main gate, and got out of the vehicle to open it.

Why would he drive such a short distance? He and I had walked it last time, and he seemed both physically and temperamentally the kind of man who'd prefer that.

He pulled the SUV through the gate, locked it behind him, and continued on through the compound to the city set, skirting the perimeter and stopping at the far end—an area that was well hidden from casual view. When he got to a low, windowless hovel made of faux stone—like the other buildings on the fringes, it looked like it had no real purpose, but was just there as background—he backed up to the entrance.

He went in through the building's rough wooden door, disappearing from my view. I couldn't see much of the interior—my angle wasn't good, and the valley floor was still dim with early-morning shadows—but from what I could glimpse, the place looked empty. What the hell was he doing in a dingy little space like that?

When he reappeared a minute later, he started unloading large cardboard boxes from the SUV and carrying them inside. The cartons looked new, still sealed, and I was able to glimpse the letters ARE on a couple of them, along with a distinctive logo of a missile rising from a launchpad against the backdrop of an American flag.

I knew that logo—everyone who'd studied science did. ARE stood for America Rising Electronics, a company that had its roots in the early space age and now was a major global supplier of laboratory equipment and electronic components.

What the hell was *that* stuff doing in a dingy little space like that?

I rose into a crouch and edged my way along the cliff until I got to another vantage point that gave me a better view inside.

Goddamn if there wasn't a trapdoor in the floor—a section of planks a few feet square that he'd lifted up and set aside. It concealed a pit dug in the earth, a vertical tunnel with a ladder inside. Kelso was climbing down it carefully, carrying one of the cardboard boxes. Was this an elaborate hiding place? It seemed that he could have come up with something that was a lot less trouble.

He apparently reached the ladder's bottom, about eight feet down, then ducked and stepped forward, once again disappearing—this time into what should have been solid earth. With his body no longer blocking my view, I finally got a relatively clear look. He'd gone through a small doorway cut into the side of the tunnel shaft and shored up with timbers. The doorway's other side was edged with corrugated aluminum. Beyond it there appeared to be a good-size space aglow with fluorescent light and glinting with metal equipment.

I lowered the binoculars, rubbed my eyes, and looked again. But there was no doubt—it was a fucking *trailer*, a fairly large one, buried under the film set.

So that explained Kelso's air of anticipation, and also why there were no security or other personnel around. He had himself a weekend hobby—building a secret underground lab. He must have had the excavation dug and the trailer lowered into place before the set construction began. Then the buildings had covered it up; no one would ever dream it was there.

All of which brought home forcefully another, very disturbing, implication—Kelso didn't have any intentions of vacating this place anytime soon. Not only had he gone to a lot of trouble and expense for this setup, he was still moving equipment *in*, not out.

After he carried the other two boxes down to his underground lair, he drove the SUV back to the Lodge, parked it there, and returned, this time on foot—and careful to close both the main security gate and the building door behind him. No doubt he didn't want to leave it there where it would advertise his presence, in case someone showed up unexpectedly.

I remembered Lisa saying that Kelso kept up his physics work in the form of constructing mathematical models and such. There wasn't any sense that he was involved in actual laboratory-type research anymore, although it was understandable that he'd still have an interest in it and maybe want to dabble.

But you didn't bury an entire trailer just to dabble.

THIRTY-SIX

Things stayed quiet for close to two more hours. Sunlight started driving the shadows from the forest and warming the granite slabs around me. I broke out a store-bought sandwich made of stuff that was imaginatively called egg salad and ate it for breakfast. Kelso remained submerged in his bunker.

Then I caught another glimpse of movement, this time inside the Lodge building—somebody walking past one of the upstairs windows, probably on the way from a bedroom to the bathroom at the end of the hall. It happened fast, and I couldn't tell anything else about whoever it was. But I figured the situation justified voyeurism, so I changed position again, this time for a view through the bathroom window. Since it was on the second story and this place was so isolated, nobody had ever bothered to put a curtain on it.

As I focused the binoculars, it was immediately clear that the person was female; I was seeing her in profile as she stepped into the shower. Her face was turned away, but she had a trim figure and jaw-length auburn hair.

Cynthia Trask, was my first thought.

That might mean that Paul was with her—although it wouldn't have surprised me if she and Kelso had a quiet affair going on; it seemed clear that they went back a long time.

I had no interest in watching a peep show; I lowered the glasses and just kept an eye on the window, figuring I'd scope in again after she got dressed. But within a minute, someone else came walking into the bathroom, and it looked like he or she also wasn't wearing anything but skin. Obviously, this wasn't Kelso. I raised the glasses again.

It wasn't Paul, either. I was looking at Dustin Sperry, the *Velvet Glove* director—the guy who'd been with Lisa when I'd first met her. And he was getting into the shower with Cynthia.

Well, well, well. Gunnar Kelso wasn't the only one who had a private weekend hobby up here. I wondered briefly if Paul knew about this, but I didn't really care, and it wouldn't matter, anyway. It seemed clear that Cynthia did as she pleased, and Paul had better like it whether he liked it or not.

Eventually, Cynthia and Sperry came out onto the porch wearing fluffy bathrobes and enjoyed their morning coffee. I got the same sense from her that I'd gotten when I left last weekend and saw her sitting in the gazebo—that she felt like the mistress of the estate.

When I put that together with Kelso's laboratory, it deepened my suspicion that they'd decided to hang on to this place, using Paul as the cat's paw. I'd scuttled that plan, along with severely cutting down his financial resources—and Kelso's riff that I'd disrupted the Gatekeepers' energy flow sounded more and more like it really meant I'd disrupted the cash flow to Parallax. He and Cynthia now had a tangible, compelling reason for wanting to draw me into the fold—persuading me to reverse my decisions.

But that still didn't come close to explaining the weird shit that had happened to me.

For maybe another hour, there was no action to speak of. Cynthia and Sperry came in and out of sight, cooking a leisurely breakfast and then settling down with laptops. A couple of times, she came outside to get something from the Hummer, which seemed to belong to her. It was a street model, not one of the full-size military rigs—but still a statement, and it fit her to a T.

I was starting to think about heading home; it looked like I'd gotten all the information I was going to, although that was a lot. Then something happened that seemed insignificant at first but got this entire scenario moving in a different direction.

The vultures came out.

The first thing that occurred to me was that it was early for them. They tended to be active later in the day, maybe because the warmer air made for better thermal conditions. And usually one or two, maybe scouts, would spend awhile gliding around in wide, lazy circles before the others slowly drifted out to join them. But now the whole flock filled the sky within a couple of minutes and quickly zeroed in over a particular spot at the base of the cliffs. Probably they already had a carcass located, and they were going for it as soon as the temperature allowed.

I watched them for a minute, remembering their aggressive behavior last weekend and looking for more signs of it. I didn't see any.

But that made me think of the cats at the college—the sudden, wildly uncharacteristic menace they'd showed.

As the vultures spiraled lower and started to land, I realized that they were going all the way down to the valley floor, a relatively open area that I could see through the glasses. I focused in on it—and got the kind of tingle you feel when you realize you're on to something, even though you haven't yet figured out what.

The meal they were feasting on was not the carcass of an animal that had died naturally. It was a very big chunk of raw meat, maybe a beef quarter, completely skinned and obviously butchered.

It looked like somebody was feeding those birds.

The spot was toward the far eastern edge of our property, well away from the Lodge and film set. I could circle around behind it overland and easily get down there without being seen.

I stuffed the binoculars in my pack and headed off for a closer look at Buzzard Bistro.

THIRTY-SEVEN

When I was sure there were no other humans around, I approached the feeding flock cautiously. There were at least two dozen of them, big, mean-looking bastards with scrofulous reddish heads and dirty dark feathers—maybe every creature has its own beauty, but it was hard to see in these—and if they did get into that aggressive mode, I'd be starring in a real-life Hitchcock movie.

They hissed like snakes and flapped their wings in agitation, but I saw with relief that they weren't going to put up a fight; they backpedaled clumsily, some winging it for short distances and landing again, other beginning their laborious climb back skyward.

The chunk of meat was relatively fresh; I could smell it, but not like it had been here rotting for days. It looked like just what I'd thought and clearly had been placed here deliberately; besides the butchering, it was covered over with heavy wire mesh staked to the ground around the edges, presumably so larger scavengers couldn't tear into it or drag it away, but the birds could reach through with their beaks.

Yet another bundle of work and expense—this time to nurture a bunch of buzzards. Somebody had to have a pretty good reason, and it had to be somebody with Parallax; none of the local residents, mostly longtime ranchers, would dream of anything like this.

I walked in as close as I cared to, within about twenty feet; from there the air was thick with flies and hornets.

Then I got another one of those tingles.

The meat was thickly layered with whitish dust, spread on like seasoning salt, and there was more of it on the ground in a rough circle several feet in diameter. This had to be deliberate, too; there were no alkali deposits around or soil close to that color that the carcass could have been dragged across.

But the real click was that the powder looked very much like the stuff I'd seen at the college yesterday, spread around the area where I'd fed the cats.

That was why this was going on. The "somebody" was using food as bait to get the animals to ingest the powder.

The clicks kept coming. Cats and vultures both turned bizarrely aggressive. But not across the board permanently—right now, the birds were normal. Maybe they were just getting their morning dosage, in which case they'd *start* getting aggressive, and it would be a good idea for me to get my ass out of here.

But another memory was intruding, and while I couldn't make it fit, I couldn't shake it off, either. The first time I'd seen Gunnar Kelso, he was watching the vultures fight—and holding a device that I'd assumed was a camera or PDA to record the behavior.

Click.

Christ almighty, what if he hadn't been recording it at all—but *causing* it? If the powder was a drug with the potential to create aggression—and Kelso had some means of sending a signal to trigger it? Was that what he was working on with such otherwise inexplicable secrecy?

And if it could be done with animals, could it have similar effects on humans? The cell phone call that made Nick snap, the VoIP calls in the previous days—were those electronic signals that were driving him nuts?

I braved the swarming bugs long enough to scoop up a cupful of the dust, hiked back out the way I'd come in, and called Dr. Ivy Shin at UCLA Medical Center. She was in her office—I had a feeling she practically lived there—and when I asked if she could spare a few minutes to look at something urgent, she said sure.

I drove straight to UCLA, and there, the answers started to come.

THIRTY-EIGHT

By midafternoon, I'd hopped on a Southwest Airlines commuter flight to San Francisco, rented a car at SFO, and was heading down Interstate 280 to the Stanford University campus. It was a pretty drive along the San Andreas Fault; a lot of the landscape was a wooded, undeveloped wildlife refuge—although the mile-long Stanford Linear Accelerator, where much of the pioneering work of atom splitting went on, was also tucked in there.

SLAC, as it was known, was linked obliquely to the reason I'd come here—to have a talk with Professor Hans Blaustein, a nuclear physicist I'd had the good luck to get acquainted with as an undergraduate. I hadn't seen him in a good ten years, and I'd hesitated to call him; he had to be over ninety now, and his health might be frail. But he sounded fine, sharp as ever and happy to talk. I'd decided to see him personally; this was too important to try to explain over the phone.

By now, paranoia was also creeping in about any kind of electronic communication. I still didn't know the real specifics, but I was more and more convinced that those mysterious VoIP phone calls to Nick had figured into his meltdown—and that Kelso's science was behind it all, with Cynthia Trask masterminding the schemes.

What I did know, or strongly suspect, was this: Ivy Shin had examined the powder I'd brought her—and quickly identified microscopic nanoparticles that were identical to the ones she'd found in Nick's cocaine.

That right there was the all-important factor that started to connect everything together.

The coke had been given to Nick by Cynthia. He'd inhaled large quantities of the nanos, probably millions, which pervaded his brain.

I guessed that Kelso had set up the vulture feeding for essentially the same purpose—to saturate the birds' brains with nanos. They weren't just eating the stuff—they were inhaling it as they fed, stirring it up as they moved around, and carrying it with them on their feathers. This had probably been going on for quite some time, as an experiment for him to refine his techniques.

And somehow—this was still the major missing link—I had to believe that he'd developed a way to use that to influence behavior. It was a big, big stretch to think that could account for what had happened to me yesterday. But—when Kelso and I had taken our walk through the film set, he'd pointedly led me into the Delphic temple, where I'd spent minutes inhaling the steamy pungent vapor. It could easily have been laced with the nanos.

That suggested that they realized I might become an obstacle, and they were setting me up in advance. Cynthia would have had no problem getting information from Paul about where I lived and worked and such, and a little covert surveillance would fill in my habits.

Then—just suppose—after I'd cut Paul off from the money, he'd called Cynthia and she went into action, maybe telling him to keep track of me until she could take over. She was out to convince me that the Gatekeepers were punishing me, and she knew I'd be more likely to believe it if I was attacked in ways that seemed impossible to explain.

She followed me to Waterton College, and she was already familiar with my workout routine. While I was in the gym, she spread the nanopowder around where I fed the cats, knowing that I'd be passing by. They'd have pounced on it, stirring up the powder and breathing it in, with the nanos immediately pervading their brains. She used electronic signals to trigger their hostility; by the time I got there, they were in a frenzy. Then she'd followed me to Lisa's, and this time she threw out a direct jolt to my own brain—causing agony rather than aggression, which carried the eerie implication that the nanos were capable of a range of effects.

It was a lot of trouble to go to—but there was a lot of money and property at stake.

After I'd talked to Kelso and tentatively bought into the smoke screen explanation about the Gatekeepers, the two of them backed off, figuring they had me where they wanted me.

Maybe they were right.

Without doubt, there was much, much more to all this. But one question in particular was gnawing at my heart.

Was Lisa involved with it in any way? Was our seemingly chance first meeting really staged? Her quick interest and affection for me, just another role? She was the one who'd planted the suggestion that I'd crossed the Gatekeepers, and then urged me to talk to Kelso. Was that all part of the setup?

The jade bracelet that he'd given her—could that conceal one of the transmitting devices? They could be of different types, working through cell phones, PDAs, and no doubt other means, and they could be tiny. That would explain my flash of rage at Dustin Sperry that first day, my euphoria when I was with Lisa, and my desolation when we separated.

It was not a pleasant thought.

I was getting close to the Stanford campus by now. I tried to put her out of my mind and concentrate on why I'd come here.

THIRTY-NINE

I took the Sand Hill Road exit off the interstate, crossed Foothill Drive into the twisting narrow streets of the original faculty neighborhood, and parked in the driveway of Hans and Frieda Blaustein's graceful old house—faded ecru stucco, built in a style that suggested both French colonial and Spanish elements, with Stanford's signature red tile roof. It had a tiny student apartment, just a bedroom and bathroom, that I'd rented during my senior year.

I'd already known who Hans was by then; besides his scientific reputation, he was a familiar and eccentric figure around campus. He was gnomelike, not much over five feet tall, with a head that looked outsize; he never drove a car, but tooled around on an ancient bicycle with a basket; and he was always impeccably dressed in three-piece suits and bow ties that looked like they were straight from the Weimar era.

Then I started finding out other things, mostly from his family and friends; he didn't talk much about them himself. He'd made a harrowing escape from the Nazis, getting out of Germany in the late 1930s. He'd promptly offered his services to the OSS, bringing them his invaluable skills as a well-connected native German and scientist. Besides desk-type intelligence work, he'd done active espionage in Europe that was extremely dangerous, especially for a Jew. After the war, he'd worked with many of the great minds of the era, had known them all, and was considered their equal.

I stood in awe of him.

The way we'd gotten to be chums was that Hans had loved doing yard work when I was living here, and he ritually spent his Saturday mornings at it. But he wasn't physically powerful, and his lawnmower was an obstinate clunker; invariably there was a struggle between this man who'd helped build nuclear reactors that burned hotter than the sun, and about the simplest internal combustion engine ever devised. As soon as I realized that, I started making a point of being around to light it up for him. That had segued into other little chores and this and that, and eventually I became a sort of combination houseboy and shirttail relative.

There was also the crush I developed on one of his granddaughters, although it was not requited.

Anyway, Hans and I had connected, in a very odd male bonding between a world-class genius who was both highly cultured and hardened by grim realities I could barely imagine, and a kid who was starting to face the fact that it was finally time to grow up.

When I rang the doorbell of the house, it was Hans who answered. He was walking with a cane now, but he still looked spry, and his huge luminous eyes were undimmed.

"Come in, Tom, come in. My, you seem even taller than I remember." He clasped my hand warmly and looked up at my face. "So long it's been."

"My fault, Hans. I'm bad about letting those things slide."

He waved the thought away. "Living in the present is demanding enough. The past takes second place." He started hobbling ahead of me into the house, then paused. "You'll wonder about Frieda. We lost her four years ago."

I winced. "I'm terribly sorry." Frieda and I had had our differences—she was old-world German through and through, and

I failed to meet her standards in pretty much every way—but she was a sweetheart, and she'd liked having me around because it gave her someone to be exasperated at.

"She was ready," Hans said. "Alzheimer's was making inroads. She knew it, and to lose herself was unbearable to her. Then came cancer—not pleasant, but relatively quick. She welcomed it as a mercy."

We walked on into the living room, hung with art that included two original Rembrandt sketches. Hans settled into his chair and gestured at a wineglass on the table beside him.

"I'm having a drop of sherry," he said. "Help yourself if you like, of course."

"I'm fine for now. Thanks." I sat on the couch across from him. "You're looking well yourself."

"Vitamin C," he declared emphatically. "Massive doses every day. You should start, Tom. Linus believed in it, and I believed in him."

I wasn't about to argue; I'd heard that Linus Pauling and Hans had been longtime cronies.

"I will, I promise," I said. "The rest of your family doing okay?"

"Flourishing." He smiled, a little slyly. "Becky talks about you from time to time."

"She does?" Becky was the granddaughter. I'd never thought I'd made that much of an impression. "She married a doctor, didn't she? An MD?"

"A good man. A wise choice for her. She was quite fond of you, Tom, but at heart, she thought of you as a project—raw material to be shaped. I must admit I played a part in persuading her that you were not shapable. You may take that as a compliment of sorts."

The things you learned.

He sipped his sherry, with his big shining eyes fixed on me.

"But you did not come here to humor an old man," he said.

I leaned forward, clasping my hands together. "Hans, did you ever hear of a Swedish physicist named Gunnar Kelso?"

His eyes turned thoughtful. "Yes, I know that name. As I recall, he was quite promising, but his career took a downward turn. I haven't heard anything more of him in quite a few years."

"He's in L.A. now—making a film, and he's also sort of a guru. He's got a philosophy that's quasi scientific; it involves quantum mechanics, energy dynamics, that sort of thing."

Hans's eyebrows rose slowly. "Do tell," he murmured.

"It gets much stranger." As I told him about Kelso's underground trailer and my suspicions about the nanoparticles, his eyebrows kept rising to their peak and stayed there.

"I know I'm swinging way wild," I finished. "Right off the top, does it even sound possible?"

He thought about it for a good minute before he said, "Yeeessss," drawing the word out hesitantly. "At least, I can *imagine* a possibility. If Kelso has found a way to activate the particles—by electronic signals, for instance—they could stimulate neurons in the brain, and it's well established that particular neural complexes affect specific emotions. This could greatly amplify those effects while suppressing normal control. I know there's been a large amount of research on accomplishing such stimulation by other means, but I haven't heard of anything quite like this." He shook his head, now looking troubled. "It brings to my mind the

strangest thought. Do you remember the story of King Neb-
uchadnezzar?"

"Just the name, I'm afraid."

"His armies destroyed the original temple in Jerusalem that
Solomon had built. According to legend, God punished him by
causing an insect to crawl up his nose into his brain. The agony
drove him mad and killed him."

FORTY

Talk about brave new world—as Hans and I talked for another forty-five minutes, he made passing references to actual research that I'd have thought was pure sci-fi.

The government had been working for years on top-secret technologies with names like Haarp, Gwen, Pandora, and no doubt others that weren't known—with precisely the object of electronic mind control. This was especially chilling because it targeted not just particular people but masses, and at distances that might be thousands of miles.

On related fronts, there was a phenomenon called synthetic telepathy, with the sender encoding thoughts in electronic impulses that were beamed to the receiver and decoded. The military was developing helmets that did essentially the same thing, reading a field commander's brain impulses and transmitting orders straight to his troops with no need for speech or other communication. Another similar process looked very promising for controlling prosthetic limbs.

Then there were the nanoparticles. Getting people to inhale them on a widespread basis wouldn't be hard. The industry was virtually unregulated. They were easy to buy or manufacture. Besides all the ways they were already being used in cosmetics and clothing that we breathed in throughout the days, other possibilities were easy to imagine. Air circulation systems in buildings, airplanes, buses.

And Hans made another disturbing speculation—that Kelso's filmmaking might really involve experimenting with specific light and sound frequencies as substitutes for the microwaves, as a means to transmit signals. If you wanted to stir up a crowd, it would be like Hitler's propaganda techniques on steroids.

With that thought hovering, Hans's gaze on me sharpened.

"I think you need to be most cautious, Tom," he said. "Not just about Kelso himself. As you can see, the consequences of this are potentially explosive. Intelligence agencies would go to any lengths to possess such technology. It's safe to assume that they haven't lost sight of Kelso, in spite of his self-reinvention; with a man like him, they don't. And perhaps other governments as well; when he was in Sweden, he very likely worked with Russians, and they are enormously interested in the field of mind control.

"Someone is bound to realize soon what he's doing—they may already know. They will want to keep this matter absolutely secret, with good reason. If you talk to anyone, even law enforcement authorities, you might put important plans at risk. It could even put you at risk personally."

Jesus—bad as the situation was already, I hadn't even thought of that.

So what *could* I do? Take the chance and talk to authorities anyway? Go on the run? Try to hide from Kelso? Start wearing a cap lined with tinfoil? I shook my head, bitterly amused. I'd always thought of that as sheer buffoonery.

Or sell my soul and give him what he wanted—my family's assets, plus my own personal obedience?

I might actually have considered it, except for Nick. If Kelso really was responsible for his fall off the cliff and maybe even his aneurysm, then it was, for all intents and purposes, murder.

"Do you have any advice, Hans?" I said. "Kelso's expecting to hear from me soon, and the choices all look bad."

Hans got up out of his chair with some effort and stumped

over to gaze out a window overlooking the garden, his hands clasped behind his back and the cane dangling from one wrist.

"When I left Germany in thirty-seven, I had family and friends who could not or would not also go," he said. "Most of them died. I have lived every day with guilt for abandoning them. But if I had stayed and died, too, I could not have played my small part in ridding the world of that filth."

When he turned again to face me, I got a glimmer of a very different man from the benign, charmingly eccentric professor I'd always known.

"My advice is that you should compromise for now and gain time," he said. "You haven't told anyone else about this?"

"Not a syllable."

"Does anyone know that you came here to see me?"

"No."

He nodded tersely. "I still have contacts in the intelligence community. Let me make a call."

After he left the room, I started pacing. Now that I had a better handle on *what* Kelso was doing, I was starting to wonder about *why*. It wasn't just for money, even a lot of it; little as I knew him, I was sure he wasn't that venal.

What made more sense was that, carefully concealed under his genial exterior, he was supremely egotistical—not in the usual petty ways, but seeing himself as a Nietzschean type of superman. He was above all laws and moral constraints; he should make the rules, and others should obey them; anything he wanted, he should get. His ego was gratified, his superiority proved, by the covert control technology that he'd been brilliant enough to develop. Probably there was also a messianic streak involved, a drive to impose his ideas on the masses; to some extent, he might even believe them himself.

But my two-bit psychoanalysis didn't offer any insights into how to deal with him.

After a very long twenty minutes, Hans came back into the room and kept on walking to the front door, motioning me to come with him.

"Someone will contact you soon," he said. "Go directly home. Keep up a pretense of normality with your family and friends—make up a plausible excuse for these missing hours. And of course, absolute silence about all this."

I put my arm around his shoulders and engulfed his frail body cautiously. "I owe you a huge debt, sir."

He smiled, but it was grim. "You are going from frying pan to fire, Tom. I hope with all my heart that this will help you, although I can't promise that. I *can* promise that you will be dealing with people who are not at all pleasant."

I opened the door and stepped outside. "Give my best to Becky, will you?"

His smile saddened. "I will—if I can think of a way to, without telling her I ever saw you."

FORTY-ONE

It was around eight in the evening when I climbed the stairs to my apartment, and I was feeling the day. On top of everything else, now the mysterious "contact" that Hans had set up was hanging over my head, without me having a clue as to what form it would take or what it would entail.

I didn't have to wonder long. I opened my door, stepped inside, and stopped, staring.

A man I'd never seen before was standing across the room, facing me, his hands folded casually at his belt. He was so ordinary looking he was hard to describe—the kind of guy you could sit next to on a cross-country flight and not recognize as you walked past him two minutes later. Maybe fifty, neatly trimmed brown hair, glasses, dressed in slacks and a light jacket. A canvas courier bag was slung over his shoulder.

"I'm not going to show you any credentials, Dr. Crandall," he said. "You can call me Venner. We'll work on a need-to-know basis. I assume you'll cooperate fully." His voice was quiet, emotionless, and it did not allow for the possibility of disagreement.

I nodded.

He set the shoulder bag on the coffee table and got out a laptop.

"Let's start with you pinpointing the location of this film set," he said, bringing up a GPS grid of L.A. and the surrounding area. I touched a square with my fingernail. He expanded the image, and I narrowed it down a few more times, until the grid showed the exact site of the Lodge.

"We'll get a better picture in a minute," he said, tapping the touchpad and a few keys—apparently relaying the coordinates to somebody or something. "Meantime, I'd like you to sketch the layout, with approximate distances. I'm particularly interested in access—any back ways in or out—and exactly where that laboratory is."

This guy was all business, and Hans had relayed the essentials precisely.

I was able to do it fast and accurately, I knew the place so well. But it was an eerie feeling; from the pointed questions he kept asking, it seemed clear that I was helping to set up some kind of raid.

When we finished that, Venner turned back to the computer. This time he brought up an overhead satellite close-up of the property; a flashing digital chronometer at the bottom of the screen showed that it was being filmed right now.

It looked like somebody was still at the Lodge; the building was lit up, with the Yukon SUV and the Hummer I'd seen earlier parked outside.

"We're trying to get a fix on who's in there," Venner said. "We think it's just Kelso and Cynthia Trask, but we don't want any surprises. Do those vehicles tell you anything?"

"That jibes. I saw Kelso driving the SUV this morning. I think the Hummer is hers, although I'm not certain. There was another man with her then and a third car, but it's gone. I didn't see anyone else, but again, I can't be sure there wasn't."

Venner nodded, then spent a minute silent and unmoving—running the computer in his head.

"All right, we want to do this without anyone ever knowing

we were there," he said. "We can handle Kelso and Trask, but if there's someone else, that could be a problem. So we're going to make you our miner's canary. He's expecting you to call him and set up a meeting, is that correct?"

Miner's canary?

"Yes," I said.

"You're going to tell him you want to come up there and talk to him right now. I'll have my team in place when you go in. You signal us with this." He held up what looked like a keychain LED flashlight, a disk the size of a quarter with a tiny protruding button. "Two clicks means it's just Kelso and Trask. One more click for every other person."

I was starting to feel shaky. "Look, I want to help, but I'm not any good at this kind of thing."

Venner did not seem sympathetic. "Just stay cool, follow his lead, and above all, don't say anything to make him suspicious. Best for us if we can get this done tonight, but if he doesn't want to meet, don't get pushy about it. Call him now. I need to hear what he says, but I don't want to bug the phone. I'm going to stand right behind you—hold it cupped away from your ear and pointing toward me."

I took a few slow, deep breaths like I used to do before a race, and then made the call.

"Well, Tom, where do we stand?" Kelso said when he picked up.

"I'm ready to have that talk, Dr. Kelso."

"Have you come to any conclusions?"

"Mainly that everything you've said makes a lot of sense. It's still hard for me to accept, and I have a lot of questions. But I'm starting to see what you mean about it being to my advantage. Tapping into that kind of power—the thought of it's incredible."

I could almost see his look of satisfaction.

"Excellent," he said. "We'll need to meet here at the Lodge, at a time when we can be alone. Tomorrow, perhaps?"

I glanced at Venner. He shook his head and mouthed the word *now*.

"My day's pretty chewed up tomorrow," I said to Kelso. "Would tonight work for you? I could be up there in an hour or so."

Kelso didn't speak for a few seconds. I waited nervously, thinking I'd somehow raised a red flag in his mind.

But then he said, "Yes, all right. Come directly to the tavern in the film set. I'll see you soon."

I clicked off the phone and let out a long breath.

FORTY-TWO

The last stretch of forest-shrouded road to the Lodge was as dark as a cellar; the night was clear, but the moon only a pale crescent just starting to show over the mountaintops. I was alone. Venner had followed me in his own vehicle but had just split off to position his special operations team, who were already here waiting. If everything went right, they would move in at my signal. Surprise was crucial—not to give Kelso time to destroy anything or escape. My job was to play along and keep him distracted until they were on top of him.

Having that on my shoulders was a very queasy feeling. I kept reminding myself fiercely what this was first and foremost about—Nick.

When I got up to the ridgetop vantage point, I stopped as usual to scope out the valley floor. No lights showed in the Lodge building now; it was just a shadowy, barely visible hulk. But the film-set city was lit with that same ghostly glow as when Kelso had first taken me there—a phosphorescence of no particular color or maybe all of them, which seemed to coat the ground like a sheen of water shifting with subtle movement. The sight had been weird enough in daytime. Now it was downright eerie.

In its midst, a single building stood out—the bar called the Velvet Glove, with its sinister neon iron fist and dim smoky windows that offered the same allure and menace as every tavern since the first one opened its doors.

I got back in the Cruiser and drove on down to my rendez-vous with Kelso.

Nervous as I already was, by now I'd started to notice an-other factor entering into the mix. Trouble was stirring inside my head again.

This wasn't anything like the violent jolt in the swimming pool at Lisa's, at least not yet—more a creeping unease, a sense that some hostile force was watching me, maybe stalking me, a vicious enemy hovering just out of sight. It was almost like an inner whispering made worse because I couldn't actually hear it—and worse still because it was so *intimate*, right at the core of my being, with no way to escape it. For the first time, I had a real inkling of what schizophrenics must suffer from their voices.

With my rational mind, I was sure it was another of Kelso's manipulations. I was physically within his sphere of influence, and he must have been sending out a microwave frequency to trigger the nanos in my brain to that particular level of disturbance.

But a deeper, more primal part of me didn't give a damn what my rational mind thought. I was scared.

I drove across the open meadow to the film set and parked. Tonight, the security gate was open. I stood quiet for a moment, listening, before I went through it; but all was still except for the usual night sounds of nature. I started walking.

As I crossed the trailer compound and then into the city itself, the tension inside my head kept rising like the flame of a burner being slowly turned up. The eerie shimmering light seemed to create half-seen shapes that flickered at the corners of my vision, streaks slithering around my ankles and shadows fading behind corners. By the time I got to the fake tavern, I was damp with sweat, my teeth clamped tight and my face feeling like a rictus. I pushed open the weathered wooden door.

The room was empty except for one person—Cynthia, sitting at the horseshoe-shaped bar with a martini glass beside her. She was wearing a short, low-cut black cocktail dress slit almost to the hip, and she looked as relaxed as a longtime regular enjoying happy hour.

"Come in, Tom," she said. "You'll be safe here." Her smile and voice were inviting, and her fingers were toying flirtatiously with an oval gold pendant between her breasts.

But I had the sudden distinct certainty that it was really a transmitter or control—and that if she wanted to, she could have me clutching my head and roaring in agony within a heartbeat.

She released the pendant. The seething in my head backed off, subsiding to a level I could just feel—like it was letting me know it was still there, barely held in check. My taut face and jittery body relaxed a little, although I stayed very aware of how close her hand got to that golden oval.

I hadn't expected to be seeing Cynthia tonight, let alone meeting her like this. I hadn't known what to expect. But I'd rehearsed several lead-ins, and I quickly pulled up one that seemed to fit.

"Cynthia, I want you to know, I didn't mean any harm," I said. "There's been a lot of strain about Nick this past week. I've been confused, not paying attention. Now I want to set things right."

"Of course—Gunnar and I understand all that. He's waiting for you." But she didn't seem to be in any hurry. She raised her glass to her lips, sipped, and set it down again. "He's impressed with you, Tom. He's going to give you special status."

That did not ease my mind. "How so?"

"He usually teaches in an arc. It starts out New Agey—sort of like using parables, but with scientific overtones. Then he clarifies the ideas over time and shifts the balance until the science aspect takes over. Most people don't have the training to grasp it right away. But you do."

All this time, her fingers had stayed on the glass stem, toying with it the same way she'd done with the pendant. She was a force, no doubt about it—relaxed but purposeful, utterly assured, and exuding her cool, compelling sexual presence.

"I'm honored," I said.

"You should be. All right, let's cut to the chase."

She pointed to a door in the rear wall, marked with a cheap, dingy plaque that read VIP ROOM.

"He's in there," she said.

FORTY-THREE

I'd held off signaling Venner up until now, wanting to be as sure as I could about who was around this place tonight. But as I walked to the door of the "VIP Room," the thumb of my free hand slipped casually into the pocket of my jeans and touched the button of the clicker device he'd given me. If Kelso was alone in there, then I was going to assume it was just him and Cynthia. There was an outside chance of someone else in the wings, but it seemed unlikely, and the clock was ticking.

I turned the knob and pushed open the door. Kelso was alone, all right—standing in front of and apparently playing, of all things, an old-fashioned slot machine. There were a dozen of them lined up along the walls, ornately handsome one-armed bandits. The overall setup was a recreation of a tawdry gangster-era back room, where the "VIPs" could enjoy illegal gambling.

When you thought things couldn't get much stranger, that was when they stomped on the gas.

I pressed the clicker button twice and then pulled my hand from my pocket as I stepped into the room.

Kelso turned to me. Unlike Cynthia, he hadn't adapted his appearance to the role; he was dressed the same as the first time I'd seen him, in a loose linen tunic and pants, and he had the same austere presence.

"Do you know of Kekulé's great moment, Tom?" he asked. Clearly, we weren't going to waste any time on pleasantries.

I nodded cautiously. The story, whether or not it was entirely accurate, was among the famous ones in science. The nineteenth-century German chemist August Kekulé devoted years to unlocking the mysteries of organic chemistry—essentially, the science of carbon, one of the fundamental building blocks of life. It didn't seem to fit the kinds of molecular behavior that had been established for other elements. One evening he dozed off in front of his fireplace and dreamed of snakes rolling like hoops with their tails in their mouths—then awoke with the all-important realization that the simple carbon molecule of benzene was a *ring*.

"Long ago, I had an experience of a similar nature," Kelso said. "It has shaped my life and work ever since."

He put his hand on the lever of the machine in front of him and gave it a pull. The cherries and oranges of the display spun merrily, slowed—and the slot at the bottom fed out, instead of coins, a single-page printout. He handed it to me.

It showed a computerized image of a human brain, surrounded by an aura. That, in turn, was enwrapped by what looked like a wiring harness, with dozens of tendrils tapping into the aura at different points. Several of the tendrils were labeled with similar but slightly different combinations of mathematical symbols from calculus and physics.

"Is this a model of the energy channels?" I said. "Lisa mentioned that you were working on these." Although she hadn't said anything about the slot machines.

Kelso's face took on a look of irony, maybe tinged with bitterness.

"Yes. When I first started, my colleagues in Europe called them 'God Schematics' in derision." His finger touched the page, tracing the tendrils to the aura. "In brief, the Gatekeepers send communications through the channels to the field of consciousness, using a form of the Pneuma energy. As we receive particular types of thoughts and emotions, it creates similar variations in brainwave patterns. By analyzing those and working backward, I've been able to approximate some mathematical properties for a few of the channels—frequency, wavelength, and such."

That sounded like pseudoscientific snake oil, although I wasn't about to say so. I concentrated on looking impressed.

"Let me make sure I understand," I said. "You're actually identifying these lines of communication, in tangible scientific terms?"

"In essence. The process is still very much in rudimentary stages. But I've also made inroads into a next step. To a degree, I've been able to *add* corresponding energy, from an artificial source, to those certain channels—to boost the signal, as it were, and reduce interference from other channels. The result is more direct and clarified communication."

I blinked, surprised in a new way. It was one thing to pose an arcane theory and bolster it with supposed scientific research so rarefied that only a few people on the planet could understand it. But this was a much more concrete claim.

"Are you saying you can demonstrate this?" I said.

Kelso nodded and laid his hand on another of the one-armed bandits.

"The energy source is built into this machine—if you pull the lever, that will activate it, and it will attune to you," he said. Then he gave me his craggy smile. "These old slots make for an odd format, I know, but I've always been fascinated by them, and they seem quite apropos. The element of risk and all that."

I flashed on *The Wizard of Oz*, with me as Toto, nosing out the humbug behind the screen who was pulling the levers— roping me in with this cover for his real lab underground and his work with the nanos.

"And if I do it—what then?" I said.

Kelso's gaze became almost uncomfortably sincere.

"The honest answer is, I don't know," he said. "The inter-actions are of varying natures. But here is what's important, Tom—this is crossing the Rubicon, a formal confirmation of your choice. You are entering the cosmic struggle on a con-scious level, taking the risks I warned you of. After that, there's no turning back."

Choice? Sure. I was perfectly free to say no—and over the next days and weeks, Kelso would make my head explode, with-out ever even having to get near me.

Just like he'd done with Nick.

I stepped to the slot machine and took hold of the lever. Kelso's routine, all of this, was pure bullshit anyway—the ex-act equivalent of medieval magicians' hocus-pocus and signing a pact in blood.

But when my hand touched that cold metal, I got a tiny shock, and while I knew it was just static electricity, it triggered a flicker of uncertainty.

That's how much on edge you are, I told myself—on edge and counting the seconds until Venner and his men showed up. I was starting to wonder if they were really coming, or if they'd called off the raid and I was on my own.

I swallowed drily and gave the slot machine handle a firm pull. The symbols inside the little windows spun, slowed, and lined up—this time, all bells.

Then the weirdness took another quantum leap.

Nothing changed in any external way—no sounds, no vi-suals, no sense of being transported to another state of being. Instead, it was like a very deep, inner part of my mind became aware of itself for the first time—as if it had always been dormant, overwhelmed by a fog of subliminal thoughts and feelings, and now that was dissolving into unimagined stillness and clarity.

Still more astounding, I was aware of other presences, like a council, a group of observers—both male and female, with intelligence that was humanlike but vastly elevated. The sense was that they had always been there, like that inner *me*, but only now was I—or it—perceiving them. There did not seem to be any specific message or valence, either of approval or hostility; only the contact, and the impression that they were watching and waiting to pass some kind of judgment on me.

After maybe twenty seconds, it faded and left me again in the here and now.

I backed away from the slot machine, stumbling a little. Hands caught me and steadied me—but not Kelso's. I turned shakily to find that it was Cynthia holding me, with a look of sultry concern.

"You're in no shape to be driving home, Tom," she said. "You'll need to stay here tonight."

FORTY-FOUR

Apparently, Kelso had handed me off to Cynthia; he was no-where in sight. She led me back through the tavern and outside into the subtly creeping glow of the streets, with her spike heels clicking along the pavestones.

I got over my physical wobbles fast, but I was still reeling mentally. How the hell had Kelso managed to engineer *that*? All the earlier incidents—the jolt I'd gotten at Lisa's, the aggressive vultures and cats, the unease I'd felt as I arrived here tonight—I could account for by the nanos, a relatively basic triggering of brain neurons.

But to think he could manipulate them to create an ef-fect so specific and refined was stunning. He'd set me up with strong suggestions, but that couldn't account for it. Could he have used a process akin to the synthetic telepathy that Hans Blaustein had mentioned? The thought was wild—and wildly disturbing.

That there might have been a reality to it was not even think-able.

But as I walked along beside Cynthia, *that* reality was start-ing to sink in. She wasn't dressed like she was and insisting I stay here tonight so we could sit around and play gin rummy. I knew damned well it wasn't because she found me irresistible. She seemed voracious, and that probably figured in, but mainly, she was establishing control. I belonged to Parallax now, and that meant I belonged to her.

I'd rather have slept with a rattlesnake than this woman who'd had a hand in what happened to Nick. Much as I didn't want to sabotage Venner, he'd better make his move before that came down to the wire.

"Let's take a little detour," she said. We were just getting to the Delphic temple, and she turned us to cross the courtyard toward the tall open doorway. I followed her through it warily, guessing that the detour was going to entail yet another bizarre surprise, and maybe a kinky one—especially because the FX were turned on, with firelight flickering and the warm whitish mist swirling around. I tried not to breathe the stuff in, although the damage was already done.

Cynthia gave me a glance that was playfully arch, and yet imperious.

"It's silly, but I like to imagine myself as the ancient sibyl," she said. Then she stalked to the chasm and swung around toward me, planting one foot on each side of it, with the mist climbing her thighs. Even with her heels and cocktail dress, there was a sense of ancient pagan ritual.

"What do you think—should I take over for Lisa?" she said.

"I haven't seen her in this role."

Cynthia's lips twisted in a little moue of amusement or maybe pique. Her eyes closed, her face lifted, and her arms opened as if to embrace the sky. There was a long, dramatic moment of silence.

"I predict that you'll look back at this night, Thomas Crandall," she intoned, "and you'll realize that it was that start of a new life more exciting than you can yet imagine." She relaxed her body and turned her gaze to me again, clearly expecting a response.

"I'm sure you're right, Cynthia," I said, "but just now I'm kind of in shock. I need to take it easy for a while."

She walked back over to me with a hip-swinging stroll, this time linking her arm in mine and brushing her breasts against me.

"Come along, honey," she said, as we stepped out into the courtyard. "Let's get comfortable, and we'll work on smoothing you out."

"Not tonight, Ms. Trask," a man's voice said from the gloom.

I felt Cynthia jerk in surprise, her grip tightening on my arm.

Venner came walking forward, and several other men appeared, seeming to materialize out of nothing—wearing black fatigues and carrying Uzi-type assault rifles on slings.

"Dr. Crandall, move away from her," Venner said.

As I wrenched my arm free of hers, she gave me a look of fury unlike anything I'd ever seen on a human face. It stayed on me while the soldiers cuffed her wrists behind her.

"Check out that pendant she's wearing," I said to Venner. "My guess is it's a control for the nanos."

He nodded and stepped to her to lift it off her neck. She didn't speak or struggle, but her fierce glare tuned on him.

Then I realized that they also had Kelso; he'd been standing in the shadows with another pair of guards, his wrists also cuffed behind his back. The men started walking him and Cynthia toward the gate. Kelso's eyes on me were calm as he passed—even with the patronizing hint of a wise man dealing with a dolt.

"There is still truth in what I've said, Tom," he said.

I took three steps toward him and got my face right in his.

"Then bring my brother back from where you put him, you son of a bitch," I said.

I had the slight, grim satisfaction of watching his gaze shift uneasily away. Then he and Cynthia moved on out of my sight—forever, I hoped with all my heart.

But a lot of questions still lingered. Whether Parallax would go with them or others would step in to carry on. Nick's health, and Paul's reaction to the changes that were coming his way. What was going to happen to the movie project. Whether Drabyak or Hap would ever come back into the picture.

Where Lisa and I stood.

PART FIVE

FORTY-FIVE

Most of a month had passed before I went back to the film-set temple again. This time it was a sunny afternoon, and for a reason as much cheerier as the weather. The actual sibyl scene for the movie was scheduled to be shot today. It starred Lisa, and she had invited me to watch.

The cameras were due to start rolling any minute, with Dustin Sperry directing. While I waited, I was sitting on the courtyard wall—carefully staying clear of the equipment and crew making feverish last-minute adjustments—and looking through a copy of the script that she'd given me.

```
INT-THE VELVET GLOVE TAVERN-ETERNAL
TWILIGHT

Uther steps warily through the door, still in
shock from his battle with the Nhangs. The
bartender is alone inside, polishing glasses.
He barely glances at Uther; the sense is that
he's seen all this many times before.

Uther: Where the hell am I?

Bartender: The Velvet Glove. Just like the
sign says.
```

Uther: I mean the city, country, all that.

Bartender: People just call it "here."

Uther: How did I get here?

Bartender: Nobody knows about that.

Uther—played by arrogant, young Chris Breen—was the soldier who had been ambushed and awoke in this strange world. He immediately encountered a mysterious, hauntingly beautiful woman—Sophia, played by Lisa—who was just as quickly abducted by the *Nhangs*, a vicious clan of thugs who were really demonic shape-shifters.

Uther put up a desperate fight, killing a couple of the *Nhangs*, but couldn't save Sophia and was nearly killed himself. He watched in horror as the dead *Nhangs* reverted to their true shape—reptilian, blood-drinking monsters. Uther then made his way through the city to the tavern, with the bartender played by a veteran character actor named William Stubbs. That was the scene I was reading now.

The fact that filming was still going on at all was a testament to how bizarre this real-life drama had been—and to how high-powered Venner's agency was. I still didn't know their actual identity, only that they were top-secret federal spooks; they were in the business of obtaining information, not giving it out, and they weren't interested in answering my questions. But their signature was that they'd gotten the job done with lightning speed and scary efficiency—besides nailing Kelso and Cynthia that night, they'd raided his lab and hauled away all the equipment inside—and the cover-up that followed was equally impressive. Nobody who wasn't directly involved in the events knew anything about what had really happened, and Venner's people kept the film project going because suddenly shutting it down would have attracted too much attention.

One thing that couldn't be hidden was Gunnar Kelso's absence. A cover story had been created there, too; supposedly he'd gone back to Sweden to tend to a dying relative, with the story supported by fictitious e-mails from him to Parallax members. I was sure that in reality the government intended to keep him working on his nano research under their supervision, and they would treat him quite well. He was an extremely valuable mind.

In other words, the harm he had done to Nick and to others would go unpunished. It was hard to accept, but there was nothing I could do. It helped a little to know that he would essentially be a prisoner.

But what graveled me almost worse was that Cynthia had also come away untouched—and was still holding her job as Parallax Productions CFO. I'd gotten at least a little reassurance from Venner on this point; it was only to avert attention, like the filming itself; he was keeping her on a tight leash, with the Lodge strictly off limits from here on, and once the movie was finished, she'd be quietly spirited away. But they obviously weren't going to press criminal charges against her; that would have required publicizing the matter. If she disappeared and stayed out of my life, that would be the best outcome I was likely to get.

There was a lot of dust yet to settle on other levels, but things were edging in that direction. I'd been keeping steady tabs on Nick; his condition was unchanged. Paul hadn't been in touch; if he was going to make any waves, there was no sign of it yet.

I hadn't heard anything from or about Hap or Drabyak, either. I hadn't pushed anything on any count, just left it all alone and quietly started teaching my summer classes. And Lisa and I were still seeing each other, at least for now.

I turned the next page of the script.

```
Uther strides to the bar and grips the rail
with both hands.

Uther: There was this woman. These
creatures kidnapped her. I've got to find
her.

Bartender: Lot of women in this world, kid.
That one's trouble.

Uther: What? You're saying I should just let
her go?

The bartender shrugs and nods his head
toward the bar's rear exit.

Bartender: Your call. You walk through that
door, you'll get a chance. Or you can go
back out the way you came in. Trust me, it's
a much smoother ride.

Uther stares at the rear door.

Uther: What happens if I find her?
```

Bartender: You'll find more trouble along
with her. How it turns out depends on you.
It's all about guts and brains.

I glanced up from the script to see Lisa walking toward me. She looked every bit the pagan priestess in gold sandals, a tiara, and her long glossy hair streaming down her shoulders, the only caveat being that for the moment, she was wrapped in a dressing gown over her tissue-thin tunic.

"Remember that guy Joe Bob, who used to rate drive-in movies by how many breasts they showed?" she said.

"Yeah?"

"Good luck keeping count. Come on, it's time."

I smiled, and we started walking back to the temple. But the personal space between us was one of the areas where a lot of the dust was hovering. She still seemed to want to keep the relationship going, and I still felt that powerful draw toward her. But my doubts about her hadn't gone away; on the contrary, they'd festered deeper. I couldn't bring them out into the open, or tell her what had happened with Venner that night, or even that anything had happened. I'd had no choice but to lie to her—tell her that I'd never met with Kelso, that I'd called him a couple of times but got no answer, and then found out he'd suddenly left for Sweden.

The strain of uncertainty and secrecy was growing.

She hadn't pressed me about it; she was under a different kind of strain from another source, which was keeping her distracted. There was serious tension on the film set. Sperry was a competent director, but it was clear by now that Kelso's calming presence and authority had been the glue that held the overall effort together. His sudden absence put Sperry under a lot of extra pressure, and he wasn't handling it well; he'd taken to making last-minute script changes of questionable value but which threw everybody off-balance, and he'd gotten more and more abrasive with the cast and crew.

In particular, he tended to target Lisa, her refusal to jump in bed with him no doubt figuring in. Her fear that he'd get her fired hadn't materialized, at least; maybe he'd made a behind-the-scenes attempt that failed, or maybe he realized he had troubles enough and backed off.

But now she was worried that the film itself was going to suffer. With the hostile working atmosphere, morale was low and the performances had an off-base feel—undercutting the zest, spirit, *life*, that were all-important to a good production. She was doing her best to hold her own, but her hopes were fading that this role would be the springboard career move she yearned for.

Who do you have to fuck to get *off* this movie? was the grim old joke that kept coming around.

It was another thing that hurt and yet that I couldn't touch. She'd made it clear that she didn't want me getting into it with Sperry personally—as with a domestic dispute, that would only make things worse, and she was plenty capable of handling him herself. On a business level, she potentially had much more serious backup—agents, production people, investors, all with a tangible interest in success—but while I didn't know much about that aspect, those voices seemed oddly muted. It was almost like a sort of jinx had sprung up, with everybody subconsciously sensing that something was really wrong, to the point where they were willing to let this project drift away downriver until it disappeared from sight.

"How's the scene shaping up?" I asked Lisa as we walked across the courtyard.

"It should go okay—not much nuance in this one. Although Dustin's being pissy even for him."

I slipped my arm around her waist. "Hang in there, baby. A few more weeks."

"Oh, I'll make it. I just feel sort of worn-out instead of worked up. Not only me, everybody."

She left me at the temple entrance and went on in to join the cast. I stayed just inside the doorway—remembering all too clearly the night when it was Cynthia who'd led me inside and playfully straddled the vapor-spewing chasm.

The fires were lit, the mist machine on full blast—without Kelso around to add in the nanos, the vapor was harmless—the place was warm and damp as a steam bath, and Lisa hadn't exaggerated the feminine charms on display. Besides her, a dozen other lovely priestesses were taking their places in a ceremonial lineup, a spectacle pretty much like I'd imagined it—a sort of ancient civilization wet T-shirt contest. It was actually quite tame, a little eye candy to spice up a familiar, and hokey, kind of scene.

The setup was that Uther's search for Sophia had brought him here to the temple. By now he knew that she was a demigoddess, and that the city's rival factions warred constantly with each other to enslave her so they could use her power. He'd fought battles and had narrow escapes, made dangerous mistakes but also honed his survival skills; he was getting accustomed to this world and learning how to cope.

But at this point in the action, he'd been captured and his future looked short. He was hanging by his wrists from a rope, hovering over the chasm. The sinister high priest—who, of course, lusted after Sophia besides wanting to usurp her powers of prophecy—had devised a fiendish way to torture them both.

She would be forced to cut the rope, plunging Uther to his death in the smoldering depths of the earth.

Instead, she would cry out mysterious words that started the temple trembling, and she would manage to cut Uther's hands free. He would live to escape—but alone. As the building collapsed on the panicked assemblage, with flames and lava spewing from the chasm, the high priest would spirit Sophia away through a secret exit.

This would leave Uther facing a new enemy—doubt. Sophia *seemed* to have fallen as ardently in love with him as he had with her. But each of his daring rescue attempts ended with her being torn from his grasp at the last second. He was starting to fear that she might be contriving this somehow—toying with him for sport while luring him on to disaster—or even that she might really be one of the treacherous *Nhangs*.

The *Nhangs*. The guys playing those parts were definitely not part of Parallax; they were extras, bodybuilder types with hard eyes and lots of tattoos, and I could tell they made the rest of the cast uncomfortable. But they did their job—adding a creepy edge—real well.

FORTY-SIX

"Okay, cut," Dustin Sperry called out, with an exasperated wave of his hand.

The action—just before the FX kicked in, with Lisa about to free Chris Breen as he hung in an invisible harness over the chasm—stopped. All the momentum that had been gathering, including a lot of sweaty, quivering flesh, stopped with it.

Sperry, seated on a telescoping boom, knuckled his Aussie bush hat up his forehead and sank back, rubbing his eyes.

"Lisa, does the term 'phoning it in' mean anything to you?" he said.

Her eyes widened in outrage. "Oh, *fuck* you, Dustin. I'm right on track, and so is everybody else. You're the one who's hanging it up."

As she stalked over to face off with him, Chris Breen twisted his dangling body toward one of the technicians.

"Get me out of this thing, will you?" he said. The tech hurried to him to release him from his harness, and the other cast members broke ranks and drifted aside. There was a distinct sense of their frustration at slamming into a brick wall from a kind of spat that had grown too familiar.

"You're obviously distracted, honey," Sperry said condescendingly. "So why don't you ask your boyfriend to leave, and then let's do what we're getting paid for? Take five, everybody."

"What *bull*shit," she said. But I raised my hand to signal okay, and I walked back outside.

It *was* bullshit. I'd been hesitant about coming today, precisely because I was worried that somebody might object. But she'd assured me that having guest observers was common, she'd cleared it with the rest of the cast, and she'd also told Sperry, who'd shrugged it off like it was beneath his notice. Now he was using it as a pretext to take a shot at both of us.

I was annoyed, of course; in fact, I was thinking about how much I'd love to jerk that ridiculous fucking hat down around his ears. But I wasn't going to cause a fuss and throw another wrench into this already troubled project.

Lisa came hurrying out after me. "I'm sorry, Tom," she said. "It's just one of his two-bit power plays."

"I know—it's fine. And you'd have any audience in the world drooling into their popcorn."

She smiled, but then her eyes got suddenly serious. "You're the one who's been phoning it in."

I blinked, astonished.

"You know what I mean," she said. "I've been letting it slide, but we've got to get straight. Let's talk later." She touched my cheek, then went back inside.

Well, I shouldn't have been surprised. Of course she'd picked up on my uneasiness about her; I was no actor anyway, and if there was anybody who could see right through me, it was Lisa.

This was Friday, with the set clearing off for the weekend; she and I planned to stay here in the Lodge tonight. There was no way I could evade a close-range grilling from her. I couldn't tell her the full truth, but I wasn't about to try to lie.

She was not going to be happy, and she was right.

As I started walking out of the courtyard, I passed by several of the *Nhang* extras standing in a group, taking a break until things settled down inside. In this scene they played temple

guards; they were wearing breastplate armor and plumed helmets, and carrying wicked-looking spears. They didn't look
friendly, but then, they weren't supposed to.

Then I realized that they weren't just unfriendly—they were
all looking straight at me, with stares full of menace. A couple of
them were toying with their spears, twirling them slowly or flex-
ing their hands on the shafts.

Why the hell would they bring their spears out here on a break?

I stared back at them, my breath actually stopped in my
lungs. They were like a bomb just a hair away from exploding.

But just as my fear started to register in my conscious mind,
it was swept aside by the same kind of sudden, almost blinding
fury I'd felt at Dustin Sperry when I'd left the Lodge that first
time. In those few seconds, I didn't *care* what happened. Not
about anything, not a shred.

"If you hear somebody busting off shotgun rounds over
there," I said, jerking my head in the direction of the Lodge, "it'll
be me, tuning up my aim."

I turned my back and started away, my shoulders tensed for
the thump of a blade between them.

I heard one of them spit venomously. But that was all.

By the time I got to the security gate and left the set, my tem-
porary bravado had faded. I tried to tell myself that I'd imagined
or at least exaggerated the incident. But I hadn't.

And now I was starting to think about what had *caused* that
sudden flash of murderous rage between total strangers, over nothing whatever. The other things like it that had happened weeks
ago, I was sure, were the doings of Kelso's nanos and Cynthia's
pendant. But he was long gone, and she was nowhere nearby.

FORTY-SEVEN

I did have several guns stored in a safe at the Lodge—hunting rifles, shotguns, and some other pieces accumulated by Crandall men over the last few generations. I'd gotten quite familiar with them when I was younger, and I'd actually been a pretty good shot, although I hadn't touched one in years. But my little display of posturing had been dumb enough; I wasn't going to add to it by blasting a twelve-gauge into the air.

But I did need to work out what had just happened. When I left the film set, I kept on walking into the woods instead of going straight to the Lodge.

Spring was turning to summer; the afternoon was lovely, edging toward warm but just right in the shade of the trees. I hadn't wandered around back here much in recent years, but the terrain was imprinted on my memory from childhood. Nothing significant had changed except for the feeding site that Kelso had staked out for the vultures, and I'd come back up here soon after Venner's raid and gotten rid of every trace of it. Still, as I got close, I imagined that rotting beef smell lingering in the air. I skirted it, walked on a ways, then cut over to the creek and hunkered down to splash cold water on my face. That and the walking both helped. I started back homeward along the bank, taking my time.

There were still some other loose ends hanging around. When the set got dismantled a few weeks from now, they'd find the underground trailer, which would cause some head scratching. And eventually, people were going to realize that Kelso wasn't really in Sweden. But those weren't my problems, and once Parallax Productions was gone, I could discreetly take care of any leftover details that did fall to me. It had seemed like, on that level, the situation was coming under control.

But I'd never quite lost the gut feeling that the way it had wrapped up was simply too neat and easy.

There were all kinds of potential wild cards that I didn't know about and that still might come into play. But the one I did know about was the single thing that bothered me most, and it bothered me a lot more after my run-in just now with the *Nhang* extras.

Cynthia.

Besides Kelso, she was the first person who came to mind as being capable of using the nanos to create rage like that. What was going on with her these days—really? Everything I knew about her suggested that she was amoral and very smart in a predatory way, with a keen eye for weakness and no hesitations about acting on it.

Enough so that she was conning Venner? Allowing him to *think* he had her under control, while she was quietly running her own game?

Maybe including revenge on the guy who'd gotten her busted? I sure hadn't forgotten that look of hatred she'd given me as the handcuffs went on her wrists.

My little hike took about an hour all told; I got back to the Lodge around four. I poured a hefty slug of Bombay on the rocks, took it out to the porch, and watched the film set closing down for the weekend—the crew securing equipment, actors trekking in and out of makeup trailers, and the parade of vehicles starting back to L.A.

Lisa would be here soon.

I had one more worry that was linked to all this, and now it was back on my radar, too. She was still wearing the jade brace-let that Kelso had given her. I had wondered briefly if it might contain a microtransmitter that affected my feelings for her. But with Kelso gone, the feelings were still here; I'd assumed that he had to be around to operate the nanotechnology; and therefore, with relief, I'd decided he must not have anything to do with this.

But what if he *didn't* have to be around? Maybe the bracelet was on some kind of automatic pilot. Maybe someone else—like Cynthia—could operate it. Maybe Lisa herself.

I wanted to stay in love with her, and I was afraid to find out.

FORTY-EIGHT

Lisa got off the set about half an hour later and came walking across the meadow toward the Lodge, looking like she belonged in this century again, wearing her usual hangout attire of jeans and a sweater. I went out to meet her, made her a drink and another for myself, and we settled on the porch.

For a few minutes we chatted, mostly about how the scene filming had finished out. About the same as everything else, was her take; adequate, but it could have been a whole lot better. At least it was a wrap.

But really, we were sparring, with the tension of something brittle between us that was about to snap. The pauses got longer.

Finally, after one of them, she leaned forward and fixed me with those wonderful Mediterranean green eyes.

"You going to make me drag it out of you?" she said.

I exhaled. "Sorry. I'm not trying to be like that. I just can't find a good way to say any of this."

"So there *is* something."

"Yeah."

"Bad?"

My gaze moved of its own accord to the vultures; they'd been straggling out for the past hour and now were filling the sky.

"Pretty bad," I said.

"And it's got something to do with me?"

"I'm not sure. There are connections I don't understand."

Her hand rested on her chair arm, her slim fingers moving slightly like they were smoothing it down. Kelso's bracelet clasped her wrist—possessively, it suddenly seemed.

"You know, for a guy who comes across so straight, you sure can spin a lot of loops," she said.

"I didn't plan it that way, believe me. It's not that I don't want to tell you—I can't, and I can't even tell you why." I hesitated, but I couldn't keep playing guessing games with her. I took it one more step. "I think it's the same for you—there are things you're holding back because you feel like you have to."

A cautious tinge came into her gaze. "Such as?"

"Such as the way we met—you and Dustin at the stream, you calling me later, all that—did it really just *happen* all by itself, like it seemed?"

Her hand stopped moving, just for a beat. But it was answer enough.

"That's not what this is about, Lisa—not really," I said. "It's about Kelso, Parallax—the *underbelly*, I can't think of a better word. Whatever you know, please tell me. It's very, very important."

A long fifteen seconds passed.

Then she said, "Gunnar's not coming back, is he?"

I didn't answer. I didn't have to.

She stood up, leaving her barely touched drink on the table, and went inside. When she came out a couple of minutes later, she had her overnight bag slung over her shoulder.

I'd been braced for this, but it was still a numbing shock.

"I'll call you, okay?" she said. She'd put on sunglasses, and I couldn't see her eyes. There might have been a tiny tremor in her voice.

I stepped over to her and put my hands lightly on her waist.

"I'm crazy about you," I said. "You know that, don't you?"

Her face turned aside. "Tom—this started out simple, but now it's really complicated. I need time to think." She pulled away from me and hurried down the steps.

"Lisa, will you do one thing for me?" I called after her.

She took several more steps without slowing down, but finally stopped and half turned back toward me.

"Get rid of that bracelet," I said. "Put it in a safe-deposit box, or mail it to your mother. Just keep it someplace far away for a while."

I could see her mouth open slightly—maybe in bewilderment at what the hell I was getting at.

Maybe in dismay that I'd caught on.

She started walking again. Away.

I went inside and poured another drink, a stopgap attempt to stave off what I knew was coming—the slow spreading ache of cold emptiness, the nothing that replaced the intoxicating something, the aloneness you'd been so used to for so long that you hardly gave it a thought until it disappeared in love.

FORTY-NINE

I hadn't spent a night in the Lodge since Parallax had leased the property—I'd hardly been inside it at all. This wasn't a cheerful homecoming. I'd looked forward to some private time here with Lisa, but with her gone, it just felt empty; and it's always a little weird to come back to your place after strangers have been staying there. Even if they take good care of it, things aren't quite the way you left them, and it somehow throws you off.

But there was a task that needed taking care of eventually, and I figured I might as well get a start on it. Kelso still had belongings here—Venner's people had deliberately left them to reinforce the story that he'd be coming back—and there were probably some other Parallax remnants around. Once they finished filming and pulled up stakes, I intended to get rid of it all—wipe the place clean of their presence. First step was to look the situation over, assess what there was and what to do with it.

As I walked through the rooms, I saw that they *had* taken good care of it physically. Everything was pristine, the kitchen even emptied of perishables; probably they'd been using professional cleaners, and someone must have told them that the place would be vacant for a while.

If I hadn't known what I did about the less apparent aspects of their occupancy, I'd have been pleased.

There were a few items of women's clothing in the upstairs bedroom I'd seen Cynthia Trask and Dustin Sperry coming out of; probably they were hers, the kind of things she'd keep around for occasional overnight stays. Kelso had spent a lot more time here and occupied the master bedroom, although he didn't have much in the way of wardrobe or personal belongings, either. On that count, he seemed pretty spartan.

He'd taken over another room as an office or den; it looked more intended for relaxing rather than serious work. A small wooden troll on the mantel labeled "Maxwell," presumably Maxwell's demon, seemed intended as a scientist's joke. The book collection was mostly intellectual nonfiction like history, philosophy, and abstruse science texts in several languages. A large desk was scattered with stacks of papers and the usual computer accessories, although Venner's team had seized his laptop. They'd also rifled the room quickly, but this office was just for show, like Kelso's public persona; he'd kept anything important in his underground lab.

Well, now I had a rough inventory of the stuff to get rid of—the question was what to do with it. The best course would probably be to tell Paul to come haul it off; if he did, it would be up to Parallax from there, and I'd be out of the loop. My guess was that he'd drag his feet, but then I'd be justified in handling it myself, and if anybody complained later, too bad—they'd had their chance. The clothing and computer equipment could go to a charity outlet, and I'd just dump Kelso's personal effects; losing the books would be a shame, but there'd be plenty of other copies left in the world for the few people who could make sense of them.

I spent a couple of minutes flipping through the books, looking for papers, notes, marked passages—anything that might give an insight into his true research. I still didn't know any detailed specifics as to how his nanotech system worked, and I couldn't risk trying to get information from experts; I was under

Venner's orders to pretend the whole thing had never happened. Maybe someday down the line I'd try to do some discreet follow-up—get a spectroscopic analysis of the nanoparticles to find out their composition, then take that information to Hans Blaustein and see what he could make of it.

But I had done a fair amount of private looking around on-line these past few weeks, working off what Hans had told me, and I'd come up with some ideas that might feasibly be connected.

There was very little Internet mention of Kelso or Parallax, no indications of where he'd been for the couple of decades before he surfaced in L.A.; he must have been pursuing his research in private, and it seemed clear that he'd intentionally kept a low profile. But he had been at the Planck Institute in Munich in the 1980s, and I came across a few references to his work in resonance theory, which originally addressed phenomena like the motion of clock pendulums and the vibrations of musical instruments. But like so much else in science, it had gotten vastly more complex—and included the study of how resonators, receptive substances, could be caused to vibrate by manipulation of their subatomic energy structures.

If Kelso's nanoparticles were resonators—which he might even have manufactured himself, tailor-made for enhanced capability—and they suffused the brain's neural complexes, then their vibration, caused by a microwave signal via cell phone or other transmitter, might agitate the neurons enough to kick them into high gear. And resonance was only one of many possible mechanisms. My grasp of physics was too feeble to rate their suitability, but electromagnetism, subatomic particle spin, wave motion, various kinds of fields and the forces that operated in them, all overlapping and interacting in infinitely complicated and mysterious ways, also might be candidates for creating the needed effect.

However it was accomplished, the next crucial step would seem to be where Kelso's genius really came into play. The brain's neural structure was well mapped by now, including the complexes that influenced emotions and the wave frequencies they emitted. Kelso would have had to correlate the frequencies of his microwave signals to those of the particular nerve complexes he wanted to affect. Different signals would stimulate different emotional responses—anger, euphoria, confusion—and he'd obviously also figured out how to hit the buttons for just plain pain. He'd have been able to control the intensity of the signal as well.

And another aspect had occurred to me. Almost all humans have very similar brain-wave patterns. A broad-range frequency blast that was nonspecific might, for instance, stir up anger in any subjects it reached, including a crowd all at once. But the possibility of refinement existed if the signals were correlated to the subtle variations of *individual* brain-wave patterns—and there were supercomputers that could run those scans within seconds, from a mile away, without the subject ever knowing it. If Kelso had done that when he'd had the opportunity—with Parallax members, or me—he might have been able to create signal patterns precise enough to strongly affect the targeted subject, while someone standing right next to him might feel it only mildly or not at all. These people would all have what amounted to personal theme songs, which Kelso could play and get them dancing to the tune. That might also help to explain why he and Cynthia seemed immune—the frequencies were carefully calculated to stay clear of their own microranges.

My search through Kelso's books turned up nothing of interest—most were older texts that he might once have used, but not for many years, like the tomes that lined the walls of lawyers' offices. The desk was no more help. The drawers contained standard supplies; the papers on top seemed mostly related to the film, with a sprinkling of computer printouts, math and graphics, suggesting that he relaxed by dabbling in the realm of genius. It was all part of the display to impress the Parallax members and cover his secret work.

Then, as I was riffling through the papers, my gaze was caught by a handwritten name.

Crandall. It was followed by the number 850K.

I pulled the paper out of the stack and studied it—a memo related to the film budget, projecting expenses for the month of June. It looked like Kelso had been working out how to cover the costs, maybe talking to someone on the phone and jotting down notes. He'd written several other names, too; a couple had question marks after them, but most were also followed by figures: 500K, 1.2M, 380K.

There was only one meaning for this that I could think of. These were investors, with the amounts they were contributing toward the budget—$850,000 from Paul, and that was for the month of June alone.

FIFTY

Exactly one week later, I was sitting in a rented Toyota Camry, parked a block away from Parallax Productions' West Hollywood offices—waiting for Cynthia Trask to leave work for the day. The late afternoon was sweltering, the air thick with smog, exhaust fumes, and heat swarming up from the pavement. By the time I'd been there half an hour, I was damp with greasy sweat.

I'd been covertly keeping tabs on Cynthia for the past several days, waiting for her like this in the afternoons and then following her for the next couple of hours; I'd rented the Camry because my beat-up Land Cruiser stuck out like a bolero tie at a black-tie dinner. It was silly to play amateur detective—like representing yourself in court and having a fool for a lawyer—but it was the only way I could think of to get some sense of whether my paranoia about her was justified.

So far, she seemed to be playing her role exactly according to Venner's script. She left the office every day around six or six thirty, with a sense of unbroken routine. She didn't show any furtiveness or extra strain, just her usual cool briskness. Her life outside her job seemed just as ordinary. She was still stringing Paul along—most evenings they met either for dinner or at her place—and he didn't seem to have a clue that anything had changed, or that one day soon she would simply be gone from his life.

Most important, nothing else had happened to suggest that the nanotechnology was in use again. As the days passed, I'd started telling myself that I'd exaggerated the *Nhang* encounter far out of proportion. They'd been feeling the strain on the set, and they were surly types anyway; I'd just had my own run-in with Sperry, plus the simmering tension with Lisa; and the two anger zones had intersected.

Still, I'd decided to stay with the surveillance awhile longer. If nothing else, it helped to take my mind off Lisa.

Cynthia came out of the building a little after 6:00 p.m. as usual. I waited until she left the parking lot and gave her another couple of blocks' head start, then pulled out behind her, grateful for the cool wash of the Camry's AC kicking in.

She was wearing a casual but expensive linen dress, and this being Friday, I expected that she'd meet Paul at one of the swank restaurants they favored, places like Cicada or the Tower. But that didn't seem to be the plan, and she didn't head toward her home in Coldwater Canyon, either. Instead, she drove west on Santa Monica to Highland, cut north to the Hollywood Freeway, and got off a few miles later on Barham, headed toward Burbank. Film business, I figured; a lot of studios and offices were located around there.

But long before she got to the central business district, still in the outlying no-man's-land of commercial strips and shopping malls shoehorned in side by side, she slowed and pulled into a parking lot—one of those older minimalls that were all over Southern California, respectably maintained but edging toward seedy and perpetually struggling to survive. This one housed a Ramada Inn and a couple of chain fast-food joints, kept alive by budget-conscious tourists visiting Universal Studios.

What kind of business did the elegant Ms. Trask have in a place like this?

I wheeled the Camry into an adjoining lot and found a spot with a clear view. She was just getting out of the Hummer, now wearing big round sunglasses and with a serape-type shawl thrown over her dress. She walked straight to the motel and disappeared into the lobby.

Business? Maybe. But this wasn't the kind of place that hosted conventions or rented out office space. It looked like business that was more personal in nature—a rendezvous with a lover.

In itself, that wasn't surprising except that she would lower her standards to a no-tell motel. But it had implications. If Venner's people knew this was going on, it must be part of their plans; it didn't seem likely that they'd allow her to just go sporting around. If not, it meant she did have considerable freedom beyond their watch, and there was no telling what she might be up to.

I didn't like either version. But oddly, it was almost a relief, a sense that maybe I wasn't just swatting at thin air. I settled down to wait, hoping that she and whoever she was meeting would come back out together and I'd get a look at him.

I'd expected her to be in there for a couple of hours. But either Cynthia was as efficient in romance as in other areas or I'd misjudged the situation completely. Only about forty-five minutes later, she came walking out of the lobby again. It was a precise reverse of the way she'd arrived; she walked straight to her vehicle and pulled out of the parking lot headed back the way she'd come in.

But she also was alone again, which left me with a snap choice to make—follow her or keep watch here? The motel was getting busy, with people checking in and wandering out for dinner or entertainment. Unless her partner was someone I already recognized, he'd just be one of the crowd; he could walk out and drive away without me ever knowing I'd seen him.

Still, this was the first promising avenue that had opened up. It was worth the chance.

Twenty minutes later, it paid—if *paid* was even close to the right word. A man came walking out with several other people, a guy so ordinary looking my glance almost dismissed him as just one of the group.

But then it hit, and I sat there feeling like I was glued in place, watching him drive away in a blue Ford Taurus as nondescript as himself.

Venner.

FIFTY-ONE

An image flashed in my mind—the way Cynthia had stared at him defiantly when he'd taken the pendant from her neck, the night he and his team had raided the film set. Was she starting her seduction that soon?

I stayed right there, trying to get a calm grip on this. The first, really unsettling explanation that came was that the two of them had cut a private deal. Kelso's research was a gold mine that could make them both rich if sold to the right people, and Venner would know exactly who they were and how to approach them. Maybe she had even conned him into inhaling a dose of the nanos, and now *she* was controlling *him*.

But that didn't necessarily follow. He could still be in control, like a high-level parole officer; they'd be in contact; a spectrally anonymous place like this would be ideal for a covert meeting. Even if they were having sex, it might be something that she offered or he demanded but that had no bearing on the agenda.

I don't know how long I sat there. I was about to start driving home when my cell phone chirped.

My heart started hammering all over again. It was Lisa.

"I've got some things to tell you, if you still want to hear them," she said.

I closed my eyes. "You bet I do."

I drove straight to her house. When she opened the door, the first thing she did was hold up her wrist to show that Kelso's bracelet was gone.

I took her hand and kissed the band of paler, untanned skin that the bracelet had covered. She put her arms around my neck and pressed her forehead against my chest.

"I'm done with Parallax," she said.

Maybe the bracelet had figured into my falling for her to start with, but if so, it was like training wheels on a bike—no longer necessary. That thrill of being with her had taken on a life of its own.

Maybe the bracelet had been clouding her mind, too. As soon as she'd taken it off, she'd started to see how she had slipped imperceptibly under Kelso's influence.

"It was like his mark of ownership," she said. "Every time it caught my eye, I thought of him. After a while, I just took it for granted that everything he said was *right*, and I went along with it."

I only nodded—grateful that so far, at least, we seemed to be with each other again instead of against. We moved on into the house and settled down on the upstairs balcony, talking while the last of the evening light faded.

She told me everything she knew about Parallax. I had to shelve the Venner incident until later, and decide how much I could admit to Lisa in return.

Kelso and Cynthia worked as a highly skilled team, Lisa said, with him providing the charisma and her engineering their plans. They'd been building Parallax for years, concentrating on people with money and influence. The film crowd was largely a face, a cover; most of them were a sort of fringe element, with no real knowledge of the inner workings. But there was a very select group of others—including important public figures—who kept their affiliation secret.

The powerful draw of Parallax came partly from Kelso's psychological grip, partly from the pseudoscientific overlay that his message was rational and intellectual rather than cultlike—and largely because it promised a lot in terms of worldly fulfillment, and it delivered. On the surface, this was due to the members learning to control their personal energy and open channels that led to success.

In practice, it worked more like a Ponzi scheme. The people at the top were already very successful. Covert arrangements would be made for them to do favors for the others—financial help, career boosts—so it *seemed* like the channeling was effective.

The top initiates, in turn, were rewarded by Kelso's Übermensch promise—that they were on their way to becoming superior beings, not limited just to their personal destinies, but tapping into the forces that controlled the universe.

It all brought to mind the phone call from Drabyak several weeks ago—saying there'd been several instances of influential people suddenly and inexplicably having the same kind of meltdown as Nick.

Did that explain it? Were they Parallax members who had crossed Kelso in some way, and was he punishing them—or bullying them into compliance, just as he'd done with Nick and tried to do with me? Convincing them that they'd angered the Gatekeepers?

With Cynthia and Venner now planning to continue to run the network?

Lisa stood up and paced to the balcony railing, standing with her back to me.

"There was a lot of secrecy, especially at the high levels," she said. "Always the sense of a big power game, and those people were the players. And if any of them wanted anything, Cynthia made sure they got it." Lisa swung around to face me, folding her arms.

"Including me, a few times," she said. "And you're right, that's what happened with you. How it started, anyway." She gave the railing a fierce slap. "You talked about trust, Tom. Well, there's mine."

She stalked into the house. After a few seconds I got up and followed her, which wasn't difficult, because she'd left a trail— sandals, dress, bra, and thong peeled off and tossed on the floor as she headed for the swimming pool. By now it was full night, the patio unlit, and she obviously wasn't worried about voyeurs this time.

When I caught up to her, she was standing at the pool edge with her toes curled over the rim.

And then she dove in. It was clumsy, almost a belly flop. But it was a *dive*, by this woman who not long ago would only ease into the water timidly and was afraid to go deeper than her waist.

She came up with her shining wet hair plastered close around her head and a pleased, radiant look, like a little girl who'd just learned how to do a cartwheel.

"I've been practicing," she said.

It was really sweet, seeing her like that.

I crouched down beside the pool with my arms clasped around my knees.

"Lisa, I don't care about what happened or how. Only about what happens from here. If you want to keep going, I couldn't be happier. But if this is just fess up and good-bye, tell me now."

She shook her head in exasperation. "I *have* been telling you, you dope. What do I have to do, take out an ad in *Variety*? I admit, a couple of years ago, I'd have thought you were boring.

But now I know you only *pretend* to be boring. You're sneaky, Crandall."

I exhaled quietly, breathing out my pent-up tension. Maybe it was still an act; maybe she knew a lot more than she was letting on, even about the nanotechnology; maybe she *had* been in on conning me every step of the way, and she still was. But I believed her, and I would for as long as I could.

"You just going to squat there like a big old frog, or you getting in?" Lisa demanded.

I got in.

She'd also been practicing her eggbeater kick, it turned out, and wanted to show that off, too. But after a minute or so her legs ended up slipping around my waist.

"That's kind of cheating," I pointed out. "Not that I'm complaining."

Awhile later, lying in bed with her curled up beside me, I was sipping a drink and feeling like a new man when she nudged my shoulder with her chin.

"I just remembered something else I wanted to tell you," she murmured.

I braced myself, abruptly afraid that this new revelation would, after all, bring my momentary contentment crashing down.

"One time—this was a year or so ago—I heard Gunnar and Cynthia talking when they didn't think anyone else was around," she said. "But they weren't speaking English. And it seemed, like—*natural* to them, like what they'd fall into when they were alone."

I was relieved, but here was a new puzzle. It made sense that Kelso would lapse into Swedish with another native speaker. But Cynthia seemed as American as apple pie, or more accurately, devil's food cake.

"Could you tell what it was?" I said.

"Not for sure—I don't know other languages. But actors are sponges. We pick up words, accents, just the general way things sound.

"What it sounded like to me was Russian."

FIFTY-TWO

My cell phone rang at precisely six the next morning. I longed to ignore it, but a call that early would be important, especially lately, and even if it wasn't I didn't want the damned noise bothering Lisa on one of her rare chances to sleep in. I stumbled out of bed to her living room, where I'd left the phone, just managing to grab it before the voice mail kicked in.

"Tom, I'm sorry to bother you so early," my mother said. Her voice was shaky with strain. "I made myself wait until now—I've been up most of the night."

"It's fine, Mom—what's going on?" I tried to hide my alarm.

"Erica had a driving incident last night. Not a wreck, and she wasn't hurt—she's upstairs asleep now. But it scared her badly, and—and things just seem to be falling apart. I'm not feeling well, either. It would help if you were here."

"I'll come over right now. Easy on the coffee, and a Valium wouldn't hurt."

"No—no pills."

What? Audrey had never abused drugs, but she sure wasn't shy about sedatives when her nerves were on edge.

"Do *you* need to see a doctor?" I said.

"We'll talk about it when you get here."

"I'm on my way."

Lisa had stirred at the phone's ring but drifted back off to sleep again. I stifled my urge for a kiss and scribbled a note, then got my clothes mostly on and eased out the front door, tucking in my shirt as I strode to my rented car. I opened the door and started to swing in behind the wheel.

Then sprang violently back away, as spooked as if I'd seen a rattlesnake.

An open newspaper was lying on the front seat, neatly spread out for me to see. I had not left it there, or left a window open. The car had been locked up tight, and it had an antitheft system—not to mention that this was a high-end gated community patrolled by security guards.

I leaned down cautiously to look at the paper. It was the early edition of this morning's *L.A. Times*, folded open, to the lead briefs of national news. My gaze stopped at a prominent subhead, right at the top of the page.

Stanford Physicist Blaustein Dead at 96

I straightened up again and stood there looking around helplessly, then forced myself to scan the article. Hans had gone into a coma two nights ago; he'd been alone at the time, and the speculation was that he'd fallen down and injured his head. Late last evening, he'd passed away.

Fallen down, hell. The paper hadn't been put here to tell me that.

He'd been murdered, by someone skilled enough to disguise it.

Who would have reason to kill the gentle old genius?

Venner. Cynthia. The two of them working together. Hans was a threat because he knew about Kelso's use of the nanos.

My skin was crawling with rage, fear, and guilt. If he hadn't died *because* of me, it wouldn't have happened *except* for me.

Ugly as that was, there was also a clear message attached—it could have been me instead, done as easily as they'd put the newspaper in this car. I was a child, playing a fool's game. They knew I'd been following Cynthia, knew I was driving the rental, knew where I was and when.

I tossed the newspaper into the car's trunk, got in, and started grimly negotiating my way toward my mother's house in Pasadena. There was no straight shot from Hollywood Hills, just a hectic network of boulevards and freeway interchanges, with traffic brutal even at six thirty on a Saturday morning.

Along with all the other stuff seething around in my head, a thread kept running around like a song you can't get rid of—that Lisa had overheard Kelso and Cynthia speaking a language she thought was Russian.

There was no mystery about why Kelso would be fluent in it; as Hans had pointed out, Sweden was practically next door, and he'd probably worked with Russian scientists.

But Cynthia? It was possible that she'd learned it in school, or by traveling or working there, and spoke it with Kelso to keep in practice.

But it seemed far more likely that she would lapse into it naturally because it was her native tongue—which turned up the scenario another big notch. She'd have been born when the Soviet Union was still firmly under Communist control and the Cold War was raging. For her to seem so utterly American, without a trace of accent, almost had to mean that she'd been trained intensively, probably from a very young age. Her identity was obviously solid enough for her to hobnob with powerful people, including in government circles—which almost had to mean that it had been very carefully established.

Those things taken together almost had to add up to espionage.

I'd read a history of modern Russia a few years back, and I remembered that the KGB trained female agents known as "swallows," taking them very young from their homes or orphanages and immersing them in the world of international intrigue. Often—and especially with those of beauty and ability—the object was to plant them in foreign nations as moles, where they might make their way to high circles of government, finance and industry, intelligence—and scientific research.

FIFTY-THREE

My mother looked every bit like she'd had a sleepless night, with waxy skin and dark, bruiselike hollows under her eyes that she hadn't even tried to disguise. She was still in her robe, sipping herbal tea. She'd made coffee for me; I poured some of that, then got her to stop fussing around and sat her down in the dining room, trying to focus on this new development.

"Erica went out with friends last night," Audrey said. "She was on the Golden State, going home by herself, and somebody ran her off the road."

"But she didn't actually get hit, and she wasn't hurt?" I'd looked Erica's car over quickly as I came in, and it seemed intact.

"No. She skidded onto the shoulder, but she was able to stop all right."

"Did she call the cops? Go to a hospital?"

Audrey shook her head unhappily. "She just came here instead."

In other words, Erica had been drinking and probably had drugs with her. Her brush with the near disaster of her hot tub video didn't seem to have slowed her down any.

"She still should see a doctor," I said. "She might have whiplash or an internal injury she doesn't know about."

"I told her the same thing, but she wouldn't listen. Maybe she will to you. I just checked on her, and she does seem fine; she's even snoring a little."

"I don't suppose she got the other car's license number?"

"No, she barely saw it. It came up behind her fast, bright lights in her mirror, then swung around and cut her off."

It made my fingers tighten with the urge to get them around the asshole's neck, but it was one of those things you just had to live with. There were plenty of those people out there pulling that kind of shit, and L.A. had more than its share. Thank God Erica had had the presence of mind—or sheer good luck—to keep her car under control.

"Let her sleep while we talk. Then we'll see how she's feeling," I said. "Now, what about you?"

Audrey leaned forward with her elbows on the table, pressing her fingertips against her temples and closing her eyes.

"Just these past couple of days, I've been getting these blinding headaches," she said. "Not really even *headaches*—they're like sudden flashes. They only last a minute or two, but the feeling is so awful. I've never had migraines, and I don't think this is like that, anyway. I'm starting to wonder if it's a tumor. Or—after what happened with Nick, you know—if there's some kind of genetic weakness in the family that's suddenly showing up."

She opened her eyes again. They widened when she saw my face.

"Tom—what's the matter?" she said, reaching out quickly to clasp my hand. "You look like you're about to fall over."

FIFTY-FOUR

I clamped down on myself and convinced her that I was fine, only concerned about her—the last thing she needed was for *me* to melt down—and I stayed there another hour and a half, putting on an acting performance that Lisa would have been proud of.

Eventually, Erica came downstairs, scantily clad as usual in a thin wrapper. She assured me that she'd been wearing her seat belt last night and hadn't banged against the steering wheel or anything like that, and that her Audi had an excellent headrest. Still, I insisted that they both go in for medical checkups ASAP, and Audrey promised to make the appointments Monday. They both seemed steadier when I left, not because I'd actually helped but just from having someone else around.

I wasn't doing any better. There was no doubt in my mind about what had happened—this was another warning message.

Audrey was getting headaches because somebody had slipped her a dose of those goddamned nanoparticles. They'd had plenty of time and opportunity to do it. She brought in fresh flowers from the garden almost every day, inhaling them deeply as she clipped them; she regularly went out to lunch with her women friends at restaurants where the air was filled with perfume and food aromas; the supplies of the weekly cleaning lady could have been spiked. They might have given Erica a noseful, too—God knew that would have been easy enough—but the threat to her was more direct, a way of driving it home that they could operate on that plane, too.

But with my mother, it meant straight out that Cynthia—or whoever she really was—did still have access to a transmitter that would activate the nanos.

Everyone who had inhaled them was at her mercy.

I could try going to authorities, but I was sure she was on the alert for that and ready to strike at the first sign of it. Drop out of sight, and persuade Audrey, Erica, and Lisa to come with me? Realistically, it would be almost impossible to pull off to begin with, and how long could we hide from Venner?

I even thought seriously about just flat killing her—staking her out with a deer rifle or shooting her point-blank with the unregistered snub-nosed .38 that my old man had half jokingly called his throw-down gun. But even if I could bring myself to do it, even if I got the chance, it was a near guarantee that I'd end up dead or in prison—and no guarantee that Venner or someone else from that shadow world wouldn't retaliate against my family.

I was starting to feel like a character in a Greek tragedy—that I'd brought a curse on my entire line, and we were doomed to be hounded by furies until we were ground out of existence.

I was coming to the end of the long driveway at my mother's house, about to turn onto the street, when my phone rang. The caller ID was Lisa's.

"Hey, baby," I said, trying to sound perky. "Sorry to bail on you—things seem settled down now."

"I'm glad to hear that, Tom," a woman's voice answered.

It wasn't Lisa. It was Cynthia.

My jaw clenched so tight I could hardly get more words out.

"Where's Lisa?" I said.

"She's not available right now. If you and I can come to terms, you'll hear from her later."

"What do you *want*?" I exploded. "I'll do anything I can. Just leave my family *alone*."

"You sound so much more reasonable than last time we met," Cynthia said mockingly. "All right, you do have something I want. If I get it, I'll consider the score even and I'll never trouble you again. Go straight home and wait for another message. Don't even think about doing anything stupid—no stops on the way, no phone calls, no nothing. If you do, I'll know."

The phone clicked off.

I drove on home, and for the rest of that interminable day, through the afternoon and into the evening, I waited.

Finally, with night settled in and the city again a vast grid of lights, my cell phone made the pinging sound of an incoming text message.

It was from Lisa's phone again.

I'M ON FILM SET CANT EXPLAIN BUT THINGS VERY WEIRD
PLEASE COME

I opened my safe, got out my father's old S&W .38 Terrier, and loaded it with five short thick rounds. Then I headed out the door.

FIFTY-FIVE

Tonight, when I drove my Land Cruiser up onto the ridgetop overlooking the Lodge, the valley floor below was completely unlit. I could still see fairly well—the sky was clear, the moon edging toward half full, and I'd driven the last couple of miles with my headlights off to let my eyes adjust. But there was no hint of where Cynthia was or what to expect.

I'd gone through dozens of scenarios in my mind, and thought long and hard about sneaking in on foot. But in the end, I had to believe that she had surveillance set up to anticipate any move I could make, and that I'd only get somebody hurt—maybe Lisa and definitely me.

There was nothing to do but keep going. I eased the pistol out from under the seat and slipped it into my back pocket, then drove on down the last stretch of road, trying to keep my breathing slow and calm.

I was just starting across the meadow when a little red dot of light appeared on the dashboard in front of me. It moved from there to my chest, shoulder, then out of my field of vision. I could almost feel it crawling up my neck.

Cynthia's voice came from the woods nearby through my open window.

"That's just what you think it is, Tom. Nothing stupid, remember? Cut the engine, leave the keys, and get out."

I couldn't see her—she seemed to be off in the trees to my left. Her tone was as matter-of-fact as if she were a nurse telling me to make a fist while she probed for a vein to draw blood.

I did what she said. The red dot of the laser sight danced almost playfully around my upper body as I got out and stood up. The pistol felt like a lead brick in my pocket.

"Turn on the headlights and walk in front of them," she said. "Undress and put your clothes on the hood."

I did. It was one thing to be at somebody's mercy like that. It was another to be there naked.

"Not bad," she said, with a mocking edge. "It's a shame we don't get along. Now walk forward ten steps, lie facedown, spread your arms and legs."

I did that, too. With my face pressed against the cool, weedy earth, I watched her shape emerge from the shadows of the tree line. She was dressed entirely in black leather—boots, pants, and jacket, her motorcycle outfit—and carrying a wicked-looking, high-caliber Parabellum automatic pistol with a sound suppressor on the muzzle. She was also wearing latex surgical gloves. She went through the clothes with her left hand, keeping the gun trained on me with her right, all with practiced ease. It only took her a few seconds to find the .38.

"Really, Tom," she said, shaking her head in exasperation. "If it wasn't so pathetic, I'd be angry."

I was finally jarred into speaking. "What did you expect—I'd gift-wrap myself?"

She walked over to me with unhurried, measured steps, and stopped between my outstretched legs. Then she moved her boot toe up against my ass and pressed it down on my testicles—not hard enough to crush them, but plenty hard enough. My lips peeled back from my teeth and my fingers dug into the ground.

"That should give you some idea of what a bullet there would feel like," she said. "Any more surprises, you'll get one—that's a promise. So tell me now."

"Nothing," I said through clenched teeth.

"Nobody knows you're here?"

"No."

She stepped away. "Get dressed."

I lurched to my feet and clumsily pulled my clothes on. While I did, Cynthia faded back toward the tree line.

"You know, Tom, I've really liked being in the film business," she said. "The ordinary world can be so dull and predictable, but in movieland, anything can happen. This is your chance to be a hero and save a damsel in distress. You'll find her at that little bridge over the stream, right where you first met her. Don't keep her waiting."

FIFTY-SIX

The throbbing in my balls was easing off, but it still hurt to walk and hurt more to walk fast. I did my best, half striding and half trotting through the shadowy woods. The rushing sound of the stream rose as I got close; the spring runoff was down from its earlier peak, but there was still plenty of it and the water was high and swift. The pond above the bridge was high, too, with turbulent swirls and wavelets lapping at the granite boulders that ringed it.

As I broke out of the trees into the clear moonlight, I could see two figures on the bank. One was Lisa, stretched out on her back on a flat rock, with her dark hair spread around her head.

It took me a few seconds to recognize the other one, a man crouched over her.

Dustin Sperry.

What?

My first wild thought was that he'd snapped under all the pressure on him and brought Lisa to this lonely spot to take out his rage on her, rape or even murder her.

"Get the fuck away from her!" I yelled, breaking into a run.

He straightened up and took a couple of steps back, but he didn't speak or otherwise respond, just stood there with his hands at his sides. If anything, he seemed confused, and I started to realize that this had to be staged, part of Cynthia's setup—just like the first time I'd encountered Lisa and Sperry here. Still, whatever was going on was *wrong*, and there was something dangerous about his vacant, troubled face and his stance; even his backsteps seemed to be more repositioning than retreat.

I knelt beside Lisa, keeping him warily in sight. She was dressed in the thin gown she'd worn in her priestess scene. Her eyes were open, but her face and body were as still as the stone she lay on. I put my ear close to her mouth and found the carotid artery in her neck with my fingertips. Her breath and pulse were both okay, slow but steady, and there was no visible blood or other signs of injuries. It looked like she'd been drugged, and while she didn't seem to be slipping away in an overdose—at my touch she responded slightly, lips twitching and eyelids flicking like she was trying to focus—I couldn't be sure.

Or was she faking, with this just another part of the act?

"How long has she been like this?" I called out to Sperry, raising my voice over the sound of the stream.

He still didn't speak, but his eyes were changing as if his blank mind was coming to life—and it wasn't a pretty look.

Abruptly, he convulsed, with a strangled howl bursting from his throat. He clapped his hands against his temples, his body jerking and his feet frantically stamping the ground.

I stared, frozen with shock. It was like seeing Nick again on the Malibu cliff—right before he'd attacked me and damned near thrown me over the edge.

And in that instant, I understood what Cynthia was doing. She had lured or forced Sperry up here, same as me. She was sending signals to enrage him into attacking me. If either of us survived, she would adroitly finish us off. When we were found, it would look like a fight between two men who were known to have a grudge over a woman they both coveted.

Sperry's head swiveled toward me, and the rest of him came right behind it, lunging at me with his fists windmilling ferociously, big sloppy swings that would have dented a car. I scrambled back, rising to my feet and running for the pond. In the water, berserk though he was, I could handle him.

I'd had time for only the briefest glimmer of wonder as to why Cynthia wasn't sending the rage signals to me, too. I should have known better—her timing was perfect. A blinding jolt seared through my skull, like the one that had hit me in Lisa's swimming pool but even worse.

I staggered, knees buckling, and then Sperry slammed into me. His weight threw us both into the numbing cold, roiling pool. With the sickening writhing in my head, my strength and motor control were gone. I could only thrash feebly while he clenched his fists in my shirt, drove me under the surface, and held me there. The pain kept coming in vicious waves, and the need for breath tightened like a vise in my chest. Spots started flickering at the edges of my vision and expanding to fill the field—the final warning sign before I blacked out and my lungs sucked in their last fill—of water.

I had never imagined that I would die by drowning.

Then, in that timeless half-dream state, I felt a distinct inner presence—infinitely distant and yet right there at the core of my being, utterly alien and yet as hauntingly familiar as my mother's voice from birth.

It was the same sense I'd gotten when I'd pulled the lever of Gunnar Kelso's mad scientist slot machine—that a group of august, otherworldly entities was watching all this and passing judgment. As suddenly as it came, it was gone.

And so was the agony in my head. Just like *that*, I was in control of my body again.

I got my feet under me, found the bottom, and burst up through the surface with my head under Sperry's chin like an uppercut that snapped his teeth together and his neck back. My lungs were so desperate for air that it shrieked in my throat as I sucked it in, but I managed to drive a fist up under his nose, my knuckles crushing into it and his upper lip. He roared with pain and let go of me, his hands flying to clasp his face.

Now I had him.

I dove away into deeper water and kept backing up, luring him deeper still as he came after me wild-eyed with fury and with the dark glisten of blood streaming down over his mouth. When his feet lost touch with the bottom and he started paddling clumsily, I dove down and grabbed his ankles to pull him under. He kicked like a son of a bitch, but he was no strong swimmer, and his rage just wore him out faster. A last few seconds of frantic struggle dwindled off into spasmodic twitching.

By now we'd gone most of the way across the pond—and a flicker of chance had appeared in my mind. Cynthia was expecting me to drown. She had to be at least fifty yards away, and the water was dark and turbulent. If I stayed under and Sperry came out alone, she just might let down her guard and assume I was dead.

I came up behind him, keeping my body hidden, and got his face above the surface while he hacked and sputtered his lungs back into working order. He'd pull through okay, but he wasn't going to be in shape to cause more trouble anytime soon. I kept us moving toward the far bank, thrashing around to make it look like there was still a struggle going on. When we got to where we could touch bottom, I started hyperventilating, the longest, deepest lungfuls I could take in.

Then I let him go and dropped to the bottom, shoving off the rocks back toward Lisa. I made it about twenty yards, clawing my way along on my belly like a lizard, before my aching lungs forced me to flip on my back and cautiously raise my face just high enough for a breath and a quick look around.

Sperry was dragging himself up onto the far bank. Lisa was still lying motionless on the rock. I couldn't see Cynthia.

Which meant that she might, after all, have seen me.

I went under again and made it almost to the bank, in water that was only knee deep and a few yards from Lisa. When I came up this time, Cynthia's dark lithe figure was striding across the bridge—toward Sperry and away from me. I got my feet under me, ready to move, but I waited; every step she took increased the distance between us.

As she reached the opposite bank, her hand rose to point at him, but she wasn't holding that big, bulky pistol.

Then he flopped back into the pond, letting out a shriek that carried sharp and clear over the sound of the rushing stream. It was a transmitter that she was aiming at him—shocking him with the same agonizing jolts she'd used on me, driving him mercilessly farther into the deep, swirling water. Exhausted and panicked as he was, racked by blinding pain, he'd sink like a stone.

Much as I disliked him, it sickened me. But there was nothing I could do for him.

With Cynthia focused on murder and the pistol not in her hand, now was the best chance I was going to get. I came up out of the water on the run, scooped up Lisa in my arms, and kept on running in a crouch for the woods.

FIFTY-SEVEN

The gunshots started within seconds, muffled *whump*s at quickly spaced intervals, but by then we'd made it to the nearest trees and Cynthia was on the other side of the pond, a good sixty yards away. Even so, she didn't miss by much—the bullets crashed through the branches around us, and one blew a chunk out of a pine trunk so close I felt bits of bark sting my face.

Then the shooting stopped. She was coming after us.

We had the head start, and I knew the turf, but Cynthia was going to move a lot faster than me carrying Lisa. We had to disappear.

I ran on to a place where the stream was only calf deep and cut sharply across it, then along the base of the cliffs to a deer trail that led up a ravine. It was just a track, barely visible even in daylight, and the rushing water covered the sound of my footsteps as I scrambled up it. After a hundred feet, I stopped and collapsed, panting, behind a rock outcropping. If Cynthia hadn't caught sight of us, we still had a chance.

Lisa was starting to stir, and her eyes had gone from glazed to scared and confused. Her mouth opened like she was trying to speak. I touched my forefinger to her lips—the sound of a human voice would carry far more than footsteps.

"Not a peep," I whispered into her ear. "You understand?" Her eyes stayed wide, but she gave me a tiny, tentative nod.

Voices carried, all right. Cynthia's cut through the night air like a whip.

"I know exactly where you are! If you try to run again, you won't get three steps."

My body jerked, and I felt Lisa shudder, too. My arms tightened around her. It sounded like Cynthia was still on the other side of the stream, but I couldn't be sure.

"Don't make things any worse than they already are," she called. "Come out. We'll get this over with—quick, painless, and that's the end of it. But if you drag it out longer, I'm going to get very angry. You *know* what that means for your family."

Very, very slowly, I eased my face to the edge of the outcropping until I could get a glimpse down to the streambed. Long seconds passed before I could see her, a shadow moving stealthily along the opposite bank—a single measured step at a time, holding the pistol outstretched in front of her with both hands, sweeping it in a searching arc.

But still searching. My eyes closed briefly in thanks—to whom or what, I wasn't sure.

I eased back to look at Lisa and gave her the *all okay* sign with my circled thumb and forefinger. She answered with another tiny nod, but it was firmer this time, and her eyes told me that she was starting to grasp what was going on.

We stayed as still as the rock that hid us while Cynthia worked her way upstream. She was silent for the next couple of minutes, then called out her threat again, her voice now muffled by the water.

It was time to move. She was bound to realize that we couldn't have made it much farther and start coming back.

Lisa was still too unsteady to climb up the steep, rough trail, so I gave her a whispered apology and carried her the rest of the way slung over my shoulder, uncomfortable for her but easier on me and leaving me a hand free to help pull us along. Fear and adrenaline gave me the strength to make it, but barely. When we got to the cliff top, I was so drained I thought I might pass out. I unloaded her onto the ground as gently as I could, then half fell down beside her and pulled her close again. My clothes were still sodden, and I'd gotten her wet, too, but I was giving off heat like a furnace and she was cold from inaction. Next step was to get her moving on her own, as soon as I could get myself up off the ground.

"Do you remember what happened?" I murmured to her.

Her voice was weak and halting, but it still managed to convey sheer feminine outrage.

"She had a gun. Made me come here with her. Made me drink a roofie. Then I went blank. That *bitch*."

Despite how insane and terrifying it all was, my lips actually curved in a smile of relief. Lisa was still Lisa, coming right back and fighting mad.

"Can you walk?" I said.

"I think so. I might need some help to start."

I got us both to our feet, then steadied her while we paced around for a minute or so. When she seemed okay, I told her to keep going and went to the cliff edge, staring down at the dark valley floor and trying to figure out what to do next. I wanted to keep moving; I didn't think Cynthia would look for us up here, but I couldn't be sure and there might be wild cards in the mix, like Venner or other accomplices who would join the search. The nearest phone was at a neighboring ranch, a good four miles away over the rugged mountain terrain. It would be tough on Lisa, but it looked like our best bet.

Then a sound erupted into the quiet night—the throaty roar of a high-powered motorcycle starting up. I'd heard it before.

Cynthia's motorcycle.

The bike was already moving fast when the headlight flicked on, a tiny glow like a shooting star, and it kept gaining speed as it headed up over the ridgetop toward the highway.

She could make it to L.A.—and to my mother and sister—in an hour.

Now I needed a phone fast.

FIFTY-EIGHT

We still couldn't risk going back down to the Lodge; she had probably cut the landline and taken my cell phone from my car, anyway. But my gaze stayed on the city set. If the security system was breached, it would instantly alert a central office, and they would dispatch sheriff's deputies. It would take more than lobbing rocks at the fence—the sensors would be set to ignore minor bumps like small animals brushing against it. But a big animal—like a man—would do the trick, and the cameras would pick me up, too.

And if Venner was down there waiting, or Cynthia had dumped the bike and come back on foot, so would they.

I strode over to Lisa. She was looking better, her walking stronger and more controlled.

"I've got to go take care of something," I said. "Don't worry. I'll be back in twenty minutes. But just in case I'm not, you've got to get out of here. Start walking that way." I pointed northeast. "Stay up here on high ground and follow the stream, you can see it below. After a few miles you'll come to a ranch. It's a rough hike, but be careful and you'll do fine."

There was no describing the look she gave me.

"Okay, Tom," she said, "but promise me one thing. Don't ever say 'Don't worry' to me again."

It had probably taken fifteen minutes to climb the trail carrying Lisa. Going back down alone took three or four. I crossed the stream and trotted quietly through the woods to the rear of the film set. At the tree line, I crouched to watch and listen for anyone moving. There was nothing—yet, anyway.

I took off in a sprint for the chain-link fence and jumped up onto it, shaking it furiously like an enraged ape in a cage. The entire area lit up instantly with powerful floodlights, along with a shrieking *wheep wheep wheep* like a megadecibel smoke detector. I waved furiously at the nearest camera, a beckoning *get the hell over here* gesture. Then I dropped to the ground and raced back to the woods, zigzagging like a broken field runner. This time I went right on past the deer trail—if somebody was following, I wasn't going to lead them to Lisa—and kept going another few hundred yards before I hid again to watch.

Mercifully, it looked like the area was clear. I gave it another ten minutes to be safe, then climbed a different trail back to the cliff top. Only a few minutes later, we saw the first flashing red and blue lights in the distance, coming our way fast.

The deputy was on the scene and starting to search the area, pistol in hand, by the time we got to him. He assumed, understandably, that we were the ones who should be arrested, and it took some fast talking to keep us from getting cuffed and thrown into his car. But he smoothed out when he realized who Lisa was—and he started taking our story a lot more seriously when I led him to the pond and showed him where I guessed Dustin Sperry's body would be, trapped by currents against the base of the dam.

The deputy's flashlight beam was powerful enough to pierce to the bottom and pick out the pale face and sodden shape, moving with eerie gentleness as the currents tugged him this way and that.

He got on his radio, calling for backup, arranging for L.A. cops to escort my mother and sister to a hotel—and putting out an APB for Cynthia Trask. Within a very short time, there were a lot of law enforcement agents looking for her.

But by morning, it was becoming clear that she had vanished.

EPILOGUE

The summer faded into autumn, and the madness faded with it until, at least outwardly, things seemed pretty much back to normal. Lisa and I had been seeing each other steadily; we kept our separate lives, and she was working on another film, but we usually spent the weekends together and a couple of nights in between.

My mother seemed to be fine; Erica was married; Paul was home being a husband and father again. Hap had finally checked in from Singapore, sending a short note that was outwardly an apology for his abrupt departure, but was really testing the waters to see how much trouble he was in. My mother hadn't answered, and I didn't know if she ever would. I still hadn't heard from Drabyak.

One evening in November, Lisa and I took a drive up to my family's Malibu property. It had recently been put up for sale, so this was probably my last visit there, but there was no sentimentalism involved. I could have done without ever seeing the place again. It brought back all the pain about Nick, the more so because Nick was gone.

Our mother and I had made the decision to take him off life support at the end of August, when it was clear that he was already dead in all the ways that mattered. I couldn't really articulate this, but I knew that Audrey felt the same—what it came down to more than anything else was dignity.

It was Lisa who'd suggested that she and I come to the Malibu house while we still had the chance. By now she knew

the whole story, and she wanted to walk around the property—
where, in an important way, the events had started—and see if
any impressions filtered into her mind. She had kept that door
firmly shut over these past months; the last thing either of us
wanted was more weirdness inside our heads. But as the immediate nightmare had eased off, our need had grown to try to make
sense of it.

Especially because we had good reason to believe that it was
still going on, hidden, around us.

We got to Malibu as the last daylight streaked the horizon
and the long electric arc of the coastline was coming aglow. I
pulled the Land Cruiser in through the security gate and parked
beside the boarded-up old house. Paul no longer had any claim
to it. Auditors were still looking into how much family money he
had siphoned off into Parallax, but it was on the order of several
million, and we had taken back this property as restitution. It
would go on the market soon, and whoever bought it wouldn't
waste any time tearing the house down. But right now everything looked the same as when I'd come here for him that night
last May.

"Sure you're okay with this?" I asked Lisa. She nodded. Most
likely nothing would even happen; as she'd told me before, she
couldn't control her ability, only invite it. Still, we were both nervous, feeling that maybe this was a sleeping dog we should let lie.

"Let me wander a little, try to tune in," she said. "Then show
me where you and Nick were."

We got out of the car and started walking; I kept pace with
her but stayed out of her way. She moved slowly, arms folded and
head bowed; although she was wearing dark jeans and a hoodie,
there was the sense of a gothic heroine on a bleak moor, mourn-
ing a lost lover or brooding over the sin that had brought her to

ruin. Gradually, we worked our way toward the cliff edge and then to where Nick and I had tangled. The gouge where the chunk of earth had broken off under my foot still stood out like a fresh scar.

It was an eerie feeling, being at this place again.

"He was standing right about here," I said, tapping the ground with my toe.

Lisa came over and turned seaward. We stood there unmoving, with the wet salty breeze in our faces and the mesmerizing pulse of the surf in our ears.

Then she said quietly, "It's like—there's something that's keeping tabs on us. Sort of hovering, waiting to make a move."

"Cynthia?" It was the thought we dreaded most—that she was still very much a threat to us, and she'd only been biding her time until she was safe in a new life.

"Maybe—I can't tell," Lisa said, looking wary, "but I think we're going to find out."

It was only an impression, she was clear about that; she could have subconsciously manufactured it from anxiety, of which we both had plenty.

But it didn't exactly lighten the mood. We walked back to the car and started home.

There had been a media circus after Dustin Sperry's death, of course, but it wasn't nearly as bad as it would have been under other circumstances. Right away, the same spectral agent types as Venner stepped in—although he himself was conspicuously missing. They grilled Lisa and me, but very little information was publicly released; they forbade us to talk to the press and came down on any of them who got pushy. No doubt there was more of that pressure from other sources behind the scenes—the secret, influential Parallax members who wanted no part of being associated with this. The story died out of the mainstream with surprising speed; even the paparazzi and tabloids that targeted Lisa backed off.

We didn't find out much from the spooks in return. Cynthia and Venner had disappeared. If they ever got caught, we'd probably never know it. The sense we got was that he was a rogue American agent who'd compromised and endangered his colleagues—about as popular with these people as a plague-infected rat—and we'd be wise to forget he'd ever existed. Cynthia was more of a cipher, with her history concealed by a careful smoke screen; the hint of her Russian origin was tantalizing. It seemed likely that they'd left the country and they might or might not still be working as a team. My own guess was that Venner had found out he was just as expendable as everyone else to her, and by now "they" were down to just "she."

There were still people looking for her, but there wasn't much doubt that she would sell the mind-control nanotechnology—probably already had—and not just for money but for security, the protection of a foreign government or powerful private interests. With that kind of a safety net, she'd have plenty of time and opportunity to take revenge on us. In that case, our best hope was that she didn't want it badly enough to go to the trouble.

In any event, the nanotech horse was out of the barn, and it was bound to be ridden hard—by whom, for what purposes, and to what effects, were the questions. With that on our minds, Lisa and I had started noticing bizarre news items that we hadn't before.

Sheer paranoia on my part? Sure. Most likely they were random and unrelated, the result of real mental disturbance, drugs, or too long a time in some psychological pressure cooker. Or *was* somebody still using the nanotech?

There's something starting up that we're going to see more of, and we might be looking at a real problem, Drabyak had said.

But Parallax had essentially vaporized. The production company had closed its doors, the movie remained unfinished, and there were no signs of the organization itself—but there were people with a lot at stake. Would they just walk away quietly, or were Lisa and I particular threats because of what we knew? Was somebody only waiting for the right opportunity to arrange an accident?

The nanos were in our brains to stay. If anyone knew of any way for us to shield ourselves, they weren't saying so. Trying to hide out seemed as unrealistic, and futile, as ever. And besides being vulnerable ourselves, someone who wanted to target us could easily set up a situation to zap a total stranger or even an animal into sudden hostility—and themselves never be suspected of having anything to do with it. Every time Lisa or I glimpsed a menacing face, heard a dog burst into sudden furious barking, saw a vehicle in the rearview mirror coming up fast, we got a sickening jolt of fear.

I knew this was edging into "careful what you wish for" turf, but a part of me had started thinking that if somebody was going to come after us, then for Christ's sake, let's get it over with.

I woke up out of a dream with my cell phone ringing. The clock read 3:17 a.m.—the exact same time as when Nick had called that night last May. This time I couldn't remember the dream— it was only a jumble of images—and Lisa was beside me. But the sense of déjà vu was still all over this.

I grabbed the phone off the bedside table and strode out of the room, raising it to my ear as I went—waking up fast.

"Hello, Tom. Don't hang up," the caller said. I didn't recognize the voice—it was male. It sounded somehow disembodied, like it might have been digitally modified.

"All right," I said hoarsely.

"You need to answer a question, and be very honest. Let's start by refreshing your memory."

Then it came—that ugly wrenching twist inside my head, like millions of insects suddenly coming to life and writhing around.

I staggered, but I managed to hang on to the phone instead of throwing it like everything in me wanted to do. After a few seconds, the sensation eased off. I tried to calm my gasping breath, then slowly raised the phone to my ear again.

"Still there?" the voice said calmly.

"Yes."

"Good. Here's the question. On the night you were almost killed—when you were in the water, fighting for your life—you got bombarded with those same kinds of signals. But you blocked them. How did you do it?"

"*I* didn't do it," I said. "It just happened."

"That's not really an answer, now is it?"

I clenched the phone tighter in my sweaty palm, expecting another searing prod to my memory. But the eerie calm remained steady, and I groped for the right thing to say.

I'd spent endless hours thinking about that particular mystifying part of the overall madness. The only semirational explanation I could come up with was that my brain had somehow manufactured a defense for those few seconds of extreme duress—a sort of neural brownout that was the product of terror, adrenaline, and the need for instant self-preserving action. My subconscious, working in its own bizarre ways, had linked that to the suggestion of "Gatekeepers" that Kelso had implanted in me.

But that edged into the realm of a "rational" explanation weaker than the irrational one, however wild it might be:

That the Gatekeepers really had stepped in to save me.

I inhaled deeply and let the words go. "Maybe something protected me. A power from outside myself."

"Very interesting," the voice mused. "Did you summon this consciously?"

"No. I never even imagined it could happen until it was over."

"Could you do it again?"

"If I could, I'd be doing it right now."

I thought I heard a hint of laughter.

"Why did they help you, do you think?" the voice said.

"I don't know. I sure didn't do anything to deserve it. Maybe it wasn't about me at all—they had a completely different reason, and I was just in the middle of it. Or maybe—" I hesitated.

"Maybe because they have another use for you in the future? A fiercer beast to throw you to?"

I sagged. "Yeah."

"An excellent guess. What will you do about it? Just wait and hope?"

"What else am I *supposed* to do?"

"Remember that Gatekeepers guard gates," the voice said, still maddeningly calm. "Find those and smash through them. There'll be beasts at each one, and they'll tear into you—but you'll learn to bite back."

It was sinking in that, bizarre as this had started out, the turn it was taking was far more so.

"How do I find the gates?" I said. "I don't even know what they are."

"You've been given eyes that see. If you're fool enough not to use them, then fool you remain."

And that was it. I was left standing there in the dark, holding a silent phone.

Then I realized that Lisa was watching me from the bedroom doorway, with her hands pressed flat against the jambs like she was bracing herself for support.

"Are you done?" she said, in not much more than a whisper.

I nodded shakily. "I don't know who it was. Maybe Cynthia, fucking with me. Maybe somebody else. I—I don't know."

Lisa came forward and put her fingertips against my chest, a light, soothing touch.

"Tom. It wasn't anybody," she said, still speaking very quietly.

"It—*What?*"

"I was awake the whole time. The way you grabbed for the phone and rushed out here—it seemed so strange, that was why I followed you. The phone never rang. The line was dead. No voice coming from the other end—nothing."

I stared at her. "I *heard* it ring. That's what woke me up."

She shook her head gently. "Sorry, hon. You must have dreamed that."

"I know I wasn't dreaming that I heard somebody talking back."

"Here, let's check." She pried the phone from my numb hand, brought up the received calls list, and held it up for me to see.

The last one had come from Lisa herself at 4:53 in the afternoon, as she was leaving her house to drive over here.

I dropped down to one knee, then the other, then fell sideways on the floor and rolled over flat onto my back. She stretched out beside me, propped up on an elbow.

"You think you're losing it?" she murmured.

"When you talk out loud to somebody who's not there, but you're sure they *are* there, that's a pretty fair sign."

"You didn't sound crazy at all, Tom. I mean, you weren't ranting or anything—it's like you *were* talking to somebody. So what did they say?"

I told her. "I seem to have some talent, anyway," I finished. "As hallucinations go, that's a pretty impressive piece of work." I must have manufactured it deep in my subconscious—with most of it bearing a suspicious resemblance to things Gunnar Kelso had said.

"But it *does* make sense in a way. There's an arc, right?" Lisa traced a curve in the air with her forefinger. "They started by scaring you—let you know they could fry your brain if they wanted. But they didn't. Instead, they reminded you that you stopped it once. Brought that around to the Gatekeepers. Then—"

"Then they called me a fool," I muttered. "Being crazy doesn't feel too bad, at least so far. But I sure hate being stupid."

She gave my ear a sharp little nip with her teeth. "What they told you was that *I'm* your eyes that see. You fool."

"You really think it *was* the Gatekeepers?"

"Yes."

"You're not just saying that because you really do think I'm nuts?"

"If you start getting messages like the alien spaceship is coming to pick us up at midnight, or like religious people who say *everybody* better believe this or else, then I'll start getting nervous," Lisa said. "But let's face it—Gunnar did something to our brains that we don't have a clue about. What he told me about opening up new channels—it happened with me, so why not you?"

The jury was going to stay out for a while about that. On the one hand, my rational mind still assured me it was a psychotic episode. On the other, if I accepted that it was real, I'd sure have plenty of company—probably most people believed in otherworldly powers, and many, that they'd had some form of contact with them.

But this had a stunning implication that set it apart.

Gunnar Kelso had destroyed his own credibility by sinking to the level of sordid deceit and manipulation—no doubt under the guiding influence of Cynthia Trask.

And yet, *had* he succeeded, at least to some extent, in what he claimed—building a bridge by means of science to the realm of mysticism? Discovering the dynamics of a hidden energy system that would someday be recognized, just as the invisible workings of atoms, microbes, forces like gravity and magnetism had come to light in the past? Proving the existence of other intelligent life in the universe, but not in a distant galaxy—in another dimension that intermingled with ours?

There is still truth in what I've said, Tom.

"So what are you thinking?" Lisa said.

"That all this scares the shit out of me."

"Well, *yeah*. But we *are* in it, like it or not. And—I know I'll be sorry I said this—in a way, it's exciting."

I rolled over onto my back again, this time pulling her across my chest. She made a little *umph* sound like she was slightly surprised, but she didn't seem displeased.

"Okay, here's my from-the-hip take," I said. "We call this a peculiar kind of *folie à deux*—we might be insane, but we both know it. We keep it strictly between us, go on with our daily life just like always. But we start looking at things in this light. If it just fades out, so it goes. If it seems to shine on something, we try that."

She nodded solemnly, her hair tickling my skin, but her lips twitched in a smile.

"We might be insane, but we both know it?" she murmured. "That's the sweetest thing a guy ever said to me."

Los Angeles Times, **November 30**

Cloud of Industrial Material Released in Fire

A fire whipped by Santa Ana winds tore through Stoddard-Line Shipping Co. in Fontana late last night, gutting the complex of warehouses and transport equipment. Firefighters battled through the night to keep the blaze from spreading. No injuries have been reported, and the facility did not store materials classified as hazardous.

However, concerns are being raised because Stoddard-Line is a major transporter of bulk commercial and industrial materials known as nanoparticles. At least several tons of the particles in powdered form were on site at the time, with most released into the atmosphere by the fire and wind.

"I hardly even know what those things are, but it's weird having them up there floating around," one firefighter commented. "Kind of a perfect storm for spreading them all over L.A."

A Stoddard-Line company spokesman gave assurances that the nanos are harmless, citing both industry and government sources.

The cause of the fire is under investigation.

ACKNOWLEDGMENTS

As always, my wife, Kim, and our families and friends; Carl Lennertz, Jonathan Burnham, Kathy Schneider, and their colleagues at HarperCollins; Jennifer Rudolph Walsh, Lauren Whitney, Anna DeRoy, and colleagues at William Morris Endeavor; Roger Hedden, Drs. Barbara and Dan McMahon, and Andrew Schneider for providing invaluable advice in their fields; my mother, Georgia Knotts McMahon, for being the marvel she is; and many others who helped in many ways—my apologies for oversights.

ABOUT THE AUTHOR

Neil McMahon holds a degree in psychology from Stanford and was a Stegner fellow. He has published ten novels, in addition to the bestselling thriller *Toys*, coauthored with James Patterson. He lives in Missoula, Montana, where his wife directs the annual Montana Festival of the Book.